The Spymaster's Redeemer

Book one of the series
'Dreda's Men'

Alexie
Bolton

ISBN-13:978-1999 853303

CHAPTER ONE

Officers and dragoons were moving from house to house, searching all the rooms, the nooks and crannies. Chaos ruled! The sky seemed to reflect the humour of the city; dark, misty and moody; then flashing red streaks of lightning, carving open the heavens; emulating the dragoons' dogs when they caught their prey, tearing at it until the men capitulated.

The leading officer Dreda wore a shallow helmet shielding his eyes and protecting his ears. Slenderly build for an officer, this belied his strength. He was all muscle, agile and had been lithe in battle. He was retired now from the army but worked for the State Security Bureau as second in command. He dominated that shadowy, secretive organization, rooting out enemies of the state and enforcing retribution, deterring future rebellions by brute force.

His men knocked sharply on a door and it opened very slowly as a small, feminine face peered through the gap.

"Let us in! We need to search your house for an escaped prisoner, a traitor," commanded the Lieutenant.

"Come in. We have nothing to hide."

Dreda looked her up and down, a spark of interest showing in his eyes. Most young females would have shivered with fear at the thought of being arrested for treason by association with a prisoner discovered in their house. This one showed no fear; it was almost as if she was challenging the officer to do his worst, knowing full well that his men would find nothing.

"I'll take this one," he said, moving forward and pushing the door slowly and firmly open. The girl stepped aside and let him in. He introduced himself. "Officer Dreda, Mistress, of the State Security Bureau."

She curtseyed, "Lady Felea Whelani, Officer. If you follow me I will show you the rooms from the attics down to the cellars." She headed for the stairs. He put his hand on her shoulder and halted her, not liking the way she had taken control of the situation. Her muscles felt like those of a young girl. Then as her eyes flashed a warning to him to keep his hands to himself; he realized he was dealing with a woman. Never able to resist a challenge he took his hand away but grasped her wrist and led her and his men down to the cellars. She tried to wrench her hand away from his grip but gave up realizing resistance was futile and humiliating as he moved her quickly downstairs in front of him.

"Open that door," he ordered.

She picked from her waistband a huge bunch of keys and he

was puzzled and yet again intrigued. She looked no more than seven and ten years of age but was acting like the chatelaine of the house. Unusually, her blue-black hair was tinged with mauve and deep auburn. Her eyes were a misty green with golden flecks like a tigress.

He let his men go ahead of him down the stairs but asked one of them who this house belonged to.

"Whelani Sir; you remember last year he was imprisoned for criticizing the proclamation cutting free speech and association when a security alert was issued. This is his only daughter and he has vanished, possibly with the escaped prisoner who was his friend from his university days."

"Is she suspected as well?" he enquired.

"The father said she was not involved but we think she has passed messages on behalf of the state's enemies."

He pushed the girl in front of him and they found themselves at the bottom of a dark, dank cellar. He kicked a few boxes and they collapsed, mouldy and useless. He knew he was on a wild goose chase this time but an instinct that had saved him from dangerous situations in the past kicked in and he sensed this house held secrets that the security forces needed

The girl leaned against the wall waiting for him to admit the search was useless. He sent his men up to search the rest of the house and proceeded to fire a series of questions at her. He admired her composure; other women would have quaked under his piercing stare and barrage of questions. He would play her at her own game. If she wanted to be treated like a mature lady he would refer to her by the formal title of Ma'am as he would the mistress of a household, a warning she would be treated as a traitress if arrested by him.

"Where is your father, Ma'am?"

"I don't know, Officer?"

"That is hardly likely. A father tells his daughter where he is going unless he has something to hide!" he said moving closer to her, pinning her against the wall, his stone blue grey eyes piercing hers.

Most women would have been intimidated by his height alone; but his commanding presence seemed to have little impact on this petite wench who merely stood her ground. With a degree of irritation as if she was humouring a little child she said quietly, "I repeat, I don't know. My father left quickly without informing me of his destination. He is absent-minded, a typical academic and sometimes forgets to inform me of his goings on."

He changed tack. "Has Gremeniz been here?"

"Not to my knowledge and I have been here most of the time.

The servants would have told me if my father had allowed him in when I went to do the marketing."

"You know he is a traitor," he said sternly, watching for any change in her visage. Her face was shuttered, and she stared impassively back at him, silently challenging him. Only her expressive eyes showed any emotion, her green gold eyes daring him to prove her wrong.

"Anyone helping a traitor is committing a crime punishable by death." This time he watched her pupils widen as she absorbed the implications behind his words. Still, she merely shrugged her shoulders. "I do not know his or my father's whereabouts."

"When will your father be back?" She shrugged again. He felt like shaking her out of her supposed indifference. Most women made an effort to impress him or even to attract him. This one merely tried to rid herself of him as if he was a nuisance. It was if she barely knew of his reputation or cared! He framed his last question. "Is your father a member of the insurgents or merely angered by the recent reduction in freedom and of liberties?"

"I know my father is angered by the loss of liberties and freedom but I don't know if he is a member of the insurgents," she said carefully. "He tells me little of what he involves himself in."

He believed all her answers but the last. Her father had told her as little as he could to protect her but she definitely knew more about the rebels than she was prepared to admit. He could almost smell the evasion on her breath.

He decided to let her go, to find out if she would lead them to the insurgents. He hoped she was not heavily involved as her life could be forfeit and he would not want to arrest such a spirited young woman.

"You are free to go," he said casually; then taking her arm in his he led her up the stairs, the gentleman again. He touched his helmet and bowed, "Until we meet again Lady Felea!" To the astonishment of his men, for he was not usually a ladies' man and was very discreet in love affairs, he took her hand and kissed the back of it.

"I sincerely hope not," she countered.

"It is a certainty Lady Felea." He smiled and turned away to the street. She was no match for him in guile; he had many years of dealing in deceit; she was but a novice.

She shut the door and bolted it quickly. She had been holding her breath and trying to keep her expression stony so that he could not read it easily. She knew without being told he was dangerous. She shivered, allowing her emotions to be released at last. He knew she had lied. Her father was up to his neck in the insurgents' business, which is why he had escaped the city last evening. Would Dreda set his men to watch her for fear she engaged in treasonable activities?

Her father was opposed to violence but would use his linguistic and code breaking skills to send messages for the insurgents and help others hide their escapees. There were secret tunnels under the house which led to caves in the hills behind the walls in the city. He had trained her to break codes and she could speak seven languages but like most girls she had not had the opportunity of a qualifying for a degree at university. Very few people knew her skills and her most important distinguishing characteristic, her telepathic powers.

Like her late mother, she foresaw visions about the future. Her powers were limited and often unreliable, their most useful purpose the warning of danger to herself. She therefore rarely mixed with noble society; she socialized with intellectuals like her father who sympathized with the insurgents and would not betray their secret.

She now felt sick and shivered. She had tried to block her mind to the officer but it was a struggle. From the moment he had put his hand on her shoulder she had felt a frisson of awareness, a connection with him that she could not explain. She should have been revolted by him! His reputation went before him; a ruthless, cruel man who had ordered the torture of insurgents who had tried to form an uprising the year before. He had personally ordered the execution of one of her father's friends.

Handsome men had tried to court her without success and she had no trouble matching her wit with them. With this man, she felt vulnerable, emotionally and intellectually. She had no doubt that she was his at least his equal in intellect but there was something else he had garnered; experience and wisdom gained the hard way in battles and in making his way to the senior echelons of the militia.

At the end of the interview she could block him out but to do this one had to be totally invulnerable to the other person's emotions or to be able to assess and undermine their vulnerability and find their weak spots by delving into the deepest recesses of their mind. She had no desire to get close enough intellectually or emotionally to this man to access his mind.

Every man and women had his weaknesses but she felt this man was very strong physically and psychologically and she did not want the challenge he presented. If she faced him again she could steel herself and block him out but she kept remembering that kiss and his promise to meet her again. She could not even remember his face; just that he was blond, had sharp chiselled features and was incredibly strong, used to being obeyed and he saw her as a challenge.

Before her mother had died she had warned her that her powers could bring her great happiness or great sadness and her looks would attract most men. Her mother said her husband would need to win her respect. She did not tolerate fools easily and a weak husband who she could bully would not suit her. She was slow to anger but when her anger was raised woe betide the man who annoyed her.

She was nine and ten years of age and had nearly two years before she attained her majority and seven before she gained her full fortune. If her father died the Emperor could easily force her into a marriage if her trustees betrayed her. He had said he wished she would troth herself before he died. Her father had wisely kept her away from the court and unwanted male attention since her mother had died.

Her loyal servant Lucia joined her. Dreda's men had questioned the servants separately and none had given any secrets away, but she said they were scared. Felea, told her servants as little as possible to protect them. Lucia noticed her wrist; where a bruise had appeared as a result of Dreda's over firm grip when she had resisted.

''My Lady, has that officer hurt you!'' she exclaimed.

''Not at all, I merely tried to resist his hold.'' Lucia knew her mistress well and could recognize she was troubled.

''Best avoid that one, he could bring trouble to this house,'' she said sagely, "he's too handsome and assured for his own good.''

''You are so right!''

Lucia left her mistress to her bleak thoughts. She knew when not to interfere. Felea could be headstrong but was usually cautious and thoughtful. She was worried though. She had never seen her mistress react to any of the men who flirted with her with anything but cool dismissal or mischievous flirtatiousness. She had easily countered unwanted advances, but this officer today had struck a chord with her mistress; there was a meeting of minds at some subliminal level. Anyone could observe that he was deeply interested in her and she was trying to deny her awareness of him.

Felea went to bed and tossed restlessly, waking during the night; expecting to see a sharp featured face leaning over her. She woke at dawn and got dressed hurriedly and started coding a message to her father. She sent one message via her servants who passed it on to a pigeon keeper at the market. A decoy; if read it spoke of innocent things like the wedding she would be attending and was designed to make the authorities think she was a frivolous girl, her head filled with trivialities and balls and gowns.

The other, the important message, was handed to a friend of her father. She had recently found out he only used this man's pigeons to transmit messages between the rebels and their supporters. Soon the pigeon would be taking the story of last night's events to her father. She had to warn him to stay away until she could reach him. She knew Officer Dreda would try to get him to come back and capture him and she started to prepare for a journey should she have to go to him.

Dreda as always slept heavily. He had fallen asleep on rough ground covered in his cloak so often a soft bed was always a luxury he made the most of. He was dog tired after searching houses until midnight.

He woke up smiling, remembering the slender girl with blue black mauve hair and smouldering green gold eyes challenging him to touch her. *She was fierce, by God!* He needed to find out more about the family and how deeply the father was involved in the insurgents' network. Despite his reputation for ruthlessness he had saved some families from torture and execution. He had them exiled if they were merely passionate fools caught up in a web of intrigue they did not understand and were being used by brighter men than themselves.

He was not sure if the girl's father was like them. He remembered seeing in the square a man eloquently denouncing the latest decree of the Emperor before he was dragged away. The old fool had been let loose after questioning but hadn't the sense to keep his head down after the caution he had been given. His daughter seemed a different kettle of fish; secretive, calmer.

Felea; he ran the name over his tongue. Named because of her stunning cat like eyes, she had watched him, assessing him in that way a feline would, assessing a predator much stronger than herself. He wondered if she had taken after her mother in personality as well as looks, her father being tall and blond haired with blue eyes. She had not inherited her stunning colouring from him, but she had clearly inherited his intelligence and thirst for knowledge.

Dreda had always avoided blue-stockings. He wouldn't suffer a fool or a featherhead in his bed, but intellectual women always asked too many questions of a man; wanting to know what made him tick and demanded more of him than he was prepared to give. No, he stuck to beauties whose skills in the bedroom were legendary and demanded a comfortable lifestyle but wanted as little commitment as he was prepared to offer.

There were women a plenty queuing up to take what he offered, and he could cherry pick the best. With a toss of an elegant shoulder and a pretence of indifference they drifted out of his life when he tired of them. That is how he liked his life; no tantrums, no complications nor long term commitments from his carefully selected ladies.

He called his clerk in. "I want Denman in now! Get him out of any meeting he is in." Peter Denman entered the office after a few minutes in his usual leisurely manner.

Denman was open, relaxed and carefree, rarely taking life seriously, except when pursuing his militia duties. A ladies' man, he spent his leisure time at balls and soirees, hunting out his latest conquest while his friend buried himself in the Bureau with details of spy networks and criminal activities.

"What's the rush? You asked me to leave a meeting."

"I went to the house of Whelani last night; you know, the Professor of Mathematics and Linguistics. His daughter let us search the house but denied knowing where her father was and whether he was aiding the insurgents.

'She clearly didn't know where he was, but she was lying when she said he was not involved with the insurgents or the escapees. I need to know how heavily the family are involved and if they have aided the escapees. I don't know if they are fools on the outside or part of the web to undermine this city state."

"I will arrest them and bring the family and servants in."

"No, I want this done discreetly and carefully. I want them watched, particularly the daughter, and any information that can be gleaned about the family including their servants past and present accessible to me as soon as possible."

"Any reason why we are to be cautious?"

"I don't want any innocents to be harmed."

"Innocents amongst a family of traitors?"

"I particularly want to know more information about the daughter. A subtler approach will gain more from this girl than brute force. She was resisting me forcefully during my short interrogation. There was no fear in her eyes. Her father has told her little to protect her and she adopts the same approach with her servants. For the moment, I want intelligence rather than action. Present me with the facts tomorrow at this same time please."

Denman knew that when Dreda was in this mood it was no use arguing with him. He accepted his dismissal and found his most trustworthy men and sent them searching for information from their informers. He was intrigued; the less he had said, the more it was obvious it was the girl Dreda was interested in, but he had no doubt that Dreda's first loyalty was to the Emperor and if the girl was a traitor she would be put on trial.

Next morning, a file sat on Dreda's desk and Denman was identifying the most important points.

''The father is one of the professors at the forefront of his field. He studies and teaches linguistics and mathematics but what is interesting and not well known is that he is an expert code breaker. His wife had the same skills but less is known about her. They retreated from noble society when a rumour about the mother delving into sorcery was put round.

'She died during childbirth and left a young daughter to be brought up by servants and the father. The father being eccentric treated her like a boy and taught her the same subjects boys would learn. She is proficient in mathematics and speaks seven languages and is quite a beauty to boot, I understand.''

He paused and looked up to see if what he had said had had any impact on his friend. Dreda merely answered, ''Yes, she is fiercely proud and beautiful. Intelligent and a linguist as well. Well what a surprise!'' He frowned, his worst fears realized, his instincts were not often proven wrong. It was likely the whole family were aiding the insurgents.

''We need to step carefully. Who are the friends of this girl and where do her father and she socialize?''

''They meet a very tight group of intellectuals but are friends of the von Magnitz family and will attend the wedding of the eldest son in two days' time.''

''Get me an invitation. I need to talk to the girl again.''

''That won't be difficult. Von Magnitz has relatives working in the militia but surely you don't want her to know we suspect her.''

''She knows that already. She doesn't know what we know, and I want to make her nervous if she has something to hide and she may slip up. ''

''A battle of the nerves. Watch it! You may enjoy this too much.'' A tight smile appeared at his friend's mouth. ''I don't think I am going to enjoy it at all.''

CHAPTER TWO

It was very dark outside but inside thousands of candles and the light from the chandeliers brightened the hall. As Felea entered the hall the cheerful interior lightened her mood. The last two days had been tense. She did not want her father to risk his life by coming back to ensure her safety. She had warned him that they were under suspicion but had couched her words carefully, to encourage him to take care but not to hurry home. She had adopted a mask like her fellow dancers and wore a rich velvet marine blue dress and mauve cloak which reflected the highlights in her hair. She felt like a young girl again without any worries and intended to dance all night.

She sought out the bride and the groom to be, hugging them and giving them presents she had bought. She was not aware of being watched by a tall, slim figure in the corner, a glass of wine in his hand, waiting silently like a panther for her to take her dance card out; ready to claim the first dance. He was surprised, she seemed very relaxed despite her family circumstances.

The groom to be put his arm around her and swung her in the air as if she were his sister. The familiarity and the ease with which the girl flirted with the men around her amazed the watcher. This carefree creature bore no resemblance to the watchful, intense girl whose house he had searched. She was like the ladies of the Emperor's court appearing flirtatious, vacuous and boring; clearly a creature of conflicts and contrasts!

"Quite beautiful, isn't she and wealthy also!" said Denman, watching Dreda carefully.

"To whom are you referring?"

"Your little spy in the marine blue dress which matches her hair. She bears no resemblance to the description given to me by my informers. You would think she doesn't have a care in the world."

"She could just be acting like the young girl she is."

"Well, old enough to have been married off by now. I am surprised she is still unwed."

"Intellectuals give their daughters more freedom than others do, and she is never at court, so she can choose her own way to behave."

She took out her dance card and the men started to gather round. The father of the groom, von Magnitz, well primed in advance, broke through the circle and taking her arm gently he led her to the watching men.

"My dear, here is a gentleman who would like you to honour

him with the first dance.''

Unwilling to upset an old valued family friend she smiled and turned laughing to offer her card to the stranger in the mask but froze in the action. She felt numb. She sensed she had met this person before, but she didn't recognize him in the mask and black ball clothes. His dark clothes were a stark contrast to his bronzed skin and pale hair making him look severe, almost sinister. A shiver went down her back at the knowledge that this man knew her, about her, but she knew nothing about him. *Where had she met him?*

He took the card from her hands and wrote his name in the card and gave it back to her. He had taken three dances and signed the name Danitz. She could not refuse, it would offend von Magnitz; so, she curtseyed and thanked the stranger and went back to her group. The stranger didn't take his eyes off her for a moment; she felt them boring through her back. Those blue eyes barely visible behind the mask had pierced her as if they read into her very soul. She no longer felt relaxed and wanted to go home but she plastered a smile on her face and played her role as a flirtatious lady again.

She felt a little faint as if one of her visions was coming, brought on by the presence of this enigmatic man. She felt she was in danger and someone was warning her she was to be careful. A message flashed before her eyes, but she did not know from whom. It just spelt out the words, ''danger! The one who watches!'' How could anyone outside the room tell she was being watched by this man.

Nevertheless, she thought the saints must be watching over her and warning her about him. She would tell him as little as she could about herself. Three dances he had taken. Three dances usually meant a commitment from a man, a desire to know her intimately but she could not even put a face to his name. He must have some other reason for wanting to dance so often with her, a reason she had no desire to find out!

Soon the musicians started the music for the first dance and she felt a hand placed on her arm. Smiling, the watcher in the mask led her to the floor and to her surprise began to dance in an assured and graceful way, familiar with the steps of the dance. She was an exceptionally good dancer and would have enjoyed the dance if she hadn't dreaded every step.

She now recognized the grip on her arm although it was gentle this time and the eyes that sparkled were the same eyes that had pierced her two days before. Why had he singled her out? There was a silence between them that seemed to go on forever until he broke it by saying, ''You seem to be very familiar with the von Magnitz family, have you known them long?''

''All my life, we are like brothers and sisters. I am to be a bridesmaid at the wedding. Do you know the family well?''

''Not at all, one of the members works for my unit and I was invited out of courtesy.''

Pretending to be light hearted and frivolous, she commented, ''She will make a beautiful and serene bride tomorrow.''

''Matched only by her beautiful bridesmaid.''

Nonplussed; not expecting compliments from this man who had been so severe on the last occasion they had met, she raised her brows, curtsied a thanks in reply and changed the subject immediately.

''They will be so lucky to live here after they are married. The lake looks so calm and beautiful.''

No longer prepared to fence with her he got to business. ''I asked you before in your house where your father had gone. Tell me now and when he is coming back.'' They faced each other, and she repeated what she had told him before, adding, ''All I know is that he had heard of a tribe who speak a language we thought had been lost for years and he hoped to glean from them the speech patterns. He is a renowned linguist you know.''

''As you are also!''

Why does he always bring the subject back to me? ''I am not in the same league. For me it is a hobby, for him a profession.''

''Until you marry?''

''Why do you ask that?''

''Are you scared of admitting your proficiency because most husbands would not want a wife more educated than themselves?''

''I have no intention of marrying most husbands.'' Her eyes flashed a warning that he was intruding on private matters and he should back off. She pulled her arm as far away from his as was considered polite, but he pursued the subject further.

''Your father will give you the choice?''

They had come to a point in the dance where the gentleman threw the lady up in the air and caught her again. As she was pivoted in the air they came face to face, the lady stiff and backing as far as was possible and the man pulling her close to his chest and dropping her lightly on her feet. For a moment, she felt suffocated by his closeness, his sharp eyes delving into her soul.

''What is it to you who or if I marry?''

''A husband could keep you out of trouble with the militia and out of my way.''

''You chose to confront me here. You asked about my

proficiency. Compared with my father I do not have the interest nor the constancy to practice enough to teach.''

"But you can translate and interpret seven languages? Are you a proficient mathematician as well?''

These were not innocent questions; he was trying to trap her into admitting she could write codes. She merely tossed her head and retorted airily, "My mother was the linguist and my father also the mathematician. I am my mother's daughter and have her skills.''

"Including powers of sorcery?''

At this, her blood did run cold. Her father had left court because cruel people were jealous of her parents' position and influence and had accused her mother of delving in black magic. She could herself be executed for appearing to be a black witch.

Again, she was tossed in the air and had a moment to think. She decided to be equally confrontational. "Why did you ask to dance with me when you barely know me? Why did you not ask me to go to your office if you wanted to ask me personal questions?''

He did not answer her but still watched her intensely. She carried on, determined to remain on the offensive. She refused to allow him to intimidate her by his silence. "Are you asking me in your official capacity or merely out of interest? You seem to want to know many personal details about my family.''

Again, he seemed to hold her a minute longer than was necessary, closer than was needed, as if he was trying to intimidate her physically. He put her on the floor, took her arm in his and guided her to the side of the hall where the waiter held drinks ready for them. She could not reject the wine but sipped it very slowly, scared it would loosen her tongue.

"Whether I am working in my official capacity or not I can dance with a beautiful woman.'' He observed the bruise where her sleeve fell and took a sharp intake of breath. "I am sorry. I don't always know my own strength. In the future, I will be more careful.''

Then he went on to warn her. "Ma'am, you and your family are playing a dangerous game. You may not be aware of how dangerous it is. I would hate to see you lose that beautiful neck.''

She shrugged her shoulders nonchalantly, as if she had not a care in the world and stared at him boldly. "I know not what you refer to Sir. My father has gone on a work trip and that is all I know.''

He then ground out harshly, "Your father is a selfish fool if he allows you to get involved in treasonable activities.''

"My father is no fool, nor is he selfish. He is an honourable man, something you would not understand!''

The dance at an end, she curtsied and swiftly left him for her friends. He let her go feeling he had needled her enough. He admitted to himself that she had got under his skin when she demanded to know why he had not interrogated her formally. If he interviewed her formally it would be recorded and permanent. For her safety, he had chosen to talk to her here, but the conversation had become more personal than he intended.

She was right. It was of no interest to anyone whether she intended to marry. God help the poor man she married! She would be sparring with him more than making love. On any other occasion, he would have enjoyed sparring with her, but this situation was too dangerous. He would try another tack later. He was looking forward to another dance with this wilful girl. She danced delightfully.

Felea spoke to von Magnitz. "That man who danced with me. He signed his name Danitz, but I know him as an officer named Dreda in the Security Bureau. "

"That is right, Danitz is his father's family name but in his professional capacity he goes only by his mother's family name. After his colours were bought he was determined to gain rank in the army by merit, not by patronage. He only uses his noble name on exceptional occasions. I was surprised he sought you out. He is rarely seen with women in court. Not that he doesn't get involved with women! He is a man of the world but very discreet. Very few people know what makes him tick.

'He asked to be invited to this ball and I wondered why. Now I know. I will watch out for you. If you do not want the last dance, we can make some excuse." He was like a father to her and he could see she felt hunted by this man. He had heard of the house search and her father's disappearance and had put two and two together.

He found Dreda on his own, brooding. Dreda smiled. "It is a poet's evening, beautiful and mysterious."

"It is a lover's evening, too good to be wasted on old men like me. A word with you my friend, on the terrace if you please!" Dreda raised his eyebrows quizzically but followed the older man. They stood overlooking the lake.

"Felea seems upset by your conversation. I am acting in place of her absent father. I heard you searched her house. I can assure you that that girl is not a traitor, nor is her father; a stubborn old fool who has sympathies for the wrong side maybe but that is common knowledge. I would hate to see that child endangered by her father's conduct or by suspicions about what she might do in the future."

"You know I cannot discuss security issues with you, but I can assure you that I have no intention of placing her in any danger. It is she who places herself in danger by not admitting the truth. I think the matter will come to a head when her father comes back which he must do soon.''

And he will come back because he knows you have intimidated his daughter at this ball. You are deliberately flushing him out, knowing his friends will report back the events of this night to him, you crafty devil!

''Very well. I can rely on you to behave the gentleman.''

Raising his brows and bowing Dreda left him in pursuit of Felea. She had been teasing two young men who were overwhelmed by her beauty and she flirted outrageously, hiding coquettishly behind her fan. She was clearly a brilliant actress. Searching in a room for a missing friend, she was surprised to find the boy come behind her and close the door.

Dropping on one knee he declared undying love for her and demanded her hand in marriage. Blaming herself partly for flirting with him she tried to let him down gently by reasoning with him, but he grasped her hand and tried fumbling to kiss her. She struggled with him and was about to slap him when she found herself released and the boy flung across the room.

''Now apologize to the lady and leave us!'' ordered Dreda. The boy's hand moved toward his sword, but he was too slow. Dreda's sword point was at his throat, pinching him until a spot of blood appeared.

''If you value your hide, I would leave now,'' whispered Dreda menacingly.

Felea was torn between embarrassment and gratitude. First, a traitor and now a loose woman; an outrageous flirt! Her reputation could not fall much further in the eyes of this man. She swallowed her pride and thanked him for helping her.

He shrugged. ''He was only a mere boy, overwhelmed by your beauty and your encouragement by flirting with him. He will soon see it is only his pride that is hurt, and it was not worth fighting over. Very few women are,'' he commented wryly to himself.

She went bright red and turned on her heel, but he put out his hand and shut the door before she could reach it. He stood in front of it and watched her. Then he walked slowly and steadily up to her and held her chin in his hand, staring into her eyes.

Cat like, her eyes were slightly slanted, gold flecks surrounding centres of green. He was drawn to them; it was like looking into deep fathomless mysterious pools. She tried to move away but he held her there motionless as if trying to divine her thoughts. She stiffened and blocked him out, helped by her anger. She rarely flirted but she had been trying show a different persona.

At last he spoke. ''My dance I think. Ma'am, be careful! I may not always be here to ward off enthusiastic young boys. It could be a dangerous man in future. If I were your father I would not let you flirt in this way.''

''I take your warning sir. Now release me if you please?''

''You take after your mother's side? A witch! Bewitching young men!''

It was said as a jest to lighten the situation, but he saw the light go out of her eyes and he had struck a nerve. *By God! Was that the answer? Had the mother been a witch and had the girl inherited her powers?* If so she was more dangerous to herself and to the state than he had thought. It also explained her resistance to his questions and her coolness. A rational man, he didn't believe in witches or sorcerers but in his travels, he had seen many things which couldn't be explained by science and kept an open mind on these things.

Felea withdrew mentally, trying to block this man from invading her thoughts. She never talked about her mother to strangers. She had come to terms with her mother's death, but she missed her dreadfully. Her father had locked himself in his study losing himself in his documents and codes. Her mother had been vibrant, sociable, a bright light in society until her self-imposed banishment. She wished she was here now to give her sound advice. How much did this man know about her family?

Dreda had no desire to hurt or upset her. He was just doing his job, albeit in an unusual way. He took her arm and opening the door he led her to the ballroom and they started to dance.

''You enjoy dancing. That is unusual for a man and soldier!''

''If it is energetic, I don't like the slow dances unless they are waltzes. My parents used to hold many balls.''

''You chose to leave society and join the army instead. Were you bored?'' She thought she would ask him a few personal questions and put him on the spot.

''Boredom and too much energy and a desire for adventure. The time was opportune, and the army gave me what I needed, structure and the ability to challenge that energy into something worthwhile.''

''Killing people!'' she countered.

''Discipline, ensuring the safety of the state and travel as well, what many young men need.'' He looked at the young man who had pestered her, who was drinking heavily and making a fool of himself.

He lifted her with ease in the next turn of the dance. Clearly, he still kept fit despite having a desk job. There was not a spare inch of flesh on him.

"What do you do with your spare time? Pore over dusty documents or sew?"

"You clearly have a poor image of an educated person and intellectual. Some of the documents my father researches reveal fascinating details of the tribes who lived around here. More interesting than the gossip I hear around the kitchens." She continued, "I do help him translate some of the literature he finds but some of it is too complex and I leave him to it. I teach Latin for a few hours at the convent. I garden, and I paint, and I play music. When I can I ride and take the horses into the hills."

"On your own!" He was astonished.

"My servant comes with me."

"That old woman gives you little protection. The hills are dangerous, bandits are there."

"I have always been safe."

He knitted his brow, frowning at the way this girl had been brought up. Not cloistered, cosseted and feminized by loving female relatives but looked after by an old woman and allowed to roam the hills freely, filling her head with nonsense from books. He loved books himself and was as well read as anyone who had gone to university, but he was practical and knew this girl would find it difficult to fit back into society if her father died and she was forced to marry.

"Your father would be better introducing you into society or remarrying and finding you a mother to help you find a suitor."

"Why do you assume I need a husband?"

"To keep you out of trouble."

"That is his role?"

"Amongst others."

"How boring! I am glad you are not choosing my husband. I prefer to stay single." The same thing went through their heads. Neither of them would want boring spouses. They were both free spirits, their own persons.

"Why have you not taken a spouse? You are old enough and your house must need an heir."

"My brother can provide the heir. I don't want any chains around my neck and wives can become bored."

For once uncomfortable, Dreda didn't like talking about himself and she had touched a raw nerve. The damn witch! Did she know about his family history? He was not ashamed of his family but the affair between his mother and another courtier had been common knowledge and the family arguments had been one driver for him to join the army at six and ten. Beautiful and bored, his mother had caused a scandal and later his parents had reconciled for political reasons and stayed together but lived separate lives.

His parents had made a marriage of convenience, but his mother had needed affection. His father was cold and had driven his mother away emotionally. He still loved and spoke to his mother but was suspicious of women. He had had a short romance with a younger woman whom he had loved deeply but he had found she was attracted more to his title and fortune than himself. This had finally made him cynical about women and reluctant to trust any society beauties. So, he romanced and left older women or ladies from the demi-monde before any affair became serious.

Needling him more, she continued, ''Why did you leave the army?''

''I had seen and done enough and didn't want the politics a high-level appointment requires.''

''Many people would think your job is political now. You decide their fate.''

''It is but in a different way, less frivolous. I protect this state. I answer only to the Emperor and my Commander.''

''Being involved in intrigue must make one suspicious of people.''

''I have good friends I can trust. Enough of me, when are you going to cooperate with me? I need answers; the whereabouts of your father and his date of return or I will soon have to investigate you formally. You would not appreciate that, and it would endanger your extended family, friends and servants if they are involved in any suspicious activities.''

''I have told you what I know about my father's whereabouts.''

''I need to know what he has been translating and if he has been helping any of the insurgents We know they will twist the arms of friends to give safety and rest to their members who are on the run.''

''You would want him to betray his friends.''

''I want him to save himself and you. The last rebellion caused so much bloodshed I don't want it repeated. I saw many unfortunate men and women executed for being caught up in something they didn't understand.''

''Yet despite the unnecessary executions you still work for and support the Emperor.''

''Sometimes the end justifies the means and we have no

choice."

She did not understand this cold, complex man. He was admitting he did not like the political situation but would work within it despite the human casualties. Her father had gone too far this time. He had deliberately told her only part of what he was doing but he had clearly embroiled himself too deeply. Leaving had only cemented the suspicions around him instead of alleviating them.

She was in real danger. Perhaps it was time for her to vanish as well. She would send messages out to her friends in neighbouring states asking them for sanctuary and warning her father not to come back under any circumstances.

"If my father and I left the state and he worked away for a few years would the Emperor then see him no longer as a threat?"

"Possibly, but he would want to know why he had left so suddenly. It could lead to permanent exile."

The dance came to an end. When they left the floor, an older man came to her and kissed her hand. "Lady Felea. And Officer Dreda," he acknowledged with a bow. "I didn't know you attended society weddings."

"If I am invited and the family are friends." Even in the mask he had a presence and had easily been recognized by some.

"Felea, I have been looking for your father in the reading rooms without success." Felea was wary of this conniving academic. He was not a friend of her father, rather the opposite; a man who tried to buy his way up the university promotion ladder and was jealous of her father's hard-earned position. He had tried to insinuate himself into her father's good graces without success and had asked for the hand of Felea in marriage.

She would rather marry a snake! His comment about the whereabouts of her father in front of Dreda was designed to alert that officer that something suspicious was happening and to make her feel vulnerable. Already bets were being traded about how long it would be before he arrested her formally and his appearance at the ball had added fuel to the fire. She wondered if Britiz had been the watcher her message had warned her about. He had clearly been regarding her; waiting until he could catch her at an opportune moment with Dreda so he could inject his suspicions into the officer's mind.

Dreda felt her discomfort and disliked the man on sight. He was a weasel, a man to be avoided at all costs; the sort his men paid frequently for information. Like him, this toad had been watching her all evening. He had waited until it was the right time to slime his way over and insinuate himself into their conversation; and try to poison

Dreda's mind against her father.

"I think he must have gone somewhere to do some research. You know how impulsive and absent minded he is."

"Yes, I have been telling him he doesn't look after you and you need to a husband to do this."

Dreda intervened. "I am sure her father will return soon, and she has trustees to look after her interests."

"We must hope so!" The man bowed and left quietly, leaving the doubts he had created in their minds.

The jackals are starting to circle her. We must finish this business quickly. If her father doesn't come back the Emperor would want the trustees to find a family who would introduce her to court and marry her off safely. Somehow, he felt she would not approve and he felt discomforted at the thought of this spirited, beautiful creature being married off for convenience in a loveless marriage for a fortune. She would be stifled and could become like his mother, a bored gossip.

He thought she would bolt soon to avoid her father coming back. That he didn't want. He needed the situation resolved. He would investigate her formally. Anyone who was being officially investigated could not leave the state without permission from his office.

"That man wishes my father ill."

"And he clearly wants you for himself."

"Possibly." She evaded the issue. She turned Britiz's comments over in her mind. He was the danger she was warned about.

"Is there no-one you can live with who could guarantee your loyalty to the state?"

"Most of my father's friends are under suspicion or want to stay alive and are distancing themselves from us."

"The latter are not true friends then. Are there not any men who have expressed interesting in courting you?"

"There were in the past, but I was not interested when my mother was dying and now I am surrounded by mere boys." She looked at the boy who had tried to kiss her earlier.

He followed her gaze. "He would not be a match for you. You would bully him."

"You have a poor idea of my character."

"I merely know you as a woman who knows her own mind and would not respect a weak boy. You need to marry a strong man. Denman, my second in charge. He is strong and resourceful. He would not bore you and would not let you bully him. Let me introduce you."

She was irritated by his determination to find her a suitor but wanting to humour him she allowed him to lead her to Denman.

Surprised at the introduction, he bowed and spoke to her while Dreda got them a drink.

Felea observed the two men. Friends they might be but different characters nevertheless. Denman was also tall and imposing but he was even featured, energetic and easy going in the extreme; the opposite of his secretive, brooding friend. He wondered if his role was to pump the girl and started asking her about her interests. A shutter came down over her face as she closed her mind again.

She turned the tables. "You were in the army with Officer Dreda?"

"Yes, we were boyhood friends and decided to join and fought in the same regiments. We left at the same time as well and joined the militia. He has risen faster than me. His personality is more suited to the intrigue than mine."

She made a mental note of this. "He is very interested in my business, unnecessarily so!"

"It is his job. He has no choice. He is protecting you. If others questioned you they would have to make a formal report which could be acted on."

"He seems interested in marrying me off if my father doesn't return."

"It would be for your own safety."

He turned the conversation to easier matters and then a dance partner took her off for a third dance. Dreda returned.

"Did you enjoy your conversation with the little rebel?"

"Not at all! She wouldn't open up to me. Our friendship intrigued her. Why did you bring her over?"

"I wanted to introduce her to a wider circle of men than intellectuals or immature boys."

"God, you don't see me as her potential suitor, do you?"

"You could do worse, a fortune and beauty and a noble house, a good match!"

His friend looked horrified. "Married into a rebel household and my neck in danger. Besides her tongue is too sharp. If and when I marry, I will want a wife with a softer tongue to comfort me, not dominate me."

"You would be bored in five minutes."

"Stop matchmaking, she is more suited to you. You both enjoy sparring and intrigue. You knock sparks off each other. I haven't seen you so interested in a woman in years. She is not one of your sophisticated paramours who bore you in a month. This one is flesh and blood, too much red meat for me but would suit you. You would enjoy the chase and the capture.''

They watched the prey, relaxed for once with a trusted friend. ''I have no desire to wed but I must solve this puzzle. One more dance with her and if she doesn't cooperate I will interview her formally.''

''You may regret taking formal action. You said we should go slowly.''

He sighed. ''Sometimes the interest of the state must take priority over the interests of the individual. The rebels are rising again. I received a message that we may soon have another attack on the city. She may have to cooperate faster than she would wish.''

He made his appearance at her side and they danced again. She had withdrawn into herself and he decided to confront her. ''We have heard that the rebels are going to rise again. That is why so many people are under suspicion and why your father must come back and cooperate. I am warning you now that unless you cooperate with me tonight I must ask you to come for a formal interview tomorrow.'' She now looked alarmed. A formal interview meant an Attendance Certificate was issued and then she could not leave the state. She must try to avoid this at all costs, so she could leave when she needed.

''What information do you need?''

''Any places your father visits regularly on his travels and the houses and inns he stays at. I mean all of them, not a few designed to put me off my track,'' he warned. ''I am used to subterfuge. Don't try to trick me. I need a list on my desk by nine o'clock Friday morning.

'Next, I want his files going back five years and the keys to his university study.

'Finally, I want your research and files going back five years and a list of friends and places you have visited during that period. That includes any suitors and lovers you have had contact with who could be insurgents.''

Aghast at this invasion of her privacy she felt like telling him to disappear. ''The last are not necessary. The only suitors were before my mother died, two years ago, except for that weasel you met earlier. I have had no lovers. My life is quiet.''

''Friday morning then.''

''Now let us enjoy this dance in peace without wrangling for once.'' He became a charming sophisticated companion, a natural athlete who enjoyed dancing with a lithe, elegant woman.

A slow waltz was played, and he held her in his arms and guided her through the dance with assurance. He directed the conversation into easier channels; art and literature and she was surprised how well read he was and that he could speak several languages fluently. He had had good tutors before he entered the army.

She in turn could analyse a book or artwork easily and had visited many exhibitions and musicians with her father on his travels. They were well matched in mind despite their differences in sex and age and background. When they stopped, they smiled at each other for a change and he bowed and kissed her hand.

''Until Friday,'' he said and went back to his friend.

''Well?''

''She appeared to acquiesce but time will tell.''

They continued to talk about a horse race forgetting matters of state for a while. Felea did not enjoy the rest of the wedding celebrations. She made a beautiful bridesmaid and received more compliments from Denman and Dreda who were there, but the cloud of potential arrest still hung over her and she knew Dreda hadn't finished with her yet. After the wedding, she went back to prepare a list of people who she knew were loyal to the state and could not get into trouble and a list of houses her family had visited.

CHAPTER THREE

Dreda was dismayed. He had arranged to meet Lady Felea on the Friday but the message he had just been brought by messenger confirmed his worst fears. Not only had she passed on messages but she had had given monies to the rebels. She would have difficulty in evading the noose if she couldn't prove her innocence to him.

He summoned her again. She stood in front of his desk and with one brief hand motion he signalled her to sit down. He read some papers very slowly and signed them with his careful signature without even looking up at her. It was a sure and proven way to intimidate and unnerve his suspects. He noticed she sat quite still, not wriggling like former suspects, determined to appear at ease; although he detected a slight tremble in one gloved hand in which she tightly gripped her reticule.

A veil covered her delicate features hiding her expressive eyes from his scrutiny.

"Good morning Lady Felea," he said at last putting his papers down. "Perhaps you would do me the kindness of raising your veil. I like to know what my interviewees are thinking, and you have such an expressive face!"

Her eyes darted upwards, challenging him for a moment, giving him stare for stare but then after lifting her veil she dropped them down, as if passively regarding her skirts, pretending innocence; the picture of a demure damsel, a milk and water miss. He smiled, remembering the images of her in her house and at the ball, her eyes sparking fire at him. She had clearly changed her strategy, thinking honey on her tongue would gain her more from him than waspish barbs.

This was no passive maid obedient to a man's will. She was fire and ice. The man who could melt that surface ice would discover a fiery passion underneath and use that passion to sate himself. She would be as exciting in bed as in his arms when he had danced with her.

This was clearly going to be a war of wills and wit, a challenge he relished, and he would take up and win. Rarely did he find he had to pit his wits against such an intellect. Tied up in such a pretty parcel too!

Felea kept her eyes down, trying not to let him read her face. He was right. Her mother had said she showed her feelings too much to the outside world and she had learned to develop an icy reserve, to remain impassive and to guard her unruly tongue in the presence of potential enemies. Lucia said everyone was to be treated as a potential enemy until she was sure of them, particularly when her father was up to his tricks. An informer could put them in prison with several malicious words.

He came around his desk and stood in front of her, bent his head and lifted her chin in his hand. "Look up at me Ma'am!" His voice was soft, but the words were a command to be obeyed. One ignored this man at one's peril. She stood up to look up at him; green gold eyes meeting blue grey eyes, speaking volumes. No longer was she the demure, impassive girl; her look challenged him to ask what he will.

"That is better Lady Felea," he mocked. "That prim and prissy look does not become you!" He watched her beautiful eyes widen and spit fire at him. By Christ! He enjoyed baiting this girl. She rose to the bait so delightfully. Mature for her age, she seemed calm with others, but he knew which buttons to press; to anger her, to ignite her fire.

He was shocked by his own reaction to her; his need to challenge and tease her; make her discard her icy mantle and show him the passionate creature underneath. There were girls even more beautiful than this one, but there was something special about this slim young thing that made him want to divine the mystery that was Lady Felea. Felea kept her eyes down, trying not to let him read her face. He was right. Her mother had said she showed her feelings too much to the outside world and she had learned to develop an icy reserve, to remain impassive and to guard her unruly tongue in the presence of potential enemies. Lucia said everyone was to be treated as a potential enemy until she was sure of them, particularly when her father was up to his tricks. An informer could put them in prison with several malicious words.

He came around his desk and stood in front of her, bent his head and lifted her chin in his hand. "Look up at me Ma'am!" His voice was soft, but the words were a command to be obeyed. One ignored this man at one's peril. She stood up to look up at him; green gold eyes meeting blue grey eyes, speaking volumes. No longer was she the demure, impassive girl; her look challenged him to ask what he will.

"That is better Lady Felea," he mocked. "That prim and prissy look does not become you!" He watched her beautiful eyes widen and spit fire at him. By Christ! He enjoyed baiting this girl. She rose to the bait so delightfully. Mature for her age, she seemed calm with others, but he knew which buttons to press; to anger her, to ignite her fire.

He was shocked by his own reaction to her; his need to challenge and tease her; make her discard her icy mantle and show him the passionate creature underneath. There were girls even more beautiful than this one, but there was something special about this slim young thing that made him want to divine the mystery that was Lady Felea.

Felea now regarded him cautiously. The odious man enjoyed provoking her, baiting her. Her demure expression had been a façade designed to win him over. He had understood her strategy and defeated it. Other men she could brush off with a frosty stare but not this one. Blue eyes had mocked her! Had dared her to meet his stare. She had resisted but only for a moment as his eyes had drawn hers to his own.

With his mockery, he angered her and melted the icy reserve she worked so hard to preserve. This man was dangerous! He might pretend fine manners, but he was no gentleman. Under his fine uniform and refined manners and accent was a primeval man, a predator; a hunter who focused on his victim, who netted it and wouldn't let it go. All at once she felt the room grow smaller as he dominated it with his presence, his iron will. In his lair, she felt trapped, suffocated suddenly and unsafe, at his mercy. Sweet Jesus, would this man ever let her return to her once peaceful life?

Intense blue eyes speared her, as if he was trying to read her, to comprehend her thoughts. She retained his stare but closed her mind to him, focusing on other things, blanking him out as she had trained herself to do. He saw her eyes glaze over. What was the little witch up to? He had won the first battle of wills with her, but she was detaching herself mentally from him now. He must maintain his control. He could not let a young chit win this psychological battle. The stakes were too high for the state and for her.

She regarded him, trying to decide what kind of man he was. Only by divining his true nature and his way of thinking would she survive this interview. She now feared for her life and must manipulate him; Dreda, the ruthless officer, spy and master manipulator of men. She divined deep into her personal reserves, trying to second guess what he else he knew.

"Please sit down but look at me Ma'am." She sat down and waited for the interrogation to start, for an interview it was not. It was an interrogation and she felt sick inside. Damn her father for putting her in this invidious position! He had tied her up in knots.

Dreda threw some missives on the desk. "Please look at those and tell me if you wrote them," he asked softly but she could not miss the menace in his voice. Trying to control the slight tremble in her fingers she opened the beribboned packages and read them one by one. It was no use denying she was the author. The handwriting was the same in all the letters and one of them had been signed by her.

She nodded. "Yes, I am the author!"

"I am pleased you do not deny your authorship. It will make my job and your position much easier," he said coming around and sitting on the desk in front of her, relaxing a little at last.

She was wound up so tight she could burst. Blast the man; he was enjoying dragging this out, tormenting her. She now knew what evidence was facing her. Those letters could be misconstrued, read in several ways. It was for her to convince him she was not a traitor.

She had heard he could be a fair man and would negotiate rather than execute a person if they cooperated. Many spies were forced to act as double agents for him. She suspected that might be what he wanted of her; to work for him and betray the rebels who had trusted her father. She waited for him to speak.

He played with a pair of manacles in his hands for a moment before he spoke. He was the sort of man who weighed up his every thought before he uttered a word. He took one letter and read the salient points out. "I donate two hundred sovereigns for this useful cause. Please send to me details of how the money was spent and if you need more." He paused and lifted another. "Three hundred sovereigns will be delivered to you at your headquarters in Vina. Please ensure it reaches the right people."

"Please will you explain these letters Ma'am and the truth; not some manufactured lies to try to hoodwink me? First, to whom were they written?"

Defiant, she replied, "I am sure you know who they were delivered to Officer Dreda or you wouldn't have them here."

"For the sake of your own health Ma'am, please elaborate," he replied, not giving her any quarter.

She expected none. He was renowned for his ruthless interrogations. She had not heard of any women being tortured but the same could not be said for his male suspects. He was tapping his fingers on his desk now, his impatience showing. "Now Ma'am," he ordered.

"The letters were sent to three places. The rebel military headquarters in Vina. The Cathedral in Rivia and the hospital in Oranche. I supplied the monies for grain, blankets and livestock to the wives and children of the rebel men who were killed or taken prisoner by Imperial troops. They were starving and freezing in the wintry rains. The livestock provided milk and there were also chickens for eggs."

"Did you visit these camps yourself?"

"No Officer Dreda. I relied on others to make sure the goods went to the correct places."

"You were misled. The monies went to supply arms for the rebels instead. What say you to that, Ma'am?" His keen glance shredded her, making her want to tell him the truth. He looked angry as if he despised her but for what? Her alleged traitorous activity or her naivety. She had trusted a friend of the rebels to do her will. He had clearly betrayed her, uncaring as to what might befall her if his actions were found out.

Dreda willed her to tell him the truth. He could usually read the characters of suspects accurately. This girl was not a natural liar. She was brave, trying to hide her fear but he could nearly feel the terror now encompassing her. Her throat had tightened. Her voice rasped as she tried to explain herself.

"I know not of any of this. I was only trying to help the vulnerable having heard of fever and malnutrition and starvation among the families. I am not a traitor Officer Dreda." The look he gave her mixed cynicism and scepticism and disappointment. He felt sickened. She was either a bald-faced liar or naïve beyond belief.

It had been the devil's own work finding information about this girl. His sources told him she rarely went into society, cloistered and closeted with a father and some servants. Perhaps, she was naïve and had trusted a blackguard who had betrayed her good offices. He would find out quickly. He knew who had received the monies and had passed them on to the rebels. He had waited to interview her before interrogating the fellow but that would happen later that day. He would soon know the true character of this wilful girl.

"The name of the man you trusted, Ma'am."

She hesitated, not wanting to condemn even a man who might have betrayed her until she knew the absolute truth. Suddenly, angry at last with her, Dreda grasped her cruelly with a slim but powerful hand. "You will tell me the absolute truth Ma'am, if you value your lovely neck!"

God how I hate him, thought Felea. She hated his cynicism with every bone in her body. He thought the worse of human kind, a natural cynic, who saw evil in everyone and denied the good in anyone. He enjoyed being proven right, so mistrustful of human nature was he. His spies were everywhere, waiting to trip up the unwary, filling the cells of the prison; many men never leaving that hateful place unless it was in an undertaker's cart.

Information given by informers sent whole families to that prison and only the intervention of the priests or powerful friends could get them out after appealing to the Emperor. The Emperor ruled this state with a rod of iron and Dreda imposed an undercurrent of fear with draconian deterrents and a network of spies that could dig out the dirt on anyone who dared to challenge the Emperor's rules. He was a man without mercy, uncaring of how his goals were achieved provided he was successful.

If I am going to go to the gallows I am going to go out with a fight, she thought, shaking his hand off her and staring haughtily at him.

"What care you for these families providing your objectives are met? They are merely pawns in your games, innocents who you barely give a thought for."

His eyes had narrowed turning a deeper blue, his only sign that he had been affected by her insults. He was not entirely impervious to her words then. Then an impassive expression cloaked his face and he shrugged his shoulders as if to shrug her insults off him.

"Well, now you have vilified me and got your feelings off your chest you will answer my question Ma'am," he snapped, pretending indifference. Her words shouldn't mean anything to a man like him, a man who enforced and almost imposed the law; a man who was de facto second in charge of the state after the Emperor.

In fact, he was lying to himself. For some reason, her analysis of his character had got under his skin. He usually cared not for anyone's opinion of him; unless it was of the Emperor or Denman his true close friend but on this occasion the accusations this girl contemptuously hurled at him had smacked too much of the truth and pricked his conscience.

It was years since anyone had dared to challenge him or worse assassinate his character. By God she had got a nerve! He rarely executed women but it would not be the first time. She was playing a dangerous game. If it had been another man she had insulted her neck could have been on the line.

Damn the man. For a moment, she had thought she had pricked his conscience but then he had stood there silently, sinister, as if her opinion meant nothing; a mere girl and rebel supporter with a traitor for a father. It was no use protecting a man who might have betrayed her.

"I had letters stating the goods had reached their correct destination, but I burnt them." she replied, knowing her words would mean nothing without physical proof.

His eyebrows raised sceptically. The bastard didn't believe her. How could she persuade him she was telling him the truth? It was as she had thought. He didn't want to believe her. He wanted her to be proven guilty for then he would be proven right about her. He hated to be wrong about human nature. It was much easier to think badly about people from the beginning and not be disappointed if a man's nature turned out to be worse than originally expected.

"Michael von Brachman was the man I charged with giving the monies to the representatives of the families," she admitted wearily. He was used to these mental engagements, but the battle of wills had tired her when she had no chance of winning while he had the evidence on his desk.

"I will interrogate the man myself and find out the truth Ma'am." He came up to her. As she stepped back he put his hands either side of her head on the wall; holding her still against it with his body when she tried to release herself.

Mocking her again, he played with an escaping ringlet, curling it around his finger, laughing out loud as she tossed her head away from his touch. He had never seen such unusual hair or eyes, the colours reflecting the sunlight, making her seem almost on fire. He had the sudden desire to see her lying in his arms in his bed, her hair splayed across his pillow.

Shocked by his lust for his suspect he reverted to harshness to cover up his desire for her.

"So, defiant still! You had better learn respect for the Emperor's officers Ma'am if you want to avoid a prison cell, even if you are innocent of paying for the rebels' arms. You could still be imprisoned on a lesser charge. Criminal sedition covers aiding the rebels in any way the court can interpret as against the interests of the state."

"Oh, it is clearly seditious to provide warmth in the bellies of starving children Officer Dreda," she mocked. "Try conspiracy also as I joined others in my actions."

"Don't test my patience Ma'am. You are walking a tightrope and could easily be pushed off! You may go now but stay within the city walls. I will summon you when I need you."

Dismissed, Felea swept out haughtily not allowing him to see how relieved she was. He cursed her fluently when she was out of his presence. When would this girl realize the danger she was in, pushing him to the boundaries of his endurance? Patience was one of his few virtues, but this girl tested him to the limits. He could think of no other man or woman he would allow to challenge him or insult him so.

He went across the square to the prison and demanded to see von Brachman. A short walk in the cool air would calm his temper. He almost never lost his temper, remaining cool and detached to the point of iciness but this girl was like no other woman he had ever met before. That mixture of ice and fire threatened to freeze and burn him at once. Naïve but mature at the same time, she was a mixture of contradictions. He believed her after that display of contempt and temper. He hoped for her sake he would not be proven wrong in his belief in her innocence.

Von Brachman was there in his cell, sprawled over the bunk, bleary eyed and sleepy, but when Dreda entered his cell he turned to him roused and wary. Dreda wasted no time getting to the point. "You received these letters," he said throwing them on the man's bunk. "To whom did you give the monies to and what were the monies used for?"

Von Brachman guessed these letters were of some importance to Dreda, more than he had originally realized, to make the great man come to his cell to carry out his interrogation himself instead of sending one of his underlings. Perhaps there were some possibility of negotiation to get himself a shorter sentence.

"Clearly you have met the lady in question Sir and know of her character; her father a supporter, aiding the rebels. I did not have much knowledge of her duplicity when I delivered the letters. Only later did I find out what they contained." He looked carefully at Dreda to see the impact his words had on him.

It was too late; Dreda got him by the throat and held him above the floor allowing the breath to choke out of him. *The Bastard! Blaming the girl for his perfidy when she was merely an innocent, trying to help the vulnerable, while he stole monies from dying children to aid the destruction of others by feeding the rebels with arms.*

He put the little conniving rat down, allowing him to collapse on the floor. "Hot irons!" he demanded of the gaoler. Von Brachman got to his knees pleading. "No, they are not needed. I will tell the truth. I was merely scared for my life and thought a woman would be treated less severely for the same crime."

"Stay yourself a minute!" said Dreda to the gaoler. He had assessed Brachman accurately for what he was, a gutless piece of shit! The young girl had more courage in her little finger than he had in his whole body. Perhaps that is what explained his unusual reaction to the man's betrayal of her.

He had met few women of any class who cared for anything but material objects; clothes, jewels or grand houses, who would trade themselves and betray others to achieve more grandeur and status. Lady Felea was loyal to a fault. She had nearly refused to betray von Brachman even when he might have betrayed her. She looked for the good in people and trusted them unlike him. It was rare to find such natural beauty, intelligence and loyalty in a woman. If she were not so bloody defiant she would be a good prize for any man.

Brachman's betrayal had struck a chord in him and made him react angrily. He rarely showed any feeling nor consideration for the sensibilities or future of his suspects. They were indispensable, merely used to achieve his ends. He wondered idly when he had stopped feeling empathy with others. For the most part, he neither cared nor showed interest in the needs of other people, excepting the few friends he truly trusted, whose number he could count on the fingers of one hand. For Denman, he would trust, risk and give his life. They had survived many a skirmish together and were like brothers. He was the only man he truly cared for; cared for more than his own father or brother who he rarely met and intensely disliked.

He was not a man given to navel gazing or introspection, preferring action but he'd had the trust knocked out of him at an early age and now believed in the evil inherent in man. He had witnessed too much in the army and the militia. He now believed that men or women rarely served anybody but themselves. Their loyalty to the Emperor came at a price.

He had found some men who could not be bought; their own money and power allowing them to remain independent of patronage and bribery. He had recruited them for his militia force, but they were few and far between. Most men could be bought with a large enough bribe and he watched his back continuously in case a bribe could be large enough to buy his assassination. The rebel forces were not his worst enemies. By trying to organize a militia force driven by professionalism and integrity instead of patronage he had made bitter enemies in the Emperor's cabinet and militia.

He brought his mind back to von Brachman. "Talk quickly for you disgust me and I want rid of your presence," he said curtly, his impatience showing as he stepped nearer the door to call the gaoler if he did not get the information he wanted from the accused.

The man nearly blubbered so terrified was he. "Lady Felea trusted me but she is naïve. She thought as her father trusted me I would serve her as fairly. I traded the monies for guns and gave them to the rebels at their headquarters in Vina. I put sawdust in the sacks the wagons took to the other locations. I paid a fellow to forge the letters from the supposed recipients to persuade Lady Felea the goods had reached their true destination."

"She is totally innocent of the conspiracy and the sedition?"

"Absolutely."

"Good," said Dreda knocking the cell door to demand his exit.

"What of me?" demanded von Brachman.

"What of you? He looked at the rats covering the floor and walls

You will keep good company with other vermin for many years my fellow. I hope they are good bed-partners." The gaoler shut the door behind him leaving the man bereft of speech.

Dreda thought of Lady Felea on his walk back to the Bureau. He had assessed her character by now. Intelligent and an intellectual kept away from court, she knew not the ways of the world and her unworldliness had led her into a trap laid by her perfidious steward. He was satisfied Lady Felea had acted without knowledge of the true destination of her monies. She was herself a pawn used by more devious people than herself.

That she had nearly ended up in a prison cell though was her own fault. Stubborn as a mule and fearless, she had made a hard road for herself by defying him when she could have placated him and persuaded him of her loyalty to the Emperor. Her challenges drove him to want to win their arguments and to tame and bend her to his will.

He was surprised, having thought she had a cool head on her shoulders. She was described by others as calm and tranquil, impulsive and passionate at times but difficult to rouse to anger. He seemed to bring out the worst in her, his cold cynicism matched by her passion. It was an interesting combination to an old warhorse like him; he was used to matching wills with men more experienced in battles than her. He wondered what other surprises were in store for him if he argued with her.

He thought he would let her stew a while. She might give more information to him then. It would do her good. Fear of him might install respect for him. She was the most wayward girl he had ever met. Even with von Brachman's confession she could still end up in gaol. Many would want to avenge their father's or brother's death if the person who had supplied money for the arms could be brought to justice.

Felea sat in her carriage and took deep breaths calming herself. She didn't understand her own actions. She had irritated Dreda knowing how dangerous he could be. He brought out the worst in her. He mocked her in those soft tones, his voice seductively tempting her to betray herself. She had wanted to throttle him. Instead, lacking any real power in their relationship she had used her only weapons, words, and had abused him verbally.

When Dreda had held her chin, she had felt the power in the man. A power both physical and emotional. A man whose will would not be thwarted and expected to be obeyed at all times. He was a man who must dominate a woman; always expecting her to passively submit to his will. He would bend her to his will until she lacked any emotional strength. Brittle, she would eventually break, like his prisoners in his cells who dared to challenge him. Under that handsome exterior was a callous, severe, insensitive man who cared not for another's feelings. He was a monster in human disguise. She cursed him richly and fluently. He would have been shocked to hear the curses she had learned from the stable lads and used only in private.

It was a shame he was so handsome. Even at his most sinister he still looked like a Greek god, blond and tanned; a man who despite his office job found time for outdoor activities and remained fit and strong. She had been held tight against the wall; his chest hard muscled like steel, pushing her back, dominating her physically.

Hard slate blue eyes had dominated her, imposing his will on her, taking all her strength to resist him when he questioned her about the letters. She had only given in because von Brachman must have betrayed her and telling the truth was her only way of ensuring her neck wasn't wrung. Translating codes and supplying arms for the rebels were enough crimes to ensure the death penalty even for a woman.

Despite her innate dislike of him she could not deny the certain charisma he carried with him. Enigmatic and quiet, he was a mysterious man who attracted women easily, his smoothness advertising his experience with women. She suspected any woman he took as a lover would enjoy intimacy with him. He smacked of confidence with women.

She shook herself, chiding herself. She did not want to react to the sensuality emanating from this man. Her skin prickled where he'd touched her, as if his gaze had sparked her flesh to life, his inherent masculinity drawing her to him. Her body had reacted involuntarily to a handsome and powerful man; her heart beat rising uncontrollably, the powerful fingers curling her ringlet tracing her skin and tantalizing her senses.

She tried to deny it but there was a chemistry existing between them lying dormant, waiting to be set alight. Her body recognized it as did his. It would only take one spark to ignite the fire that raged within them, waiting to consume them, an attraction they both mentally recognized and were fighting fiercely.

She had been courted for a few months before her mother's death by friends and allies of her family; pleasant, safe courteous men. Not like dangerous, manipulative Dreda, the predator and user of women. She had never felt the naked attraction to those men that she now felt for Dreda. It almost frightened her in its intensity. She had thought she was a cold dispassionate creature, unanimated by the touch of men, but Dreda's touch had impassioned her, forced her to re-evaluate her own character and sexuality. She knew now she was as sexual a creature as any other woman when faced with such a desirable man.

As enemies on competing sides of the civil war they could not meet in the middle. Culture and family forced them apart. She wished her father could come back and take her away from the ambit of this intimidating man. She wished Dreda to Hades; she must guard herself from him.

She was on tenterhooks for forty-eight hours waiting for Dreda's message, waiting to find out whether she would be arrested and put on trial. She feared von Brachman might implicate her in the provision of arms to the rebels to save his own neck. She had never liked him, but he had insinuated himself into her father's good graces. Her father had told her to trust him, but his sneaky beady eyes had always watched her too closely. He had listened more intently to her conversations with her father than a steward should.

A knock came on the door and she waited while Lucia answered it. It was Dreda yet again on her doorstep, inviting himself in. Lucia gave a sniff and let him in, taking his hat and cloak from him, giving him a telling look, which showed he was not welcome in this house of secrets.

"Officer Dreda," said Felea curtseying, holding out her hand for him to shake. He took it and kissed it, noting her eyes widen and her attempt to retain her composure. He was not sure if it was his kiss that made her hand tremble slightly or her natural apprehension and fear she might be arrested. Her strong personality belied a fragility; she was like a delicate exotic butterfly, its wings vibrant and shimmering in the sunlight. She was so slight he could break her bones with one swift hand.

"I cannot stay but I have some good news for you." Her face had lost its colour when he had arrived at the door. No longer wan; in answer to his words a blush returned to her cheeks. Her eyes sparkled emerald green, flecked with gold, ringed by impossibly long dark lashes. She looked alive again; no longer consumed by worry.

"Von Brachman?" she asked. "He exonerated me?"

"With a little persuasion. He was going to save his own neck and sell you down the river like the gutless creature he is I am afraid. You are a bad judge of character Ma'am."

"I did not like the man. My father insisted I used him for our purposes, Officer." She had no desire to hear what persuasion he had used to make Brachman confess. She had heard from a prison visitor Brachman had no visible marks on him, so she hoped the threat of torture was enough.

"Well you are a free woman. No charges will be brought against you this time but when you come to the Bureau with your files you will be given a formal reprimand which will be on your records for five years. If you are arrested and convicted of any other charge in that time your reprimand will be turned into a formal action and progressed in the courts. Do you understand? You must be on your best behaviour. No helping rebel orphans or the like.''

"Yes, Officer Dreda. I must thank you for your help. I am deeply grateful for your intervention.''

He smiled, mocking her again. "I thought I was an uncaring insensitive cur who used innocents as pawns to achieve my aims.''

Trust him to throw her words back at her, to rub her hasty insults in her face! She bit back a retort. "You are indeed ruthless, but you serve justice and have treated me fairly this time.''

"I'll take that as a compliment Lady Felea. It is unlikely I will get another one in a long while,'' he said wryly. "If I were you I would avoid helping the rebel families in any form or fashion. Keep your head down. There may be others who want your head on a platter if they think you have helped the rebels in any way. I may not be able to protect you another time.''

He said his adieus and went swiftly back to the Bureau. He had had no need to deliver the information personally. He told himself he wanted to see her again to reassure her she was safe and encourage her to cooperate with him regarding the matter of her father and his disappearance.

Unexpectedly, she arrived on Thursday morning at Dreda's office. He was deep in thought, reading some files made on her father and barely heard her come in. Looking up, he could not help smiling as she struggled in with some heavy files. She was too independent for her own good, refusing help from his clerk who had opened the door and stood outside.

He took them from her and asked her to sit down. "You are a day early.''

"These are only part of what I can find. I need more time.''

"How much time do you need?''

"A week, if you please. If you start reading these, you will see your suspicions are unjustified, but I will supply all the data you need under any circumstances.''

"You can have until Monday.'' He knew she was buying time and it meant she had something up her sleeve. She saw he was reading a file about herself and felt sick. He knew all her personal details. There was also an Investigation Certificate and an Attendance Certificate on his desk with her name on them waiting for his signature.

She nodded and went out. He rested back in his chair, hands folded behind his head, puzzled. It was not like her to acquiesce so easily.

'What was she up to?'' He called Denman in.

"Denman, I want the girl followed, discreetly. Give her description to the officers at the city gates in case she bolts."

Monday arrived but not more files nor Lady Felea. Her house had been searched but no-one knew where she was. Her old servant was more surprised than they were. She had vanished in the middle of the night taking one male servant with her.

Dreda was furious as she had not been intercepted at the city gates. Now she was in danger. He had to issue a warrant for her arrest. His blood ran cold at the thought of the rough treatment she could suffer at the hands of some of his other colleagues who would not be as respectful to an alleged traitress.

"Read these Sir, I am afraid she is implicated in other activities." Dreda read the papers cursorily and then swore. "The little fool! Financing the education of rebels with her own money!"

"She may have taught them herself, Sir," said Denman. "Some urchins off the streets were taken to the convent where we found she teaches. Our men suspect the children were the daughters of rebels who have slipped through the net and did not end up in the camps we created for them."

"This young woman has more nerve than we thought and the organizational skills of a drill sergeant," said Dreda grimly. "I wish she were on our side! Sadly, she is making a noose for her own neck."

Denman watched him pace his office, thinking out his next steps. Then Dreda ordered, "Clear the university offices and the house of any files and papers and sift through them for clues to their whereabouts. Put a rumour out that she is under arrest and the father may come back.

"I want my horse saddled and bags packed with provisions for a long journey. Get Thomatz and he can track her." Thomatz had been a professional army tracker who now worked with them. If anybody could track her he could.

'Damn the girl! Escaping when an uprising is possible any day."

Denman was about to suggest someone else could go but bit his words back. Dreda was not in the mood for arguments. He clearly felt this girl's fate was his personal responsibility. He had read more of the file and realized that her mother was not a witch but was telepathic and her daughter could have the same powers. She could be useful to the enemy.

Dreda cursed her naivety and obduracy and he could willingly wring her neck but he didn't trust his men with her, a known fugitive and decided to bring her back himself. Why he chose to take on this role he would not admit to himself, but he sighed and prepared himself to recapture this delightful but wilful girl.

With Thomatz's help he would have her back in the Bureau within a week and then he would have a reckoning with the lovely Lady Felea. She had foxed him, and it had hurt his ego. Her father had clearly neglected to teach her respect for her elders and gentlemen. It was about time she learnt some discipline and he was the man to teach her. Her beauty and wit would not save her this time from his clutches.

Felea had not used the city gates to leave the city but instead a tunnel leading from a friend's house. She had been followed but she had given her pursuers the slip in the tiny alleyways of the milliners' district. She had found some files her father had hidden. He had not given haven to the escapees but had found them safe hiding places. He had regularly coded messages and translated documents and had spied for the rebels. She had found letters involving him in the latest rebellion and a plot to blow up the Emperor's carriage. Enough ammunition for Officer Dreda to have his neck wrung.

She didn't want him to come back, so she had left knowing that she was now in immediate danger, a suspect. She was certain Dreda would send his troops to find her. She feared him more than any of the other officers as he had guile and could think like a spy. What he wanted he would get.

She travelled through the hills towards the next city state whose leaders were enemies of the Emperor. The authorities there would give her sanctuary if she could not stay with her friend. She rode astride on horseback, dressed in a boy's clothes, hair pushed under a hat, with only a groom to accompany her.

They slept in underground caves and tunnels. She was brown as a berry instead of pale white and they only had two more days to go. Perhaps fortune was on her side and she could reach there safely and send a message to her father to join her. She kept getting flashes which rocked her and made her struggle to sit safely on her horse. Someone was near and following them. She had to move quickly to evade capture.

There was a safe hiding place nearby few people knew about, a waterfall hidden by lush creepers with a cave hidden behind it. If Lady Fortune was with her the soldiers would not know about this place and they could rest their horses and eat until it was dark and then start the hardest part of the journey to the summit of the mountain. Over the top, it was an easy walk and ride to the track which led to the next city.

She pushed on now, her horse sometimes slipping but saving her from falls on the slippery track which was more suitable for mountain goats than humans or horses. Sensing her agitation, he snickered and rubbed his head against her.

"Hang on boy!" she said, trying to calm him. "We are nearly there! Soon we will be safe!" Animals were loyal she had come to believe but people were often turncoats, willing to twist information to please the Emperor's men.

He had been a good friend when some families, supposedly friends, had rejected her family; after her mother had been accused of being a witch.

A rumour about her mother's powers of sorcery had spread through the court circle. Felea's circle of friends had grown smaller, only three or four remaining loyal to her. Rarely had she been invited to parties then. Cold looks and malicious whispers followed her when she left a room. She was rejected by most girls and increasingly isolated, lonely and scared of what might happen to her mother who was reluctant to go to any court soirees or balls.

She remembered playing with friends at a thirteenth birthday party when four girls had cornered her. One blond girl had caught her by the arm and tugged her into the middle of their circle. She had demanded, "What's your friend's name, your familiar?" as she pretended to stroke the imaginary cat that she purported to be sitting on Felea's shoulder.

Felea had pulled away and tried to push herself out of the circle but the girls had held her tight and barred her exit. Another girl grabbed her by her fine wavy hair and pulled hard. Felea flinched but would not give these girls the satisfaction of knowing the tears smarted in her eyes. It felt as if the cruel grasping fingers were pulling the hairs out of her head.

"My Grandmother said that in the last century your mother would have been burnt at the stake. She has been seen recanting spells. She even looks like a witch with that hair and those evil burning eyes!"

Felea had been incensed. Her gentle mother had the same distinctive looks as she; those smouldering eyes; their fiery hair and luminous skin that set them apart from normal women. These women and girls were merely jealous of her family's beauty. "My mother is not a witch and you are hateful and jealous of her beauty and her grace," replied Felea with as much dignity as she could muster while the girl had hold of her by the hair, tugging her head back until she felt her neck would break.

"Soon she will be executed. The militia are collecting evidence about your family," spat another girl." Her mother witnessing this from the doorway came in and the girls fled. Later that night her parents had decided the court was too dangerous for their family and had reluctantly withdrawn from court life.

Formerly an open warm friendly girl, Felea had withdrawn inside herself, only forsaking her newly developed reserve with the few friends who had stayed loyal. Her father had recently been persuaded that she must meet more people if she was to make a successful match in the future. He had reluctantly entertained and opened his house up more frequently to his friends and those families he considered loyal but had still over-protected Felea.

She had buried herself in her books and code breaking, her intellect challenged but she yearned for more contact with the outside world. Naturally gregarious she felt starved of human company. Her father, usually buried in his study, rarely came out to see her more than once a day. She lacked female company, Lucia being her only female confidante. She felt cocooned and caged, the stories about the characters in her books a poor substitute for adventures with real life people.

Frequently bored, her sharp mind had needed an outlet. Her mother had talked of votes for women and universal suffrage. Equal access to education for women was a pipe dream for most women but her mother had been a most exceptional and unconventional woman. She had used her money to found a small school for women at the convent. There, she had taught girls the Sisters had picked off the streets before the pimps could find them and recruit them for their brothels.

Felea had followed in her footsteps but went further. She had encountered women who had been chastised physically by their husbands. She encouraged the girls to learn mathematics and book-keeping and practical skills which would make them independent of their spouses if they wanted to leave them and earn their own living. Cooking and cleaning were no longer the only ways the women could earn their daily crust.

She had tried to hide her activities from 'polite society'. She was regarded as revolutionary and rebellious by the few matrons who knew of her activities; a bad influence on women in the lower classes, making them think they could ape their betters and rise higher than their stations. She cared not. Her lovely mother had taught her to think independently and made her father promise on her deathbed he would not force her daughter to make a marriage of convenience.

Within certain boundaries she could choose her own husband or choose to remain single while her father was alive. Within her small circle of intellectuals her views were considered reasonable but outside that narrow circle she would be regarded as dangerous and too liberal; a woman who needed a husband who would master her and bring her to heel.

Felea thought these attitudes primitive and had no desire to marry if a husband was there to admonish her, to tame her and make her behave like most other women. She had not found any men worth giving her independence up for and thought she might remain a spinster.

She had not told Dreda about all her connections with the rebels. She had turned a blind eye when she had found some of the children picked off the streets were the children of rebels whose fathers had died. Their impoverished mothers had been forced to farm their children out as apprentices to harsh tradesmen. They had escaped a life of hardship, preferring to live on the streets than be at the mercy of their harsh employers, suffering beatings and starvation for up to seven years.

Felea had found tutors who would teach a child irrespective of her background and had leased a small building under another name and encouraged children in desperate need to attend and gain a rudimentary education. Only a few people knew her connection. The Emperor had forbidden anyone to help the rebels or their families in any way on pain of death.

His grip on power slipping, the militia were filling the courts with people who had aided a rebel family. Executions of families were becoming more frequent although clemency was given to those who informed on the rebels. Citizens were becoming more careful about who they could trust, mistrusting their neighbours or friends as the atmosphere in the state was becoming more suffocating under this increasingly oppressive regime.

Felea knew that if the authorities found out her school was aiding rebels and her affiliation with it her enemies would bay for her blood. Her father would not be able to protect her as he had once in the past when she had battled with a master. She had refused to allow him to take back his apprentices who had escaped his workplace and had been picked up off the streets ill, half-starved and with broken bones. She must now escape to safety before her activities were uncovered.

CHAPTER FOUR

They rode on for leagues up the mountainside, the track getting steeper and stonier. Eventually, she had to get off and lead her horse. She felt giddy as an image of a blond man in uniform solidified in her head. He was pointing up the mountain giving orders to other soldiers to follow her. She felt his presence as if he was there with her. It must be Dreda and he must be close!

She wondered if Dreda could be trusted to treat her fairly. She was not sure. He had tried to warn her about the consequences of her father's actions as if he didn't want her to be harmed and had intervened and bullied Brachman into making a confession clearing her of her alleged crime. He had personally brought her the news that she was innocent to reassure her. He was a peculiar man, sardonic and reserved like herself, mistrusting people but he was fair and merciful to her.

She shivered thinking about him, the way he had intimated her neck was at risk due to her father's alleged betrayal of the Emperor. His position in the Security Bureau must make a man suspicious of others but there was more; an innate dislike of humanity and belief in the evil of man. She feared he would have no hesitation in throwing her to the wolves if he believed she had betrayed her country.

His words at the ball hinted he was a misogynist, believing women were untrustworthy, useful for one purpose; slaking his lust. Yet she admitted to herself, that when he had smiled at the ball she had seen another man under that severe demeanour. There was a cultured, sophisticated man hiding under that impassive inhuman façade who had charmed her when he talked of topics other than her spying. She wondered what had made him so distant and cold and so mistrustful of his fellow man and especially of women.

Dreda wanted to catch her himself and ensure she returned safely without being molested by one of his less savoury officers. Thomatz had found her tracks and Dreda's troop of men were steadily catching her up but she was wily and knew places to hide and paths to take which were unknown only to a few and they lost some time going back over tracks. Dreda was beginning to admire her tenacity. She was a worthy opponent testing his investigative skills.

A group of officers accompanied him, scouting these hills as they were too big for his party. They were led by Hemani, another ex-army officer but of a different kidney from that of himself. Hemani was a womanizer, a cheat at cards and unscrupulous but he was a good fighter and was rising steadily up the militia ranks. Dreda thought he could help find the girl but then he Dreda would take over after that making sure she reached the militia headquarters in safety.

Thomatz paused. "She was here about three hours ago, look at that crushed leaf and branch, they are still damp." The track ran above a waterfall and divided into two parts, both into deep, steep glens. They divided into two parties, Hemani taking the left and Dreda the right.

Dreda followed the path down the glen leading the horse and slipping on wet moss. This girl was tough to climb this terrain. He reached the bottom and heard a cry. It was from the other direction. Hemani must have taken the correct track.

"Take my horse," he cried to his men and climbed up the glen at fast as the slippery bushes would allow.

Hemani had climbed down the cliff and was at the entrance to the waterfall. He pushed through the creepers and there were two boys hiding in the cave. He pulled them to the front of the cave and daylight and saw to his pleasure one of the boys was in fact a girl, dirty but very much a girl. He would enjoy taking this one capture. He bound their wrists while his men guarded the entrance and found their horses.

Dreda reaching the men was pleased to see the fugitives. Hemani put them on their horses and they were guided down the track to a village where there was a fort. He directed them to two cells with barred windows and locked them in.

Dreda reached the fort as quickly as he could and was relieved to see the prisoners were subdued but unharmed. A few hours in solitary might make Lady Felea more cooperative. He would have the devil's own work saving her neck after this even if she wasn't a traitor and so far, it looked as if she could be.

He heard a racket later whilst eating. He opened the cell door and found to his disgust Hemani trying to lie on top of the girl. Her shirt was torn, and she was resisting him forcefully, trying to scratch his eyes out but was no match for his strength. He held her down and was kissing her neck and moving downwards toward the v of her breasts. Dreda could not stand men who bullied women and a red mist descended over his eyes. He wrenched the officer off her and threw him so hard he hit the wall.

"Why are you interfering? I found her first. She is a traitor's whelp after all."

"Get out before I kill you."

"You want her yourself!"

"So, what if I do? She has caused me enough trouble. Get out!"

"You!" he snapped at the girl. "Tidy yourself!" and he gave her a clasp to mend her torn shirt.

"Follow me!" He turned on his heel and marched to the officers' rooms. She followed, still bound and not knowing what her fate was to be. To be captured so close to safety. This man must have the luck of the devil. Why must he pursue her when there were so many worse criminals and traitors to capture?

He opened his room and pushed her in. "You will be with me until we have rested. It is the only way I can ensure your safety. Some of my men are very rough." He undid her hands, but she flinched away from him when he sat next to her on the bed. She clearly expected him to try to violate her.

"I can assure you that if I take a woman to bed she will be willing and clean, not covered with moss and as dirty and brown as a stable lad."

"Thank you for rescuing me."

"It is a pleasure. I just wish you could keep out of trouble!" He went out slamming the door. Soon he returned with clean clothes, food and water.

"I will give you an hour and then you will answer my questions!" She realized that having been saved by him once he might be the best person to save her now and awaited the interview with caution but no fear.

He came back and sat on the bed and pushed her chin up until she made full eye contact with him.

"You did not leave because you feared my interview. You found something amongst your father's papers, didn't you? Now is not the time for dissembling if you want to save your life. Use your head!" She said nothing. He had underestimated the loyalty a daughter had to a father who had been the lone parent and brought her up.

"We have news that your father is now in the boundaries of the state and will be in a 'safe house,' tomorrow. My officers intend to arrest him and his colleagues." Her eyes widened in fear.

"You would be better to tell me everything you know instead of leaving it to me to try to get it out of him by worse methods." Torture was in widespread use by the militia and she now knew they would not hesitate to use it on her father.

Angered by her silence, he shook her shoulders until her teeth rattled. "I am trying to save your life. Your father's is forfeit already!" He left the room slamming the door in exasperation. He had told the truth.

He had sent Hemani back. Denman was in charge of arresting the old man and could be trusted implicitly. He himself would take the girl back and let her father talk to her. He might talk if his daughter was under arrest. He regretted the whole sorry episode. What a waste of a life if she was executed. The old man knew what he was getting to, but she clearly was not aware of the whole situation.

He came back. "You take the bed and I will have the chair." He threw some blankets at her. "You will need these. These quarters are cold at night."

"Thank you, I assure you this room is no worse than the caves I have slept in recently."

"I will take you back tomorrow and then we will try to find your father."

He looked at her sitting on the bed fully clothed, her arms crossed defensively across her breasts. "I will turn my back if you want to get undressed." Then rather curtly he reassured her; "I promise I will not look!"

He turned his back and when he was permitted to look at her again she had put on a big nightshirt he had borrowed for her and which to his amusement dwarfed her, covering her fully. She no longer looked as tempting as she had before. Her very damp fine shirt and breeches had outlined and clung to her slim but shapely form, leaving little to his very vivid imagination.

He cursed himself for getting involved with her predicament. This damn girl was not what he needed in his life. He wanted her back home and out of his way as quickly as possible. Women like her were trouble; they embroiled men in their escapades and before they knew it the men were entangled in relationships they could not escape from. He wanted no part of any permanent relationship with a woman. His own lifestyle suited him just fine.

She jumped into the bed and pulled the covers up over her as far as was possible. She had seen the looks he had given her whilst she was dressed in her shirt and breeches when he thought she was not looking. He had scrutinized her from her head to her toes, mentally undressing her, making her shiver under his intense gaze. He had surprised her, behaving the gentleman whilst she was undressing.

His eyes had turned from a hard-blue grey to a deep moody blue and there was something subtle there in his gaze she could not identify. She felt he was trouble; his very nearness upset her equilibrium. He was the sort of man who would love and leave his women, not giving a backward glance to see how they fared. Why need he involve himself in her business? Why could he not leave her alone?

He half slept in the bedroom chair but early in the morning he woke sensing someone was moving around the room. Staying still, he pretended to be asleep but saw out of the corner of his eyes a petite figure dressing in a man's clothes. He saw her go to the window and look out and open the door.

She saw all was clear and came back for her coat and hat and boots. Shrugging her coat on and placing her hat on her head she looked at him in the chair but thought he was asleep and moved across the room to the door again. He moved like lightning crossing the room in one stride, but she moved faster toward his sword which lay on the table and took it up striking at him and forcing him to jump back.

She knew how to use it and pushed him back until he was back to back with the armoire and the sword point was at his throat. She pushed it a little watching the bead of blood at his throat.

''I am sorry Officer Dreda. I appreciate your saving me from that officer, but I must escape and help my father.''

He could kick himself for letting down his guard and for not manacling her to the bedpost. He had underestimated her intelligence and resourcefulness again. He tried to test her by making a movement forward but all he got for his troubles was a sorer, bloodier throat.

''Stay where you are!'' she ordered. He stood as still as a statue, watching her for any mistake she might make that he could take advantage of.

''Undo your holster and place it and your pistol slowly on the ground.'' As he moved slowly she released the sword point an inch allowing him to squat down on his haunches.

''Push it over here,'' she said. ''Get up now, slowly,'' and she allowed him to rise and stand upright her sword still within an inch of his throat. She threw him the manacles.

''Put your hands behind your back and turn to the armoire facing it.''

For an instant, he hesitated, and she said quite deliberately, ''If you try anything reckless I will skewer you. Remember my father's life is at stake.'' He believed her. Her eyes had lost that smouldering, seductive look and were like hard dark pebbles daring him to disobey her. The passionate feisty girl had been replaced by a cold, hard scheming woman who would do anything required to save her father.

Removing the sword point two inches she let him turn toward the armoire. ''Put them on one wrist and then manacle your hands behind you. And do it very quickly, I am becoming impatient and my hand is less steady.'' He heard a slight tremor in her voice; she was nervous, unused to acting in this way but there was nothing he could do to challenge her at that moment. She still had the upper hand. He put the manacles on one hand and started to manacle the other. He thought, *she could get away with this.* She had planned it and was not putting a foot wrong.

"Put your feet farther apart and away from the armoire and lean your face flat against it." He did not move fast enough. A sharp sword point made him lean further in, slightly off-balance.

She was about to tell him to fasten the manacles and she would have picked his holster up when a noise at the window distracted her for an instance. The pane of glass shattered, and she had to duck when some bullets ricocheted around the walls of the room. Dreda also ducking took advantage of her lack of concentration and as her blade was lowered he turned and kicked it out of his way. It was wrenched out of her hands and he caught it moving deliberately toward her. She moved even faster noting some swords on the wall and grabbing one.

As he moved slowly toward her she dived forward trying to fence the sword out of his hand. He laughed, mocking her, saying, "Your luck is running out Ma'am. I have fenced for much longer than you and will soon have the upper hand." He could very easily out-fence this defiant girl. He would enjoy teasing her, giving her this sharp lesson and showing her who was master of this situation.

He easily turned her sword point but she held on and sliced it at his legs cutting the cloth and making him jump back, a trickle of blood running through his breeches. She pushed forward and cut the belt at his breeches just missing cutting the buttons off, leaving him still decent.

"Damn," she cursed, having hoped to denude him.

"You play deviously Ma'am," he commented and "so then shall I."

He dived forward, and his sword point cut through the second from top button on her shirt leaving the top of her breasts bare to his gaze. She gasped and hesitated for a second and then gritting her teeth she pulled her coat closer and moved forward to him again, her rapier coming under his and trying to flick his away.

"I have no choice but to be devious Officer, you have greater strength and a longer reach than I."

His answer was to withdraw his rapier for a second and then to push forward at a faster pace, showing his superior strength. The force of his thrust nearly made her drop her sword. Regaining her balance, she jumped to the side trying to reach the door and then tried to push him back again. His greater strength enabled him to stall her thrust and he pushed forward, and she was forced back against the closed door.

Seeing the determined look in his eyes; that of a predator knowing he had nearly caught his prey, she desperately tried once more to parry his thrusts. He merely said, "I have enjoyed this game very much Ma'am, but it is now time to finish it," and he thrust fiercely, twisting his sword under her blade and her rapier flew out of her hand. Sword-less and flat against the door she could only wait until he walked another pace forward and she faced his sword point at her chest.

He moved the point up to her neck making her lift her chin to look at him directly, eye to eye. He smiled a smile that didn't quite reach his eyes.

"Now Lady Felea, it is my turn to give you instructions," he said in a quiet menacing voice. "Walk to the bed and lie down. My point will be within a hair's breadth of you all the time." Allowing her a little space he watched while she slowly walked to the bed. "Lie down on your front, and put your hands outstretched on the top of the bed-head."

As she did so, he picked up the holster and once she was safely on the bed and prone facing the covers he pulled out the pistol and withdrew the sword. He swiftly followed her and sat beside her on the bed and pointed the pistol to her head. He dropped his manacle off his hand and picked it up and turning her on her back he manacled her right hand to the bed-head and locked it.

She looked up at him appearing passive. Looking closely at her he saw her breasts, easily visible through the half-buttoned shirt, were heaving with emotion and her eyes flashed fire at him. He may have mastered her physically but mentally and emotionally she was still her own mistress. He gently pushed away an errant curl which had strayed across her face and touched her mouth, feathering a finger across her lips.

"You would be wise to acquiesce to my demands Ma'am. Answer my questions and be done with all this. You cannot win this game. It is beyond your control."

He saw another answering flash in her eyes, they daring him to do his worst. He would have loved to have stayed with her and answer the challenge in her eyes; to subdue her and teach her to obey him. He turned away from the temptation and said, "You can sit up now, you can't get away." Another bullet came through the window and he saw a flare and he heard cannon fire and went to the window.

"Good God! The fort was under fire." It was one of the small forts that overlooked the city and was the first one to warn the city of danger by lighting beacons. They were frequently attacked by small groups of rebels and normally dealt with them in hours, but this was different, a more serious and dangerous situation.

He quickly fastened her coat up to her neck. In her opened shirt, her breasts partly showing to the world she would have tempted a saint and he didn't trust his men to leave her alone. He felt her trembling under his fingers as he touched her satin-like skin. He explained, "We are under fire. I will come back for you." He put his boots, his holster and his scabbath on and slipped outside. The rebel uprising had started. What a position to be in!

After an hour of fighting, despite being fierce, ruthless fighters his men were outnumbered fifty to one. He had to surrender to avoid a massacre. If they took the girl she could be saved and taken to sanctuary, so all would not be lost. He must talk to the rebel leader.

Felea lay on the bed with bullets ringing through the window. Cannon fire could be heard and the sound of guns and men getting closer. She had no doubt that Dreda would keep his word if he remained alive. She shivered at the thought of other men finding her in this defenceless position on the bed. No gun at hand, manacled to the bed, she was at the mercy of any man who wanted to violate her.

Damn it, why had he left her in this state? She tried to think positively. If these men blowing up the fort were rebels and they did secure the building she might be safe once she had persuaded them she was on their side. They might give her safe passage to her father.

She heard Dreda giving his orders, moving between his men. The senior officer there, he had immediately taken control. He was a man who had to be in the thick of things, a leader who would not take a back seat when trouble beckoned. Then to her surprise she heard him order, "Put up the white flag. Our men can't take much more of this. I want no more lives squandered." A few minutes later the cannons ceased firing and the rifle shot slowly diminished until it halted.

Dreda came in swiftly and leant over her and undid her manacle. She loosened it and took it off rubbing her wrist. "We have surrendered, and I will ask the rebel leader to guarantee your safety Ma'am." She lifted herself off the bed and asked, "And what of you? What will become of you?" He shrugged. "I am the senior officer here and must take the consequences. In a few minutes, I will be relieved of my command and be like any ordinary soldier who is a prisoner of war."

She knew his situation was much worse than he made out. Second in charge of the State Security Bureau, he was a prize the rebels had been seeking for the last few years. He had a price on his head just like the rebels had. The information he could supply would be worth a king's ransom to the rebel army and they would not hesitate to try to wring it out of him!

She would not like to be in his position, she thought but he carried himself with dignity and the arrogance of his birth; exhibiting indifference toward the rough rebel soldiers who forced open the door and pushed him hard against the wall with their bayonets. As his hands were pushed up the wall and his legs kicked apart she heard his head make contact with the rough surface.

When he was allowed to turn around his head was bleeding, the blood streaming into one eye from a rough graze on his forehead. He raised his head trying to blink the blood away and stood quietly waiting to find out his fate. His face was impassive, a silent mask hiding his feelings. No-one would have known how much danger he was in by his calm resigned demeanour.

Disarmed now, he was allowed to move further into the room. ''I need to speak with your Commander. My name is Officer Dreda. This lady was my captive, but she supports the rebel cause and was trying to escape a cell in the city. I want her safety guaranteed.'' One of the more senior men replied, ''We will talk to our Commander and take you to him soon once the battle is tidied up.''

Felea said, ''This man saved me from being violated by one of his officers. I am grateful to him for that.'' She took her scarf and tied it round his head over a pad made from her handkerchief.

''It would not do for you to die of blood loss or infection Officer. Not after you have chased me so far.'' He bowed. ''Thank you, Ma'am. I am grateful for your kindness. It was a pleasure to help you in your time of need.''

An hour later he was taken to the meeting room where the rebel leader invited him to sit down. He was not dealing with an ordinary rebel. This was the third in command, Michael Gavantz, so this uprising must be for real.

''The girl with you. Who is she?''

''Will you guarantee her safety? She is the daughter of Whelani the Professor who we think aids your cause, but she is largely innocent and was fleeing for her safety. We followed her here.''

''We will take her back to the next state for her protection. What of her father?''

''He should be in the city by now.''

''In a 'safe house.' I know the plan. He was rushing back to save his daughter, so you clearly have set a trap and will catch him tonight.''

Dreda said nothing. He wasn't giving anything else away willingly.

''You have a price on your head. Second in charge of the State Security Bureau.''

''I do my job well!''

''How many rebels have you had slaughtered?''

"I am responsible for the security of my people. I do what I have to do."

The door opened and the Felea was led through. Her eyes widened, and she ran forward and hugged the rebel leader. Dreda was perplexed.

"Have you seen your father recently?"

"No, he left the city and I have not seen him since."

"You two seem very familiar," Dreda commented angrily, feeling he had been duped.

"Michael Gavantz lived in our house for many years while my father taught him at university. He was like a brother to me."

Dreda observed sourly to himself that the look Gavantz was giving her in her tight fitting boyish clothes was far from brotherly. Gavantz placed his arm round her shoulders making Dreda feel even more uncomfortable.

"We were going to study together but then the fuss occurred with her mother and Felea pulled out." He promised Felea, "We will try to save your father if we can get to him in time. We need a map of the tunnels you used."

"And you," he said to Dreda. "You will be locked up and I will talk to you properly later."

"Get rid of him." The men led him out.

Dreda thought fast. Once in the cell he would not have a chance. As he walked past a barrel he kicked it and it rolled in front of his captors. It tripped them over and he launched himself over the parapet and jumped to the terrace below gripping it like death with his fingertips.

The rebel leader leant out the window as he was swinging himself from one terrace to the other and fired. Winged, he lost balance and dropped to the terrace below. He was winded. As he pulled himself up a rebel kicked him in the back and he fell to the pavestones in agony.

They manacled him and dragged him back to the rebel leader. Felea looked at the wound which was bleeding. Gavantz ordered, "Get him water! I don't want him dying before I can interrogate him. Felea help him! You are good with wounds."

Tearing open his shirt, she washed the wound which was only a bad, deep graze and looked worse than it felt. She should have hoped he would die but she felt grateful he had survived. He had tried to help her and had saved her from worse men. Dreda felt less than grateful for any help. He was in a jam and was not looking forward to the interrogation. He wished himself anywhere away from here.

He was left to stew in a cell for hours and then the rebel leader walked in with two of his henchmen. Two hours later they left him bruised and bloody. He had said nothing but was in a very rough shape. The same procedure went on for two days and he held out.

Felea was looked after by Gavantz and renewed her friendship but she heard screams of pain and wondered if it was Dreda. She had nightmares imagining what could be happening and the same to her father. She was talking to Gavantz when a rebel walked in and said, "It is no good, he is too strong and won't give in. We need the rack or something similar."

Gavantz said, "It is too late anyway. We know most of what he could tell us. We needed the rest by yesterday. Kill him!"

Felea could not believe this. He may be her enemy, but he was brave and had helped her. Gavantz was clearly not thinking straight. Lust and jealousy were overriding his common sense. She had seen the vicious way he had looked at Dreda when his captive had scowled at his arm resting around her shoulder. She thought quickly. "Could he not be traded for my father?"

"That could be a good idea. He is worth a lot to the Emperor. Let's talk to him."

She was shocked by what she saw. He was lying on filthy straw in his own blood. His eyes were closed and he had been burnt and had bruises in the shapes of kicks and punches over his body which had had most of his clothes ripped from it. She felt sick.

Gavantz woke him up from the first sleep he had had in two days and his bleary eyes saw the girl looking anxiously at him. He had believed he was going to die so this was totally unexpected and he let his guard down for just a moment. He smiled invitingly at her, no sternness in his expression.

"We were going to kill you but Felea has suggested we trade you for her father. In fact, there are other men on our side who have been captured and have more important information worth trading you for." Dreda was surprised and wondered who was so important it was worth trading him for; he was the second in command of the Bureau! He thanked God they believed he had not been in his position long enough for them to make it worth their while keeping him longer and continuing to torture him.

"That is the best idea you have had so far," he grimaced trying to smile.

"Clean him up and we will make the arrangements."

Despite his half nakedness she helped bathe his burns, bruises and wounds until he looked half decent. He was the first man she had seen with so few clothes on and her face burned with embarrassment as she washed him and applied salve to his muscled torso and thighs. He noted her embarrassment and thought how innocent and naïve she was even though she might be a spy and enemy of the state. Even in his semi-conscious state and pain he could feel his own body reacting to her nearness, the perfume of her soap and her silk like hair.

"I am sorry I can't stand up properly yet but thank you for saving my life."

"You'll survive," she said tightening his bandages. "I want my father back and you are his ransom."

"Sorry, I thought you wanted to save me!" he said quizzically. Being stuck in this cell and facing death had made him think clearly about his relations with her. He knew now he had chased her, not to capture her for the Emperor but because he wanted her safe for himself.

"While you are alive my father has a chance."

He dragged himself off the stool on which he sat and slowly and painfully stood up and kissed the underside of her wrist; a lover's kiss! She pulled her hand away sharply but not before Dreda had noticed her hand tremble in reaction to his caress.

He was watching her carefully, smiling as if he could read her mind. *Dammit!* This man seemed to be able to permeate her barriers making her feel vulnerable to him. She needed to rid herself of him. He was dangerous, a man who would charm a woman into giving him what he wanted without a thought for her needs.

Gavantz pushed Dreda against the wall after seeing that kiss. Dreda sagged against the wall for a moment, pain rippling through him as his wounds bled again. Then recovering his strength, he stood up straight.

"Leave her alone," said Gavantz. He put his hand again possessively on her shoulder. "Come Felea, we need to discuss your father's fate." Felea removed his hand from her shoulder and left the room.

"You touch her again and I will kill you."

Dreda turned and faced him. "You take advantage of her vulnerability and I will kill you," he promised the rebel leader. They stood like two angry animals competing for their mate. Neither would give an inch.

Outside the room Felea felt bemused. Gavantz had never shown any romantic interest in her before but then he had never had any competition. She had always liked the former Gavantz, a gentle intellectual but this rougher, tougher Gavantz didn't appeal to her at all. He was now a warrior, a cold man of steel; a man who would do anything to achieve his goals. He clearly saw her as his possession and would rid himself of this officer in a flash if he thought he was in his way. Felea didn't want to be the prize these two men were fighting over. She would make up her own mind as to the man she would wed and bed. Her father had promised her he would let her choose her husband.

She prayed Gavantz would stick to his side of his bargain and trade Dreda for her father. She could pretend she wanted to save Dreda for her father's sake but in her heart, she knew there was another deeper reason. She could not bear to see him hurt. Hard and ruthless he might be, but he was a gentleman. He had saved her from being violated by that militia officer.

But she wanted as little contact with him as was possible. That kiss had unnerved her. Her hand was still tingling from its contact with his lips. Her heart had raced when he was standing close to her. When she had tended his wounds, she had felt how muscular and strong his chest was and remembered their dance; that waltz when he had held her tight against him. He was in her mind all the time; she tried to block him out and raise her defences against him. His attitude confused her; at one time being fierce and admonishing her and at another time gentle, teasing and kissing her hand lover-like.

Dreda took another day to recover and she got to know the adult Gavantz better. He was like her father; self-absorbed and self-centred at times, totally devoted and preoccupied with the rebel cause. He would make a poor husband. She also noticed he had a cruel streak, pushing and generally ill-treating Dreda, just to make it clear who was in charge. Dreda did not complain, merely screwing his eyes in pain and grimacing when Gavantz pushed him hard against the wall or into a chair causing his wounds to bleed again.

They had to wait another day before Dreda could be tied to his horse and led down the hill to the city state. The rebels were at the city gates trying to gain entry by force. A message was passed to the authorities and they were allowed in. Felea had refused to leave her father behind and Gavantz was exasperated by her stubbornness.

Moving Dreda before he was fully recovered did not help him and he was barely conscious, but he noticed they rubbed each other up. He smiled at their conflict. He enjoyed sparring with Felea but Gavantz clearly didn't. He didn't see Gavantz as competition if Felea had her way.

He was taken to a rebel 'safe house' and allowed to sleep. Felea nursed him back to health. Now they were no longer in a power relationship they did not fight. He got used to having his bandages removed and he enjoyed being with her, smelling the clean smell of her jasmine soap. He wished he could hold her and run his hand through her lovely hair. She found it easier to be around him while he was weak, and he was no longer trying to dominate her.

The swop was negotiated after two days. She came to clean his wounds for the last time. He undid his shirt and she rubbed salve into his wounds which were healing slowly, doing it quickly and efficiently; wanting the job over as quickly as she could manage it. She felt suffocated when she was too close to him.

Running her hands over his muscled chest she could feel his heartbeat rise and when she looked up she saw he was watching her intensely. He took her hand and kissed it saying, ''Be careful when you are around Gavantz, he is not what he seems.''

She withdrew her hand as if it had been stung but she saw a look in his eyes that showed he also had felt that sensation, like a shock, that had run between them. She nodded, acknowledging he was right and he leant towards her and she thought he would kiss her but Gavantz came in and the moment was lost.

Dreda was roughly manhandled into a carriage and swopped that night for her father and one of the rebels' most senior spies. Dreda was surprised to find the rebel had been swopped given the information he could have given under duress. He would not have swopped the man if he had been in charge. Her father was delighted to see his daughter and they were quickly taken to a different 'safe house'.

CHAPTER FIVE

Dreda was still weak but he and Denman decided they were not going to let Gavantz take the city. The Emperor asked them to take control as his generals were mainly occupied in the rural areas fighting other rebel contingents. They each took control of half of the city and directed the army and the militia against the rebels.

Dreda could not ride out to fight for a fortnight and directed operations from a clock tower. The rebel forces tried to siege the city, but the militia found the hidden secret tunnels used by the insurgents and managed to bring supplies in during the night until reinforcements arrived and attacked the rebels from behind. Felea and her father escaped through the tunnels one evening with a few friends.

Dreda couldn't get near Felea, being preoccupied with the rebellion. He had thought about her continually during the quiet moments during the siege; the memory of that sword fight, her determination to win and later her eyes spitting fire at him when she had defied him from that bed. Fight it he may but that damned girl was in his blood and he wanted, no needed her. For the first time in his life he had been racked with jealousy, an emotion he hated and made him feel weak and vulnerable.

Even finding his fiancée in the bed with another man had not angered him like this. He had merely shrugged and turned away and terminated his engagement, developing a thicker, harder shell and had recently settled for less than love. He had had affairs and mistresses and treated his ladies as a gentleman should, supplying the requisite houses and jewels that came as part of the package. He had felt no guilt when the relations had ended and had never had a desire to nurture or protect any of them.

This time it was different. His blood stirred at the thought of Gavantz taking Felea to his bed and destroying her innocence. She was his and his alone! Her responses to his kissing her hand showed that beneath that calm intense exterior was a woman who would ignite into flames if introduced to passion by a man she loved. He was the one who would take her virtue and introduce her to love! Gavantz would rue the day if he tried to claim her for his own.

When this ridiculously spirited girl defied him, he felt like putting her over his knee to spank her and then taking her into his arms and kissing her into submission. He thought of her being hurt or injured by Gavantz and he knew he would move heaven and earth to help her and protect her. He admitted ruefully to himself this stirring in his blood and burning in his loins would only be assuaged by his taking the Lady

Felea into his bed and thoroughly seducing her, making her cry out for him and only him.

What he would do with her after that he had not thought about. She was innocent, and he was not the marrying kind. Now she had no father to protect her and the Emperor might confiscate her lands she might be penniless. Might she be looking for a protector? Would she accept a carte blanche or demand more? He pushed the perplexing problem out of his mind and concentrated on the fight. He would deal with Lady Felea later.

When the last cannons were fired, and rebels rounded up he said to Denman, "Now to sort out my other business." Denman looked surprised. He could only think of the girl, but she had vanished. He noticed his friend had put on his best uniform and looked even more polished than usual.

"Where are you going?"

"To the house where the Whelani family took refuge."

"They have gone."

"What!" His friend erupted in anger. "When?"

"I informed your office two weeks ago, when they escaped through a tunnel. They may have met Gavantz. They are nowhere to be seen. We have combed the streets and countryside. I thought you had forgotten her when you didn't answer my message."

His friend paced the room. "See my horse is saddled and there are provisions again. You had better stay here and look after security. I didn't get the message. I must get her back. Gavantz is a bully and violent!"

He remembered his own savage beating. Gavantz would not put up with much argument. He was already losing his patience with her when Dreda had been with them. "Her father is still blind to Gavantz's faults. If he puts pressure on her to marry him she may suffer at Gavantz's hands." He paced the room again, agitated, his sharp mind thinking quickly.

"You may not find him easily." He thought for a moment. "Whelani is clever. The house has been stripped of any valuables and you can be sure that he has them somewhere miles away but safe. He will live in luxury.

'Ask Thomatz to meet me at the city gates again. We do know which tunnels they used to escape, don't we?"

"What is your intention?"

"I intend to bring the Whelani family back alive and Gavantz live or dead. I want a troop of dragoons at the city gates, armed and ready to fight tomorrow at eight."

At the nod of agreement, he stormed out of the room, out to the yard and jumped on to his horse. He still ached but he forgot his pains at the thought of Felea in the hands of that bully.

Denman smiled. For the first time in years Dreda had found a woman who had captured his interest; enough to make him chase after her and rescue her. He had never seen Dreda so animated by a woman. Even his fiancée had not raised his passion in this way.

He knew Dreda had been hurt much more by her defection than he had pretended but he had brushed it off like another nuisance in his life and buried himself in his work, taking difficult missions and risking his life more than was necessary. The young idealistic young man who had entered the army had turned into a cynical harsh officer; a good motivator and leader of men but aloof and mistrustful of women. He spent his time mainly in the company of men, jokingly denying the need to become leg-shackled and a tenant for life.

There was no shortage of women wanting to warm his bed. Widows enjoying their new-found freedom and wives finding their complacent husbands boring enjoyed his company. He was often seen with a new ladybird on his arm at the theatre or the opera. He could afford to buy the most beautiful and sophisticated birds of fancy but tired of them quickly offering none of them permanence in his life.

Denman had thought Dreda was lost to love; doomed to remain in his solitary and lonely existence with just a few good friends for company and a stream of women moving swiftly through his life. Perhaps there was hope for his friend now he had met the lovely Lady Felea. He saw what had attracted his aloof detached friend. More than a beautiful face, she was charitable, loyal and cared for the vulnerable.

Strange, he thought. In many ways, she was the opposite of his cold, callous self-centred friend.

He had known a different Dreda before the boy had become a man. A caring, sensitive boy was raised by household staff and neglected by a cold cruel critical father and a lonely tempestuous mother both of whom rarely acknowledged him. Adventurous and energetic he had rejected the more passive diplomatic service for an army career, disappointing his father who wanted his first-born son to take on his mantel and step into his diplomatic shoes.

His father made no secret he preferred his second son and wished he had been his heir. Intimidating, always waiting in the shadows for any signs of rebellion, Dreda was compared unfavourably with his younger brother; a diplomat, who was oiling his way up the hierarchy of society, doing the pretty, saying what everyone expected of him. His brother smiled his way through society charming others. Dreda was careful not to insult those in power but he cared not a jot for the opinion of 'polite society' unless it concerned his job and the security of the state.

A man who inspired fear and respect, he quickly deterred the sycophants who fawned on him trying to win his patronage. He preferred the company of men and male pursuits to the trivialities of the salon and the ballroom and Mamas had long given up thrusting their debutante daughters in front of his nose. He attended court and balls for the purposes of pleasing the Emperor but that was all. Duty came first not frivolity. The enemies of the state were all around them, infiltrating every layer of society and the policies of the Emperor were becoming more draconian, encouraging more rebellion.

His reserve had developed into a hard shell, protecting him from his father's criticisms and his intelligence and wit had turned into harsh sarcasm, designed to ward off the unwary who might cross his path. He had learned to keep his own counsel and company, cautious, rarely expressing his opinion unless it was sought. A caring child had turned into a harsh man who only let Denman near him emotionally.

He only showed his caring side to his pets and animals, showering affection on his two overgrown dogs and his horses who idolized him. He had learnt to look after himself and rarely considered anyone's feelings other than his own. Self-absorbed, he focused on his own needs and avoided helping others when he could. He didn't want the complications of other people's troubles in his life. His work at the Bureau could be carried out clinically and unemotionally without delving into the sensibilities of his prisoners or his officers.

Denman was taking leave in a few days. He was visiting his family for a wedding. When a boy Dreda had spent more time at Denman's house than his own, the sensitive child enjoying the warm family atmosphere, the siblings' jokes and teasing and rivalry. They had become his second family.

Denman thought they had saved his friend from becoming an inhuman machine, even colder and self-centred than he was now. He thought living with a warmer family might have brought out his better qualities, for Dreda in the past had been loyal and generous to those he cared for, having risked his life for Denman and other army colleagues.

He just showed that loyal and caring side of his nature to only a few. He needed someone to bring out the warmth in him that had lay dormant so long. He wondered, perhaps Felea might draw out the caring nature he knew was hidden deep inside his friend. She might be his redemption.

CHAPTER SIX

Felea was having doubts about her father's sanity and judgement. He still supported Gavantz even after the rebellion was quashed. Gavantz had escaped with a squadron of men, leaving some of his men without any support and at the mercy of the Emperor's troops when he could have made an escape route for them. Her father nevertheless seemed to ignore Gavantz's faults and misdemeanours.

Tales of his cruelty were filtering through the rebel network. He had personally authorized a firing squad to kill in cold blood Imperial troops who had surrendered. He had made an example of them and had burned a whole village down after hearing the people had fed the hungry men.

He was becoming as ruthless as the Emperor and some of the peasants were now supporting the Emperor again. Felea had supported the rebel cause disliking the way opposition to the Imperial decrees was put down with extreme severity and violence. Now she mistrusted the change in leadership as Gavantz and others like him worked their way up the hierarchy. The new leaders were as dictatorial as the existing Emperor and she believed they would treat the populace with as much contempt as he did. She now thought it was better to stick with the 'devil one knew' than put an unknown quantity in his place.

They met up with Gavantz near the waterfall. He insisted on riding next to her and began to treat her with a possessiveness which bordered on ownership. He referred to Dreda as the reason for the failure of the rebellion and wished he had killed him while he could. She kept her distance as much as she could, but her father kept mentioning nuptials and the joining of the families. He was acting strangely, talking to himself and forgetting recent events while remembering events that occurred years before. She wondered if he was going senile.

She cornered her father in the parlour of the inn while Gavantz was bedding the horses for the night. "Father, we must talk about Michael. He seems to be under the impression I might want to marry him."

Her father looked bemused as if trying to concentrate and focus on what she said. He was looking older than his years and if she hadn't been worried about her future she would have hugged him and tried to reassure him. He blinked and seemed to come back to reality. Looking around the room he could clearly recognize where he was.

"My dear Felea, your mother and I always wanted to join our two families together. Your mother thought Michael needed to mature but she would admit if she was alive he is now a leader and will improve this state much more than our present Emperor. He will look after you when I am gone. You admitted that your trustees were not protecting you and there is no-one else to take my place.''

Felea drew in a breath and asked God to give her the patience she required to explain Gavantz's faults and cruel streak to her father. ''Father, when I was with Michael at the fort he behaved quite cruelly to a prisoner and he was impatient with me. I don't think he would make a good and kind husband.

'He may not be a good leader either. Some people say he has been as harsh as the Emperor and we are losing support from the peasants. The Emperor will take his land if his troops push into Michael's territories and he would rely on my fortune and estates which the Emperor could confiscate. I think my future could be very uncertain with Michael.''

Her father worried about this for a minute. ''You still need a husband and a strong man to guide and protect you.''

''But not Michael,'' she said, thinking of another man who was strong and had protected her in the past.

With the determination of a weak mind, unwilling to contemplate any more problems, her father said, ''My mind is made up Felea. I intend you to marry Michael and as soon as possible.''

Felea felt overwhelmed. This was not her father speaking; this weak feeble old man who was digging his heels in because he could not make other sound judgements. She would have to think how to extricate herself from this situation as she would get no help from her father. She had to admit now he was he was addlepated and needed looking after by more skilled persons than herself. She knew if she married Gavantz there would be murder committed and she didn't fancy a spell in Helmand Prison.

Gavantz came in and put his arm around her. She slid away from him, smiling, getting out of the range of his octopi like hands which seemed every day to wander over her body more and more. ''We arrive at the chapel tomorrow Felea,'' said Gavantz. ''It is one of the few towns that will have an orthodox priest. We will tie the knot there.''

Felea recognized the certainty in his voice; that determination he would get what he wanted, trampling her feelings underfoot. She was devastated, having no-one to protect her from him. She had recognized the same note in Dreda's voice. Both men would stop at nothing to achieve what they wanted.

She had heard nothing of Dreda and didn't expect him to contact her, but she missed their arguments and next to him Gavantz was nothing. If her father was going senile she would be better to become a ward of the Emperor's court than rely on him for protection and sustenance. Dreda had been her enemy but he was strangely the first person she would trust now if she needed help. Despite her many challenges and defiance, most of the time he had treated her as a lady and despite her provocation he had protected her virtue when she was vulnerable.

She had heard from one of her friends he had a dreadful reputation. Whilst in the army he had been a rake, cutting swathes through the ladies alongside his friend Officer Denman. Since he had begun his career in the militia he had avoided being blackmailed by discarded mistresses and had been discrete and selective in choosing the women he had had affairs with.

She had decided he had merely been toying with her; an innocent virgin, probably laughing behind her back at her confused reaction to his kisses on her hand. At one time, she thought he behaved as if he might have held a tendre for her, but she had given that idea up and would treat him coolly now, as if he were merely an officer of the state who might help her. She had no-one else to turn to and swallowing her pride she had managed to get a letter sent to Dreda explaining the situation and asking for the Emperor to intervene and send someone to rescue her and take her back to the city.

CHAPTER SEVEN

When Dreda entered his office that evening totally prepared for the journey he found the letter with other unopened mail. His anger boiled over. It was received a week previously but at least he knew where they were aiming for. He passed the letter over to Denman and the next morning he and Thomatz and the troops set off.

They travelled day and night over hills and mountains for four days. They moved much more swiftly than their fugitives who made slow progress on the steep tracks with horses heavily laden with their worldly goods. Then they slowed their pace, travelling only in the day after that and caught up the fugitives in a small village where Felea's father knew the priest.

The fugitives were sleeping in the house attached to the chapel, resting for several days now they felt they were safe from the militia. The priest was being given gold by her father when Felea walked into the dining room.

"We must secure your safety my dear. Gavantz has impressed on me how dangerous your situation is, you a young unmarried girl. We must rectify the situation immediately. The priest has agreed to marry you tonight."

Felea nearly had an apoplexy although she had been expecting this. Her father had forgotten their earlier conversation. Losing patience with him, she decided not to mince her words and to tell him the truth. She reminded her father that he had said she would choose when and whom she married, and she had no intention of marrying a rebel on the run who could be hunted down at any minute and had no home or prospects. Most importantly she disliked and mistrusted Gavantz. It was unfortunate that he walked through the door as she stated this.

"That is a shame but hate and love are two sides of the same coin and one can turn into another in time. We were made for each other and your parents intended this."

She remembered her mother releasing her from that engagement and wondered if during the long holidays he had stayed with them her mother had divined what sort of man Gavantz was. She was a very wise woman.

Gavantz took her hand and forced it to remain still while he put a ring on it. The priest witnessing this got his bible out. He was only interested in the money he could earn. He started reading the service and she tried to drag her arm away but Gavantz slapped her viciously across the face. He forced her arm behind her back until she screamed, making her say the appropriate words.

The service was almost over and the bride about to make her final vows when the door was kicked open and Dreda walked in and tore her from Gavantz's grip. He sent Gavantz flying with one blow and then kicked him through the open window where the rebel lay dead with a broken neck. Felea stood nursing her arm.

Dreda was only interested in the marriage service. How far had it gone? He was relieved the final vows had not been taken although the husband would have been in an immortal state anyway. He then turned to Felea. "Ma'am you are safe now and I am come to take you home."

Overwhelmed by relief she brushed a tear from her eyes and allowed him to lead her to his horse. He put her on it in front of him, using her arm as an excuse to ensure she rode with him. She did not object. For the first time in years she felt comfortable and safe. He nestled her in one arm and she fell asleep.

Much later in the evening, they stopped, and she woke up and he let her into the bed-chamber of an inn he had booked for the night.

"Sit down Ma'am while I bathe your arm. This herbal water and salve will bring out the bruise and swelling faster."

"You seem always to be rescuing me."

"It is my pleasure Ma'am. If I had discovered your letter earlier Gavantz would not have had the opportunity to assault you."

He rested her on the bed against some pillows. "Now you sleep while my men and I watch out for any fugitives. Gavantz's men are still in the area."

She took his hand and shook it. "Thank you, Officer, Dreda. I know I have been a nuisance and caused you great discomfort. I hope I can be more helpful in the future."

A peculiar look came into his eyes and he bent over the bed taking her hand and dropping a light kiss onto it. He smiled, mocking her. "Are you feeling quite well Lady Felea, admitting you are at fault?" He felt her forehead. "I think you must have a fever."

"I hope I am woman enough to admit when I have been wrong and caused problems," she said colouring.

"A few cuts and bruises were worth the effort of getting you back, Ma'am."

"Hardly a few bruises! You were brutally tortured by Gavantz."

He shrugged. "It was all in the line of duty Ma'am and the prize was worth the forfeit." Still exhausted and in pain her emotions overwhelmed her, and a few tears came into her eyes. He leant over and brushed them away with his fingers and touched her cheek gently.

Pulling away from her he turned on his heel and left the room.

Goddammit! She was temptation itself lying there even with a bruised face and arm in a sling. She was so innocent she didn't know how she could entice a man just by looking at him with those smoky cat-like eyes.

He was up early and after breaking their fast he seated her on his horse and they plodded on again over hilly terrain. He looked exhausted. She knew that this journey was taking its toll after a month of directing the militia and army whilst he was still recovering from such a vicious beating. When they stopped for a break she asked to see his bandages again. He shook his head and went to mount his horse.

"Officer, you must let me look at your wounds and dress them."

"I am well Ma'am and will be fine when I can rest in the city."

"Officer Dreda, you know I am persistent," she said coming toward him armed her with her dangerous weapon, the salve that stung like hell. "You gave me aid when I merely had one bruise. Please let me ease your wound."

Realizing she would not take no for an answer he sat on a hillock and let her undo his shirt. She gently eased the bandages and saw how raw the wounds were. "Your wounds have not healed very well. There is infection there. You ought not to be riding and should have had these tended to earlier."

She felt his head. He had a slight fever. "We must boil up some water for some herbs, so I can make another more effective balm for your wounds." His wounds stung like the very devil when she washed and balmed them but once the bandages were redone he felt more comfortable. She feared for his health as he still had several days of riding left.

He was relieved when she had finished. She was in too close a proximity to him, running her gentle fingers over his chest, setting his pulse racing. She still had no idea what affect she had on him. An experienced man and no slouch in the bedroom he could tell she was also affected by his presence.

When he had lifted her down from his horse he had felt her tense and withdraw as if disinterested in him, but her eyes had told a different story, widening and darkening when he had held her tight for too long a moment. Her hands trembled ever so slightly when he had kissed the underside of her wrist. This girl was definitely affected by his touch although she might try to pretend otherwise.

The next day his fever had worsened but they rode continuously each day sleeping in inns until they got to the city gates and then they went straight to a villa frequently leased by Dreda as a summer residence.

Denman had arranged for Anna an aunt of Dreda to live there as chaperone and the Emperor had put Felea temporarily under Dreda's protection. The rebels might see her as a turncoat and she might be a possible target in the future after Gavantz had been killed. Even whilst he was sick the rebels were unlikely to target the villa of the second in charge of the State Security Bureau. Denman had placed some officers as extra security around the villa to ensure their safety.

Dreda referred to Anna as a dragon and she was more than a match for his severe manner and sharp tongue having brought him up when his mother left home. She had jet black hair despite her advancing years and the sharp features and piercing eyes of Dreda. She forced him into bed and she made a stronger solution of herbs from the garden.

Dreda wanted to get up to make his report and find out what had happened in his absence. He found his clothes had been taken and rang the bell to ask for replacements. Instead of his valet, Felea came in carrying a tray of food and refreshments and a vial of some evil-smelling liquid.

She was no longer dressed in her boy's clothes but was in a modestly cut marine blue silk dress which exaggerated her daintiness and femininity. Her hair was down her shoulders and back, a blue-black mauve mane framing her delicate features and those amazing eyes. She looked like an innocent young girl again. Even in his ill state his blood pumped swiftly through his veins and his loins burned when she plumped his pillows and helped him up to a sitting position and put the tray on his lap.

He cursed the Emperor for putting her under his protection. He was trying to behave the gentleman in her presence, but he felt no gentlemanly feelings toward her. Lust and seduction were upmost in his mind and it was lucky he was too ill to do anything about it! He had been celibate too long.

She felt his forehead. ''You are burning up Officer Dreda. Your fever has worsened badly. Please drink this. It may reduce your fever.''

''I don't want anything except water.'' He was burning up from inside. He certainly didn't want any broth!

''I assure you the medicine is not too bad, Sir. I have used it in the past and found it tolerable. I gave it to my cousins when they were young, and they managed to bear the taste.''

Thus, implying that I am not able to suffer what children and a woman can drink, he thought taking it grudgingly. He pulled a face but downed the lot. He refused to eat the thin beef broth though.

''I am not eating that repulsive dish-water,'' he said. ''Who the devil made it anyway? No one serves it in my house.''

She lowered her head and said, ''I thought I made it tolerably well, but I shall throw it away if it doesn't please you Sir.''

Looking at the sad look on her face he felt goaded and said, ''For goodness sake give it to me then.''

He ate half of it and then looking at her rather satisfied expression he commanded! ''Come closer Lady Felea.'' He said with a gleam in his eye which belied his stern words; ''I should put you over my knee for pretending your feelings were hurt by my not wanting to eat your broth. You are either a very good actress or a consummate liar, but you won't fool me again.''

''You wrong me Sir,'' she said but backed away in case he did what he had said. He was not a man who normally made idle threats. She was in fact safe as he could not reach her. He would not get out of bed as he had no clothes to put on and was sitting up bare-chested apart from where the bandages covered his skin.

''You should not be in here with me alone in my state of undress,'' he scolded.

''Your aunt knows I am good at acting your nurse and she thinks you will not harm me. I am used now to seeing you partly unclothed.''

''Pray, get me some clothes. I need to get up. I have business to sort out.''

''No Officer! Your fever will worsen even more if you leave your bed.'' She pushed him back and he fell against the pillow as weak as a kitten. He took her wrist and said, ''You choose to command me in my own house?''

She met him stare for stare. ''Only when it is for your own good! You are too weak to get up and need to rest or the fever will not go.'' He tried sitting again and gave up, resting his head against the pillow, acknowledging she was right.

''Perhaps, I like being ordered about when a lady has my interests at heart,'' he said looking questioningly into her eyes. She looked away not knowing how to answer him. He pulled her back to face him and kissed the underside of her wrist. She flinched and tried to pull away.

He released her wrist. ''I have never found milk and water misses attractive. I have always preferred a woman who has some spirit.

''One day you may find yourself one, but I think you would want to break her like you would break in a young filly to bridle when she disobeys you,'' she said frowning at him. She was making it quite clear she would not be broken in in by him or any other man.

"I think not," he said. "The woman I am thinking of will be given plenty of freedom and a loose rein and will come to me willingly when she knows I will not hurt or confine her and will adore her and care for her."

She felt this had run on long enough and rang the bell for the maid and covered him up and went out. Out of his bedroom and in the safety of the hall she leant against the wall and took a deep breath. He talked in riddles, one-minute scolding her, the next lover like.

Her skin burnt where he had kissed it and she knew he had felt her pulse race when he held her wrist. She could barely control her responses to him and needed to be away from his dominating presence. Even while his body was weak his will was like that of iron and his piercing blue grey eyes challenged her continually and upset her peace of mind.

He lay back and smiled. He enjoyed teasing her and knew he upset her equilibrium. He wanted her off balance, so he could try to judge her feelings for him. She was attracted and aroused by him, but he did not know whether the attraction was merely based on lust or whether she cared for him more than she would for any other man who rescued her. She was a cool woman who could shutter her emotions away, but he was gradually breaking down those icy barriers she had set up against him.

For the moment, he needed to sleep. His body was shot through with fever and his head banged all the time. She was right. He needed to rid himself of this fever and then meet the Emperor to finish his business. Denman would operate for him on his behalf while he was too weak to get out of his bed.

His aunt had watched how this young girl handled her awkward, domineering nephew and approved. She was no fainting prissy miss. She felt he had met his match with this one. She would not bore him nor give into him and would joke him out of his sullen moods. It was not clear whether she loved him though. She was clearly concerned for his health and she explained he had saved her skin on more than one occasion. She was grateful for that but how much passion was there it was difficult to tell. She was a calm, intense creature like her nephew and very private.

They took it in turns to stay up for eight nights and when the fever broke she saw Felea break into tears of relief. Perhaps she did have deep feelings for this man after all, the old woman nodded to her satisfaction. She was clearly important to him. He had called her name out throughout the nights.

The next day when he woke up he looked around for her, but

she was not there. Before he could try to jump out of bed his aunt said, "She is having a well-earned sleep after eight sleepless nights looking after you." She pushed him back on to his pillows, "You are now to rest."

"I have an audience with the Emperor."

"He knows you have a fever and sent his best wishes and some cheroots. He will see you in a few days' time if you are well."

Denman had visited the villa every few days to check on his progress. He arrived one day and flourished a document in front of him. "Wardship papers, signed by the Emperor! Felea has been a ward of court this past three weeks and is under the Emperor's protection. And not a minute too soon! Her father is addle-patted, and no-one is listening to him now. I heard you sorted Gavantz out."

"Permanently and I enjoyed doing it too much! I should have brought him back live for interrogation. I got there just in time, but she wore his bruises."

"And now you have sorted the business out you can leave him to rest," said Anna.

She shooed him out of the door and shut it behind her. "We got close to losing him this time. He can't take the beatings at his age as well as he used to." Denman thought he was hardly in his adage at the grand old age of thirty-nine but nevertheless, he was no longer in training every day.

"He must rest."

"The girl is helping him. When she is there he seems to relax."

"How serious are their relations?"

"I don't know, he never talks about it, but I have never seen him so angry as when he thought he was going to lose her to the rebel leader. What does she say? "

"She is a closed book as well, but I think she is as deeply attracted as he. It is whether two stubborn people will admit it."

"She is good for him. He no longer wants to devote himself solely to work and the security of the state. She is bringing out a warmth in him I have never seen before."

Satisfied, the aunt decided to progress this relationship a little further. This nephew was a favourite of hers, never asking for favours or special treatment. Always taking his punishments without complaint he had made his own way in the world. Being a sensitive boy, he had withdrawn into himself after the rejection by his father of his mother and her abandonment of him and his little brother to nurses and female relations. Only twelve, he had been deeply devoted to his mother and her abandonment of him had made him mistrust women. At six and ten he chose to join the army; an institution where life was regulated and dependable and one relied on other men for one's life.

Both women took it in turns to sit with the man reading books and keeping him occupied as he was continually restless and easily bored. He wanted to work but they refuse to allow this, and he was really too tired to argue so he put up little resistance. While he slept, the aunt told her a little about his family history and his career in the army. Felea was not surprised to hear about his bravery and coolness under fire. She was surprised to hear on one occasion he would not leave for safety until he had managed to get all his injured colleagues out of the range of fire.

After four more days of total rest his bandages were clean, and he could get up. He was no longer as weak as a kitten and normally an active and restless man he wanted to get fit. Denman and he went to the library to fence.

"God, I ache," said Dreda. "That bed rest has made me as stiff as an old man."

"You need to practise every day. At your age, you feel the pain more," he said joking, for he was the same age as his friend.

"I will make you pay for that," said Dreda, lunging forward. Even at his best he was no match for Denman who was the best swordsman he had met but he could give him a good run for his money when he was fit.

His friend parried the lunge and they spent the next few minutes in a tight fight. Normally Dreda's longer reach was matched by Denman's superior skill. Felea watched them compete. Both men were dressed in shirt and breeches and fenced in stockinged feet, their only protection masks across their faces.

She compared them. They were two fine specimens of masculinity in their prime, both tall and broad shouldered with narrow hips leading down to firm muscular legs. Dreda was angular and as lean as a whippet, his muscles clearly penetrating the soft linen shirt and breeches. Denman was more heavily built and very muscular but was toned and barely breathed as he fenced.

Friends they were but very competitive and for a few minutes Dreda pushed his friend to the limit, both men red hot and rivulets of sweat running down their foreheads. Then his energy dissipated, he coughed, breathed heavily and put his sword up in surrender.

"I am done, Denman," he said, "I will need to do much more of this to get fit again."

He turned and saw Felea at the door watching them intensely. She blushed when he raised his brows at her watching them so carefully. Her pulse had raced when she had seen Dreda fight so forcefully, remembering how he had forced her back against the fort door and pinned her there, a prisoner to do with as he wished.

He bowed and said to Denman, "Lady Felea is no mean fencer. You should give her some lessons in the future."

"I would love to sometime Ma'am. For now, I must away to the Emperor; he asked me for an audience." He went out leaving Felea and Dreda facing each other.

She broke the silence. "You are both excellent fencers Officer Dreda."

"Denman is the superior fencer. He is a natural and can out-fence any man I know." He came over to her. "Who taught you to fence?" he asked, thinking what an unusual upbringing she had had.

"My father and cousin."

"You had good teachers. You could do no better than copy Denman's style. For a heavy, muscular man he mixes grace and elegance with energy used economically. Your styles are similar I remember. You were lithe on your feet and fast. When Denman has given you a few lessons you could fence me with me again."

"I think not Sir," she replied. "It would not be appropriate," she flushed, embarrassed, remembering that point in their sword fight when he had partly unclothed her.

"How tiresome," he said his eyes lowering swiftly to her bodice and up again, clearly remembering uncovering her bosom for his eyes to see. "I enjoyed pitting my wits against you last time. Denman tends to fight in a more orthodox style."

She blushed again thinking of their unsportsmanlike tactics. "I told you at the time you had an unfair advantage and I had to use my wits against you. Nevertheless, you outwitted me."

"You forget I have been involved in intrigue and deception for much longer than you. It comes naturally to me now."

She saw he was still breathing heavily and now gasping. She poured a glass of water and gave it to him and he drunk it gratefully. "You have exerted yourself too much Sir," she said looking severely at him. She patted him on the back and helped him to a chair. "You must rest. Shall I ring for a servant to help you back to your room?"

"That will not be necessary," he said but collapsed into another paroxysm of coughing. She saw he did not like to admit his weakness particularly in front of a woman. That was why it had been so important for him to win their swordfight and stop her leaving the fort. He would not be bested by a "mere," girl. "I will rest on my bed when I have recovered my breath."

She took his wrist and felt his pulse. "Your pulse is racing Officer Dreda. You must look after yourself Sir."

He took her hand off his wrist but did not let it go. Holding her hand, he said, "I am not used to being looked after so well."

"I owe my freedom to you Sir and merely wish to show my gratitude. I would not want to see you die."

"Even though you would have skewered me if I had got in the way of you rescuing your father."

"It would have been a necessity Sir, but I would have regretted doing it," she said truthfully.

He laughed and let her go. "An honest answer and I suppose I should be grateful that you were not more bloodthirsty Ma'am. I shall watch my back in future if I annoy you again." She did not respond to his provocation and he went on. "Did your father teach you to shoot as well?"

"Yes."

"And you are a crack shot I should suppose?"

"I can shoot well," she said and then defensively, "I suppose it is again another thing you think a girl should not learn. You think my upbringing was defective?"

"On the contrary, I told you I like a woman who has spirit and will defend herself. The capture is more interesting when the chase is more exciting, and the prey is wily!"

She looked at him. "You talk in riddles Sir, I don't understand you."

He looked at her with raised eyebrows, showing he disbelieved her. "I think you understand me very well, Ma'am."

As he walked toward her she swiftly escaped him leaving the room in a swish of silks and satin. As she left she shot him a backward glance and said, "I think you have always posed more of a threat to me than I would ever do to you,"

He stayed a few minutes while he recovered his breath and thought about what she said. "Did she hold a tendre for him or did she merely see him as a friend?" He needed to know for this cursed girl had got under his skin.

CHAPTER EIGHT

Dreda had left for the Bureau. It was good to get out to a wholly male environment full of conversation about the latest card game, horse race and mill. He felt suffocated by the feminine influences in his villa. Once it had felt like a gentleman's residence but Felea's presence now penetrated every room except his bedchamber and study.

Flowers and herbs replaced the manly scents of leather and dogs. The heavy drapes in the salon and morning room were opened more frequently and the sun shone in making the house look lighter and homelier. He barely recognized it at times although she had made no dramatic changes. She had found his study was filled with heavy masculine furniture but also novels, poetry anthologies, paintings and sculptures showing a more artistic, sensitive side to this complex man.

Denman noted he didn't spent most evenings until eight or nine at the Bureau poring over papers and then going to his club for a late dinner and games of faro. His trips to the club or gaming hells were confined to several nights a week. He still visited a small villa in a less exclusive part of town where he had situated his current lady, coming back early in the morning to change his clothes if at all. Often, he met Denman for a bout of pugilism in the ring or a match in the fencing studio and then went home for dinner with his aunt and Felea.

She a cat lover, had installed a scraggy, flea bitten, mangy animal she had found in a sack in the gutter. Despite his protests, she had made him stop his curricle and allow her to open the bag and release the frightened animal.

"You don't think that scrawny thing is coming home with us, do you?"

"The poor thing is half-starved and terrified," she said. "Please let it sleep in the stables?" Dreda could not resist those pleading eyes and had picked it up cursing when his reward was a scratched and bitten hand.

"If the bloody thing bites me again it will end up as a hat," he said menacingly but despite his protests he had found it sleeping in a box in the kitchen and the creature slowly manipulated itself into their lives. It had grown sleek and elegant and haunted her footsteps, curling up on her lap beside the fire in the library.

Felea insisted on the fire being lit every evening during the cold late spring evenings and she enjoyed sitting on the rug before the flames playing an instrument or reading a book with the cat at her feet. Her blue-black hair with mauve and auburn highlights streamed behind her, her slight figure illuminated by the fire. She looked like a goddess come down to earth. He found her more fascinating by the day!

Denman came for dinner and they sat in the garden by the pond watching the carp swim by, waiting for Dreda to arrive home. Felea drifted her hand in the water and wished it was Denman who had kissed her hand and behaved lover like. Dreda blew hot and cold confusing her. Denman was an uncomplicated ladies' man. What one saw on the surface was what one got with Denman. There was no pretence.

He admitted he saw women as just for fun, to be toyed with and he took his pleasure with a certain type of woman but explained it was because he had never found a woman he could love fully without reservation. Felea understood it was the way noblemen treated woman of 'dubious morals'; she disliked it but said nothing. He behaved more gentlemanly to women than many men she knew and was honest about his behaviour, not hiding his views like others. At least he liked her and did not criticize her all the time.

Denman had seen she was despondent and held her hand. ''You seem to be suffering the megrims my dear,'' he ventured.

''Oh, I am just a little blue-devilled. When I have met the Emperor and he settles my future I will feel less uncertain. At the moment, I don't know where I will be in six months' time.''

''He has told Dreda he will not confiscate your lands.''

''Which means he is likely to want to marry me off to a person of status to improve our state's relations with other countries. I think my position is worse than if I were not wealthy and titled.''

She took her hand away from Denman and asked, ''Do you think Officer Dreda will plead my case for me with the Emperor? He was helpful before.''

''I think he has already spoken to the Emperor on your behalf and waits his answer. You are lucky. I have never known Danitz put himself out so much for anyone, let alone a woman. You have impressed him you know.''

''Indeed!'' she replied, amazed. ''I think he regards me as a damned nuisance and wants me out of his hair. The Emperor shouldn't have placed me under his protection. He can't tell me to leave and go to the devil as much as he might want. All he has done recently is criticize me and make me aware I am not yet up to snuff. You would think I am a child. He makes me so mad!''

''I think you are reading the situation incorrectly. Danitz enjoys your company and just wishes to protect you. In his position as your Imperial protector and living here he must remain distant from you. It might be wholly different if he lived in his lodgings.''

''I think not Officer Denman. He told me he wants my situation resolved as quickly as possible. I can then set up my household.''

"Do you want to be independent?"

"I don't know. I have enjoyed living here but it cannot go on forever and I do not want to be perceived as a nuisance. I intend to have it out with Officer Dreda and suggest he persuades the Emperor to let me move out of this villa."

"I think you are misreading the situation but perhaps you should talk with him and clear the air."

"I will talk to him tomorrow night," she said determined. "The Emperor is giving him an audience soon."

Denman thought it was about time this couple had a reckoning. Dreda was making both miserable with his moods and brooding. Denman had seen them boxing clever around each other for months. Neither one of them was willing to admit they held a tendre for each other when it was clear to the world they were head over heels in love with each other.

"Watch it! Dreda is coming out looking like thunder."

"Why is he looking so angry?" asked Felea. Denman thought she was too innocent for her own good. Her father had kept her "insulated" from society for too long. Dreda was coming down the path looking as if he could murder somebody and Denman thought that somebody could be him.

"Perhaps he thinks we hold a tendre for each other," said Denman mischievously, linking his arm in hers.

"He is mad then for we are just good friends."

Dreda had reached them. He glared at Denman and ground out harshly, "Lady Felea, I would have thought you would have had more sense to come out here with Denman knowing his reputation."

"Come on old fellow, we are just good friends and who knows other than us and your aunt? No-one will think I am compromising her."

"Servants talk Denman! I would appreciate it if you would keep your hands to yourself and stay in the house where my aunt can chaperone you two."

Felea looked amazed. He was almost acting as if he could be jealous. "We have done nothing that might be construed as improper except by people with mischievous minds! Are you not acting a little petty, Sir?"

"And you are implying?" asked Dreda.

"Why nothing Sir! I haven't got a devious or suspicious mind!"

Felea dragged her arm away from Denman's and ran up the

path and into the salon to await dinner. She stood fulminating, wishing she could go out to dine or eat in her room. This man was trying to dictate to her as if he were her father. She didn't know why she was always in the wrong.

Since that day, she had watched the two men fight, he had gradually changed; remained aloof, no longer teasing and now finding fault in everything she did. Her necklines were too low, and she was too friendly to the male staff at the villa. He said she encouraged too many of the male Bureau staff to visit the villa although she was not officially out yet.

He had caught her giving Denman a thank you kiss on the cheek after his friend had kindly given her a fencing lesson. Dreda had ordered her into his study and given her a tongue lashing.

''Proper young ladies do not kiss male friends. They only kiss relatives or their fiancés Lady Felea. If you were seen by the patronesses of society, they would call you loose! Think about your behaviour in future.''

''You have no right to lecture me about my morals Officer Dreda. I hear you are not a good role model.''

''And what are you inferring my girl?''

''Lady Felea to you Sir!''

''When you behave like a lady I will address you like one,'' he retorted. ''I am asking you to explain your accusation.''

She would not back down. ''It is a bit hypocritical to take me to task for one kiss for a friend when you house a lady who society calls your Mistress!''

''Let me remind you, proper young ladies do not listen to gossip about gentlemen,'' he snapped.

''Well as you are only a nobleman it doesn't count! A gentleman would not look for the worst in a woman.''

''There are dual standards for innocent young debutantes and single men. It is expected that men mount mistresses, but young women are supposed to remain blameless. What might have been acceptable by a father growing senile and wrapping himself up in his books will not be tolerated by 'polite society'. Grow up and conform or you will be judged wanting!''

His aunt hearing the row had intervened saying, ''Danitz, you are behaving like a crabby old bachelor in your dotage. Relax before you have an apoplexy! Felea has had enough experience of men with dubious values to separate the good from the bad and to adjust her behaviour accordingly. You can trust her.

''Felea your behaviour is exemplary. Ignore my foolish nephew.

He judges all men by his own and his friends' behaviour, trusting no man.''

"Oh, and what do you mean by that Aunt?'' he said rounding on her.

His aunt was not going to be intimidated by a man she had juggled on her knee when he was a snotty brat. Sending Felea out she shut the door and stared at him making him feel uncomfortable. She had always had the capacity to make him feel like a two-year-old.

"Danitz, you are behaving like a bear. You only criticize Felea when she becomes friendly with other men. Ask yourself why you are so possessive of her.''

Leaving her nephew with that unanswered question she had gone to Felea and reassured her. "Danitz is being overprotective of you. He worries for you. You must impress the Emperor. He was saying just the day before how well-mannered and ladylike you were.''

"Well, he has a funny way of showing it, Ma'am,'' said Felea her feathers ruffled.

"Once you have been presented he will relax my dear.''

Felea thought, *tonight he has virtually accused me of being a flirt and Denman of taking advantage of me.* She was perplexed. He was always so rational with everyone except her. Why did she bring out the worst in him when she wanted him to like her and approve of her?

Just as she had been beginning to like him a lot he had turned into the harsh, bullying militia man again. He would never trust her! That comment about her father meant he was ashamed of her. She bit back the tears his harsh words had caused. She had never been a watering pot and wouldn't start now.

"Damn Francis Dreda!'' She hoped he would rot in hell for his insults!

CHAPTER NINE

"Damn the girl," cried Dreda watching her angry entrance in to the house. She could turn his words inside out and make him feel small minded and petty.

"Well, you handled that well!" Denman said sarcastically. "You made her feel like a strumpet."

"She needs to know how her behaviour could be misconstrued. She will soon be presented at the Emperor's ball and needs to be observed as demure after her recent flirtation with spying. The matrons will be looking for things to find fault in her."

"I cannot think of anyone who is more innocent than Felea. She has been too protected in my mind's eye."

"Even more reason to protect her and make her toe the line."

"Are you sure you have not got your own agenda?"

"What do you mean by that?"

Denman nearly laughed out loud. His friend, usually the last to rise to anger, known for his sang froid and even temper, was nearly asking for Denman's seconds so was he incensed by Denman's familiarity with Felea.

"Nothing really! You do anger easily old fellow. Are you quite feeling up to the mark? You seem a trifle blue devilled recently. A bit like Felea. I was merely trying to cheer her up."

"I am perfectly all right. Just a little hungover. Last night's game went on longer than I expected." He wrinkled his brow. "What is upsetting Felea? Has someone hurt her?"

"Only some insensitive clodhopper who has trampled over her feelings by criticizing her and making her think she is a nuisance and unwanted. She wants to move out of here with her own chaperone if the Emperor will let her. You are a bastard taking out your moods on her."

"How did she get that doltish idea in her head? I don't think of her as a nuisance, but the Emperor is giving me an audience the day after tomorrow and he will decide her future soon. She must be prepared to leave here and find a husband."

"Unless a husband finds her first," said Denman and then leaving his friend with that thought in his head he followed Felea into dinner.

Bastard! thought Dreda. Denman would always tell him the truth irrespective of how he would feel. That is why he was such an old and good friend. He felt guilty now. Had he taken out his rotten mood on Felea and upset her? He would talk with her the next evening.

After dinner Denman caught him over a bottle of brandy in his club. Looking carefully at his friend Denman ventured, "You have nothing to be concerned about Danitz. Once I might have tried with Felea, but I soon realized it would have been no good. For some reason, the silly girl has only eyes for you."

His friend had been staring moodily at the amber liquid in his glass. He looked up. "What do you mean by that?" he asked quietly.

"Why old fellow, she makes moon eyes at you when you are not looking. She is half in love with you although she may not know it yet."

Dreda swirled the brandy around in its glass for a minute and then snapped the glass down on the table impatiently. Denman's normally calm and patient friend looked wound up like a spring and took a moment to collect his thoughts and chose his words carefully.

"Regretfully, I think not, my friend. She is attracted to me but treats me like a friend, avoiding me if I say anything that borders on the intimate or personal. I am her rescuer to whom she is grateful but far too old for a sweet young thing like her."

Denman thought, *there is no fool like a fool blinded by love.* His friend was choosing to spend more time at home with this young girl who intrigued him. No other woman had made him want to change his behaviour before Felea. He was changing, softening toward her and other people; not as cynical as before and less judgemental, a much nicer person to know.

She had not made any demands of him. Rather the opposite. He had chosen to change his lifestyle. He had allowed her to make changes to his home. They already behaved like a married couple enjoying quiet evenings together. Denman at times felt jealous of their shared intimacy and enjoyment of each other's company.

He wondered if he would ever share that intimacy with a woman. He had never found a woman who shared the same interests as he nor made him want to devote all his non-working time with her. He cared little for most of the women he spent time with; the birds of paradise whose nest he generously feathered or widows who wanted merely a dalliance and lively companion to share their new-found freedom with. Very few kept his attention more than a month and he lately felt a little lonely as his friends were gradually becoming leg-shackled and settling down to family life.

He had been wool-gathering and shifted his mind back to his friend's dilemma. "I will say just these few things and then keep my mouth shut Danitz," said Denman watching a scowl appear on Dreda's visage. "I have never seen you so relaxed and content in a woman's company and when you are not looking she looks at you as if the world revolves around you. Your house is now a home for the first time instead of a bloody mausoleum and you want to come home to it.''

He took another swig of his drink and rammed his message home. ''You need to decide what you want from Felea, Danitz. She is too decent to be toyed with.''

''I have no intention of offering her a carte blanche Denman, if that is what you are concerned about. Once I might have thought about doing that, but I have come to realize she is not that sort of woman.''

''What will you do then? Move into lodgings and bury yourself in work again. Look old fellow; you have a wench there who is intelligent, loyal and beautiful. She is nothing like Antonia or your mother. You clearly care for her deeply. You just have to trust her and yourself.''

Dreda knew his friend had hit the nail on the head. He could not trust a woman after his fiancée and mother had been cheats. It was too much of a personal risk. He would bury himself in work. It was safer than trying to love again.

''Stow it, Denman,'' he said angrily, ''or you can drink alone. The matter is closed.'' He called for another bottle of brandy and started shuffling the cards again, pretending to be interested in the game, whilst all the time trying to push an image of a beautiful, reserved young woman who had demanded nothing of him out of his mind. He downed two more glasses and then threw his cards down in disgust, unable to concentrate on the game.

''Well I never thought I would have found you to be a coward, Danitz,'' replied Denman disgusted.

Dreda got up and excused himself. ''Damn you Denman! When I want a lecture, I will go to my father!'' Demanding a fresh bottle of brandy from the waiting lackey he ran upstairs and locked himself in his club room intent on becoming totally foxed and driving Felea's face out of his mind that night.

An hour later he lay on his bed, a glass in his restless hand, the bottle half empty. He thought of calling on his Mistress who would welcome him at any time, but he couldn't summon any enthusiasm. He was a dull dog who just wanted his home and a pleasant companion beside him. *I must be getting soft in the head or old,* he thought. He finally acknowledged to himself he missed his home and Felea. Calling himself a fool he made for where his horse was stabled and rode home.

Felea was still up, a night owl. She would say she, ''Ventured out with the frogs and the toads.'' Sitting, resting her back against a heavy armchair, she was reading a book and the cat was curled on her knees purring contentedly. She made a pretty picture of domesticity.

Hearing him open the door she made to push the cat off and get up.

"No, stay there, you look comfortable," he said not wanting to disturb the ambience of the room. His day had been vile; he had had to order the execution of some people he had known personally, who had sworn to him they were loyal to the Emperor. Knowing they had lied to his face to save their skin had made him feel sick to the stomach thinking they had been good friends of his at one time.

He was beginning to think the Emperor was losing touch with his people if he was losing gentle folk of this type in droves. The Emperor was surrounded by sycophants of limited intellect and even more limited experience of the world who told him what he wanted to hear. They knew nothing of the suffering of the peasants in the hinterlands and the people in the new dirty, overcrowded unhealthy cities where fevers rose each year killing the old and young alike. He had tried to encourage his ruler to make changes to the systems, but progress was slow, and he felt discouraged.

It was good to come home to a well-organized and tranquil house. Felea had a light touch with the servants who enjoyed working for her and he knew they were more loyal to her than him. He was always polite to those who worked for him, but he was a reserved and sometimes sardonic man and lacked the warmth that made them love Felea.

Felea's warmth generated many friends and his villa was always frequented by visitors unlike his lodgings where only a few masculine visitors had bothered to join him. He realized he had been lonely in the evenings before she had arrived; secreted in his masculine cocoon, protecting himself from the sordid world he worked in. Denman had come regularly for dinner recently, saying the atmosphere in his villa was almost welcoming to visitors now.

"A drink Officer," she asked shoving the indignant cat off. The cat ignored her after being cruelly rejected and wrapped his body around Dreda's boots, trying to insinuate himself into Dreda's good graces.

Dreda had imbibed half a bottle of brandy to himself in his club room and despite having a hard head he was more than a trifle disguised. Tripping over the cat whilst nearly half cut hadn't put him in a good mood.

"No thanks, I've had enough."

He toe-ended the cat out of his way. "That bloody, manky, feline was on my bed this morning. He is nothing but an infested fleabag." She picked the cat up and cuddled it and said, "I will give him some herbal powders tomorrow Officer."

"Better bloody get rid of him. He doesn't even earn his keep chasing rodents away."

Felea resented his tone. Wondering what had put him in such a bad humour she retaliated in kind. "Would you like to put him in the river with a brick round his neck or ask the gardener to shoot him?"

"Don't tempt me! Stop being so bloody dramatic, Woman! Find a home for him."

She hugged the cat closer. He was one of the first friends she had made since she had come back to the city. "I will find him a box and put him in the stables Officer." She pushed the cat out of the room. Tired of his bad humour, she said, "As you don't want a drink I will leave you in peace and retire now Sir."

"No Lady Felea, stay a little," he asked regretting his harsh words already. He was envious of a bloody cat getting close to her. Whenever he came close to her she was as jittery as a lamb near a wolf; yet he had caught her giving Denman that kiss on his cheek as thanks after he had given her a fencing lesson.

Denman in turn had touched her hair gently, a gesture of friendship between two good friends. He had erupted in anger and remonstrated with her, deeply envious of Denman. How he wanted that warmth and trust between himself and this young girl, but she evaded him all the time. His gut churning, he had nearly challenged his best friend to a duel. Never had he felt such jealousy cut him to the quick. He must control himself. He must quash any feelings he felt for her. He could not allow any woman to have power over him again.

He sat down in the chair and took her wrist in his hand and made her sit at his feet. "I am sorry, I had an awful day at the Bureau and that just triggered my bad temper earlier." She pulled her hand away from him and sat watching him.

"He is a good cat really. He just likes company. He normally sleeps beside the range, but like any cat he is an opportunist and will take a soft bed when he can."

"He is a traitor coming to me when you rejected him!" said Dreda.

"I can't persuade you to like cats but at least you could tolerate him."

"Give me dogs any time. They are loyal to a fault!" he said unconvinced. His dogs had followed him into the room, slumping at his feet, trying to push Felea out of the way and resting their great paws on his boots. He pushed the two great wolfhounds away and pulled Felea back into place.

"Thor, Giant. Lie still!" he commanded, and the two canine

monsters howled but sat next to him while Felea stroked their large heads.

"See, obedient and loyal!" he said pressing his point home.

"Yes, if you want unswerving loyalty but I prefer an animal who chooses to make one a friend," replied Felea. "You want certainty; I am prepared to take a risk!"

"T'is true," he said. "I don't like taking my chances with humans or animals."

"If one doesn't take risks one can miss the chance of more excitement and happiness."

"I prefer to take no risks with my personal life."

"I am surprised after you pursued a career in the army and are always working against dangerous foes."

"I try to insulate my personal life against chance," he said. "I like tranquillity and certainty at home. Risk is for the card table and the horse races, not one's home life."

Nor his love life, thought Felea. This man had been hurt by women and wanted total control in his personal life. Damaged, he would not trust easily and had placed barriers against all but his few good friends.

"Play something on the pianoforte if you please," he requested, changing the subject but wanting her to stay with him. She went to the instrument and sat down. She still smarted from his earlier insults but wanted to humour him.

When he was in a good humour she loved his company. He was the most stimulating man she had ever spent time with. He was educated, witty and charming, not to say handsome and strong. He made her feel feminine and protected and safe for the first time in years. She had been living in fear since she had first found out her father had been helping the insurgents. Under Dreda's protection she had no fear of being accused again. Only now did she understand his influence on the Emperor and the respect he was held in by society.

Dreda the man was a mystery. No-one could breach his walls and find out what made him tick. He had had little love in his life and gave little in return. She felt that if a woman could make him trust her he would love her without bounds. Getting close to him was difficult. He rarely talked about himself, changing the conversation when the topic became too personal. How she wished he would trust her and let her care for him a little. He deserved better than his lonely life wedded to his work and coming home to a house filled with solitude and shadows.

She felt sad. While he was unwilling to admit his feelings for her or to show his commitment she could not allow him close to her. She had become accustomed to his presence and missed him when he went out of town. A tidy ex-army officer, nevertheless, he left his mark on the villa; a whip here, his keys and small change there and his own brand of cologne that drifted through the rooms and reminded her of him.

He relaxed back into the chair and felt at peace for the first time that day. This woman was a bundle of energy during the day but at night when she played the pianoforte she closed her eyes and a dreamy expression came over her face. She was transported into some other world he couldn't penetrate. How he would like to break down her barriers and divine what was going through her mind. She was as elusive as the air itself and as sensuous as sin. Every night she disturbed his sleep entering his dreams. For the first time, he thought about a woman all day, every day. He could not get her out of his mind and had difficulty focusing at work.

A prize on the matrimonial market he had been used to women using every trick known to man to trap him in the parson's mousetrap. Felea was a refreshing change! She was not like any of his ladybirds nor the usual debutantes or widows he met at court. She made no effort to disguise her thoughts if she thought he was wrong. She was the most transparent female he had met, avoiding pretence and coquetry; making no effort to entice him or to trap him with her looks or winning ways. In fact, she would argue the hind leg off a donkey as the saying goes.

Used to being obeyed without question his ego had taken a knock when she had often disagreed with him showing him the error of his ways. He knew he worked too long hours for the goodness of his health. She had made sure he had food to sustain him if he did not go to his club, staying up late, waiting for him to come home and persuading him to dine on something small but nutritious. He was annoyed at her interventions but sometimes the girl was right; damn her interfering ways!

She had piqued his interest, but he still did not know how she regarded him. She was a closed book and hid her feelings well. He wondered if Denman was right. Did her supposed indifference and avoidance of intimacy with him mean she was attracted to him more than she would admit even to herself? He would have to test her feelings because he was more drawn to her than ever before. He had been harsh about the cat because he was impatient to know her intimately and his frustration had shown itself in anger.

A calm expression on her face, Felea played some Mozart. That calm mask hid a maelstrom of emotions, swirling beneath the surface.

This man so cold and detached with others seemed over the last fortnight to storm at her on the slightest pretext as if she irritated him. She barely saw the sensitive man who had kissed her hand and had gently teased her. Excepting the times when he had sat with her by the fire he had remained aloof and criticized her as if he despised her and wanted her away from him and his home. She would have it out with him and leave his home if necessary. She would not be his whipping boy.

God help the woman he eventually settled down with if she had to put up with these strange tempers. He had even sworn, something he rarely did in front of a lady, unless he was in his cups. She had smelt the brandy on his breath but was puzzled. His aunt said he rarely drank excessively being too controlled but recently he seemed to over-imbibe most nights coming home in a foul mood.

He came over to the pianoforte and turned some sheets of paper for her, leaning so close to her she could smell his cologne and soap. He always smelt masculine, that mixture of sandalwood and something spicy, with a healthy dose of leather and a hint of the stables. He was never far away from his favourite horse which he groomed personally, caring for it more than he did most humans. He had trained the horse from when it was a foal whilst in his last years of the army and it was now a chestnut stallion, fiery and temperamental but as devoted to its master as he was to it.

Dreda had forbidden Felea to go near him. The animal regarded her evilly and summed her up. She thought it was a wise decision. A good rider, she still knew this horse was a man's horse and only a special rider could tame it. Denman had called it, ''A bloody cantankerous brute,'' it having unseated him recently, but Dreda had called him 'chicken' and said he had to show the animal who was boss. Denman had declined the generous offer and said he would prefer to make some steaks out of it!

She knew when Dreda was troubled or angry as he saddled the horse himself and took off along the river, only coming back when he had soothed his soul. Fire, the horse, seemed to know when his master was unhappy and neighed and whinnied when he neared it, nudging his back instead of kicking out as he did at the stable boys.

She smelt the horse on him now. He rarely took his curricle out even in the evenings although Denman said he risked his neck coming home half-cut on such an unpredictable animal. Dreda said he liked the ride home in the sharp air and shrugged the risk off as he did most things.

Felea contrasted this risk-taking part of his personality with his cautiousness with women. His aunt had explained he had found his fiancée in the arms of another man. She had admitted she would have married Dreda for his money but then have maintained her liaison with her lover.

She had destroyed a trust in women already eroded by his fickle mother. Felea was prejudiced but she couldn't understand how that woman could have preferred another man over Dreda. He had his flaws, but he still made her heart lurch when he looked at her. His strength, his integrity and the way he protected her overcame his irritating determination to dominate her.

A man used to being obeyed without question, he was used to being master in his own house. Unused to having his will gainsaid, they had had words more than once, she refusing to give in if she thought she was right. Exasperated, he had smoothly changed the subject, but she knew one day they would have a reckoning. He was not the sort of man who would let a woman dictate to him! She did not want to face his ire. He wasn't easily raised to anger but by God when he turned his anger on one, like Gavantz, all hell was let loose on his target! Cold in anger, he was ruthless in destroying or disarming his target, uncaring what the victim suffered.

The Mozart finished Dreda changed the sheets and sang a duo with her in his strong tenor voice. Felea felt his warm breath on her neck, so close to her he could have kissed it. She shivered, and he asked if she were cold.

''No Sir, someone merely walked over my grave.''

Ignoring her protest, he put his cloak around her shoulders as much to deny himself any temptation as to warm her. He had the desire to kiss her bare shoulders and follow a path to her pert breasts. Felea had been slim but underdeveloped once but her figure was slowly maturing now, developing in all the right places; she was unknowingly a temptress!

To the devil with being a gentleman! He wanted this woman child more every day. Living with her but not touching her was pure hell! If his aunt hadn't been such a careful chaperone he would have had had her in his bed by now despite his promise to protect her.

He was shocked by his lust for her. Not since he was a callow youth had he deflowered virgins. He behaved as was expected of most noblemen, taking his pleasure when and where he wanted but he recognized his moral boundaries and did not cross them. As a gentleman and a mature man, he left innocents to the libertines, concentrating his attentions on mature widows or birds of paradise who knew their way about men and what was expected of them. Felea was the first woman in years who was testing his self-control and ethics to the limits.

She felt him pressed against her back and wanted his arms around her. Her pulse was racing. His hot and cold behaviour excited her and confused her. Standing so close to her his arousal was quite evident. She might still be innocent, but she knew when a man was attracted to her.

The song finished, she closed the sheet book ready to get up and leave. He stopped her by pulling her up and turning her to face him. Placing his hands on her shoulders, he said, "You play and sing beautifully, Ma'am. There is no end to your talents." She coloured delightfully and replied, "My skill is not above average, but I enjoy music."

"I enjoyed every minute Ma'am. One day you will make a lucky man a graceful hostess and charm his guests."

She coloured again but had no answer. She cast her eyes down, not wanting him to read her expression. It was the first time he had complimented her since he had recovered his strength. She could suffer his bad temper but this charming Dreda was putting her off her stride. So close to her was he, she could feel him look down into her eyes. His eyes drew hers as if she were hypnotized, an expression in them she couldn't define. It was as if he was assessing her again, as if he was trying to make up his mind about something.

Her heart lurched as if it did not belong inside her. She did not understand this strange, difficult man and feared if she allowed him too close he would break her heart. Leaving his house would be the most difficult thing she had had to do. She felt as if she belonged there with him. Those evenings quietly reading or playing chess with him had been the happiest she had experienced since her mother had died.

She had wanted him to kiss her neck and shoulders. Through his cloak, she had felt his gentle fingers. They sent sensations she didn't understand down to her waist and lower. Her body had been warm and receptive, drawing back against him, wanting greater intimacy, not wanting to end this closeness with him. Her womanly instincts in the presence of a handsome and virile man were now wide awake and aroused, demanding she satisfy both of their needs. She held back, knowing without a commitment from him loving him would be a lost cause.

She could not be his mistress. She had inadvertently seen him with his former paramour. Polite and courteous to this lady, he had nevertheless treated her as a beautiful appendage to be deserted and disposed at will. Cold and indifferent to her plight, his needs served, she was now dispensable, passed on to another less discriminating fellow until he also tired of her. Felea had to leave this household while she still had her sanity, her self-control, respect and her heart intact. If this man controlled her without making any commitment she would no longer be her own woman, merely a pawn to be played with until he tired of her.

Dreda pulled her closer and stroked her hair. "It is like fire," he said winding a strand around his finger and stroking her head lightly. He put her away from him and just stared at her for several moments. Unnerved by his touch she could not tear her eyes away from him. She supported him staring at her and then asked, "What is wrong, Sir? Have I something wrong with me?"

Dreda grimaced at her then stiffened dropping his hands to his side. "There is nothing bloody wrong," he snapped angrily, surprising her. "You are just the most alluring woman I have ever beheld," he said, turning on his heel and slamming the door hard behind him, stunning her with his violence.

Shaking, Felea sat down, her legs unable to support her. She would have to tell him she wanted to leave. This maelstrom of emotions was unsupportable. She was too inexperienced to cope with such a virile and dominant man who could twist her emotions until she didn't know where to turn. She was woman enough to know she wanted him as much as he did her. Her heart was still pounding! He had only to touch her and she went up in flames.

Dreda went to the pond. He drew out a cheroot, smoking it until the end was just a stub and his pulse had slowed. Denman was right; Felea meant much more to him than just a woman he was protecting for the Emperor. He had grown accustomed to this girl; one day gentle and kind, the other a wildcat he was desperate to bed and tame. He once would have offered her a carte blanche, but he now knew that was no longer possible.

She would take any such offer as an insult and he admitted to himself she meant more to him than his usual barques of frailty to whom he offered short term liaisons which could be terminated with ease. She had insinuated herself into his heart and life, but he was not sure he was ready to commit to anything permanent. His blood ran cold at the thought of marriage. Trust was at the heart of matrimony. He still remembered the sniggers behind his back, the embarrassment of knowing that he was tricked when others knew the truth. After Antonia, he did not feel he could ever trust a woman again.

At boarding school, he had had to bear bullies taunting him about his mother. "Your mother's a whore, a harlot!" had cried one lad. For one term Dreda had needed to use his fists against the sordid mouthed youths. Denman had aided him, always in the background; helping deter the groups of bullies who looked for any sore spots they could put their finger on.

Finally, the taunting and physical assaults ended as Dreda proved to his fellows he was a better, more skilled fighter than they, but the scars were left. When he went into 'polite society' he felt his family was being judged by his mother's failings.

He could not easily show his feelings. Even to Antonia he had hidden behind a cold façade. When Antonia had been discovered by him naked with her lover her words had devastated him, shattered him!

"You are handsome, rich and titled Danitz but you cannot give a woman what she wants; warmth and affection, intimacy; caring for her." She was right. He had caged his feelings, distancing himself from people after his mother had left him. Antonia's deceit had made him withdraw further into his shell. He had sworn never to love another woman again and let her have power over him.

Reluctantly, he admitted to himself Felea was unlike Antonia, the only woman he had thought he loved. He realized he had merely been infatuated with Antonia, entranced by her superficial beauty and intrigued by her coquetry. In his mind's eye, he compared the women. Both were beauties, but Antonia was mercenary. Felea liked the balls and the fripperies most young woman admired but still enjoyed the simple things in life; quiet evenings by the fire and the affection of that flea bitten feline.

Antonia was devious using people, manipulating them for her own ends. Felea was strong-willed but generous and loyal, sticking her neck out for her father. She was honest to a fault, often to the detriment of his own ego when she told him he was in the wrong. Antonia was cold and detached. Felea was calm and intense but passionate about the things and people she loved, like that little scrawny, feline spitfire she had nursed back to strength who reminded him so much of her.

He must make up his mind about her and decide if she was the right woman for him to spend his future with. He would give his mistress her congée the next night. A lovely passionate lady he couldn't summon any desire for her anymore; she deserved better than him. Felea had spoilt all women for him!

Felea had tossed and turned all night. Eyes dark circled and red rimmed she looked a mess. Dreda's aunt took one look at her at breakfast and summed the situation up. Her charge's mind was troubled. Like her nephew Felea kept her problems to herself.

"I slept badly. I must have eaten something which disagreed

with me.''

''Witch hazel will help and then later a nap.''

''Has your nephew gone to the Bureau Ma'am?''

''No, he also awoke late having slept badly. Perhaps you both ate the same bad thing,'' said his aunt raising her eyebrows sceptically.

''He is in the study working on papers but in a bad humour. Go there at your peril!'' she warned ironically.

''He will make time for me,'' said Felea, determined to confront him.

She knocked on the door and slipped in without waiting for the order to come in. She was giving him no opportunity to avoid their discussion.

''I thought I told you I was not to be disturbed!'' snarled Dreda over his shoulder. Lack of sleep, an army shooting in his head and a sick stomach ache made him foul tempered. He needed to catch up his work or suffer the harsh tongue of the Emperor.

''Charming! Who got out of the wrong side of his bed?'' He looked worse than she did; his eyes red and bloodshot; his hair askew; he was unshaved and looked as if he had slept in his clothes.

''I am not going to the Bureau today. I am working on these papers and then going back to bed!''

''A strong coffee and a ride in the fresh air would do you more good!''

''I was not aware I asked you for your opinion on my state of health,'' he retorted, angry she had seen him in this state. He was always fastidious in his dress and rarely foxed. This last few weeks had been an exception. He had been driven to drink by frustration and despondency. He did not want her to know she was the reason behind his change in behaviour. That sort of knowledge gave a woman power over a man.

''I need to discuss a matter with you Sir.''

''Can't it wait until tomorrow? I am not in the mood to discuss inconsequential matters.''

''It is not inconsequential. It is of great import to me!''

''Oh, very well,'' he agreed grudgingly. ''Sit down!''

''So, gracious of you!'' He raised his eyebrows at her impertinence. He was a man used to being obeyed by people without hesitation or complaint!

''I prefer to stand,'' she said, feeling less intimidated than when she was sitting down.

''As you wish,'' he said churlishly. ''Make it quick. I can give you five minutes of my time.''

It was not a great start but Felea thought she would not get a better opportunity. Resisting the urge to smack him with his heavy reading lamp she stiffened her backbone and confronted him.

"Sir, I realize this position of my protector was foisted on you by the Emperor against your will."

He had shut his eyes, resting his head on his hands behind him, trying to stop his stomach from turning and to ignore the banging in his brain. His eyes shot open at her words and narrowed.

He said carefully, "I won't say it hasn't been damned inconvenient, but we have made the best of a bad situation and it should soon be over."

"That is what I want to talk with you about."

"I thought you said it was of great import. This discussion can wait until I have seen the Emperor." He closed his eyes trying to avoid the bright sunshine piercing through his brain like a sword impaling him.

"No, it can't," said Felea firmly. "I know you think me a nuisance and want me out of here, so I want you to ask the Emperor to get me a new chaperone and place to live. I think we would both be happier living in our separate households. We rub each up too much to live alongside each other." There she had said it and waited for his answer.

"So, you want to leave," he said. "You are not happy here?"

He felt shocked! Hollow inside! Soulless. Cold and dead; hungering for something he could not identify! He had expected her to leave one day but he had not contemplated it being so soon. She had become part of his existence, making his evenings happy as Denman had intimated. He would not show how much her leaving him would affect him. That would show her his weakness, how much he really needed her.

Damn, he was making this so difficult, thought Felea. As usual his face was impassive, his emotions so difficult to read; for a moment, she had thought him shocked, even a little hurt but then a shutter had come down on his face again and he sat silently, waiting for her to explain. No wonder they called him Vulcan at the Bureau. What would shake this man?

"I did not say I was unhappy all the time, but I seem to anger and irritate you and you leave the house to avoid me. It would be better if I left and gave you back your home. You are always criticizing me and saying I am not up to snuff. I don't want to show you up when I am presented at court."

Dreda breathed a sigh of relief. All was not lost; he could make her change her mind. He had been a bear and Felea had borne the brunt of it. She had been brave enough to beard him in his den, a difficult thing to do for such a young woman and himself such an intimidating man. He would apologize and make it right although it went against his grain to apologize to any young woman.

"Lady Felea," he said moving from behind the desk. "I am sorry if I have given you any reason to think you are a nuisance. Chasing and rescuing you was worth every minute. I have enjoyed my evenings here with you. You are the most intelligent, interesting woman I have spent my time with."

He moved closer to her, wanting to be near her, to persuade her to stay with him. "I have no desire to rid myself of your presence Ma'am, despite your turning my house upside down and making it smell like a lady's boudoir, and installing that flea-ridden bag of fur you call a cat. Which slept with me again last night, on my face, nearly suffocating me!

'You do not hesitate to pull me down if I become arrogant. You challenge me if you think I am wrong. What would I do without my little termagant to put me in my place? If I have been irritable you must blame this situation which has been quite uncomfortable for both of us."

He placed her hands in his and smiled a gentle smile that made her heart turn over. "Stay with me until the Emperor has decided what to do with you and I promise not to take my bad humour out on you."

She pulled her hands gently out of his and said, "If you are quite sure Sir. I don't wish to inconvenience you."

"You have grown on me Ma'am!"

"Like mould," she said self-deprecatingly. He smiled and replied, "I am going to the Emperor soon with you and then we will discuss your position further. You have the Emperor's ball to go to tonight and must look your best. Get some sleep and I will see you this evening. I must work and make myself look presentable."

"I have a receipt which is good for hangovers," said Felea. He pulled a face. "It is as bad as the other potion I expect?"

"Worse but my father said it was effective when he imbibed too much." Dreda suspected her father hadn't downed one bottle to himself but he would do anything to make himself feel and look respectable for the ball that evening.

"Bring it on," he said, "and then leave me to my work please." He wanted to do the work quickly and sleep the headache off until the evening. He felt like the dog's breakfast! His bloody wolfhounds had found the cat on his bed last night and were damned jealous and had howled the place down until he had rung the bell and asked his valet to remove them before he shot the bloody pair.

His life was calm and regulated before Felea had entered his life. Since then he had been shot, tortured and no longer controlled his home. He had had the opportunity to send this girl packing. She had volunteered to leave but at the last moment he had backed down and she was here to stay indefinitely. He must be mad!

He worked through his papers swiftly drinking copious cups of coffee and water until Felea sent him a potion that was so vile he vomited the contents of his stomach up. Promising himself not to get foxed again in a long time he washed his body and dragged himself into his bed to sleep.

He woke up at four in the afternoon. To his relief his stomach had stopped turning and he could move his head without any pain. He could not move his legs though and found to his disgust three pairs of eyes watching him. Enormous as the bed was two giant canines and one cat jealously guarding him had him pinned there.

"Buggar this!" he said and called the valet. Felea appeared with another potion smiling at the picture he presented.

"You can stop laughing! This all your fault! Those dogs were well behaved until they met your cat! Now they are canine delinquents!"

"Call it sibling rivalry," she said giggling but dragged the two dogs off by their collars. Surprisingly they behaved, cowed by the petite woman. Evicting the cat was more difficult. He pushed it away and was rewarded by a bite and scratch.

"That cat is going to be a muffler in a minute," said Dreda nursing his hand. "Tell my valet I need a bath. You look better. No dark circles or red eyes. At your age, you can take a few poor nights" sleep." Felea took the protesting cat, threatening it with a few of her own choice words until it behaved.

"Unladylike but pardonable," said Dreda. "Who would have thought that a sweet lady could curse like that," he teased.

"You would be surprised what a lady can say if she is angered sufficiently," said Felea.

"I wait that with anticipation then," said Dreda. "You know I don't admire milk and water misses. I admire a lady with a little fire."

"Just hope you don't get burnt then," was Felea's parting shot, good humour restored between them at last.

CHAPTER TEN

The Emperor's equerry had said that the Emperor wanted his aunt to introduce her to the court at a ball. Dreda would take them both and later for a private audience with the Emperor himself when that man came back from a short visit away.

She had her hair dressed in the classic style, a ringlet artfully curling down her neck. She wore as befitted a debutante a satin dress with a modest neckline but in an unusual shade of marine blue, spiked with mauve streaks unlike the normal whites and pale pinks the girls normally wore. Her creamy shoulders were almost bare, with tiny set back sleeves cupping them.

He walked her in with his aunt and noted the room stood still, everyone wanting to know who this new woman was. The Empress was acting in place of the Emperor and Felea curtseyed low before her and then went back to his aunt. She was the most beautiful woman in the room. As soon as she took her dance card out men clustered around her, wanting to dance with this alluring woman.

Dreda had gone to take a drink and seeing her card filling up quickly he walked across the room to her. The crowd moved out of his way, his reputation having gone before him and he took the card out of her hand and wrote his name against two dances. He then bowed and walked away again to the card room.

His aunt said to herself, ''Making sure everyone knew he wanted her.'' Dreda barely ever danced with a debutante. He did not want to raise the hopes of match making mamas and their offspring and only danced with them out of duty at the Emperor's instructions.

Felea felt uncomfortable, she had felt him watch her from the corner. He looked sternly at her when she flirted with the young men and raised his eyebrows when a young man tried to hold her too closely.

Good God, he is acting as if he is my guardian. She had warned him not to interfere in her life the night before. She did not want her actions criticized by another domineering man after escaping the clutches of Gavantz.

She waited for the dances with him with equal measures of excitement and trepidation. She remembered her last dance with him; his strong arms holding her almost too tight in the waltz. She had waited so long for him to hold her again but feared her body would act traitorously and show how she felt about him.

He came over and took her arm in his and bowed to her and they started meeting in the middle where he lifted her and turned her round. He was enjoying her closeness, but she felt uneasy, trapped, not knowing what this dance meant to him. Breaking the silence, he said, "You are an instant success, I knew you would be. Your looks and demeanour will attract most men."

She made a brief curtsey in thanks and said, "It is good that I may meet more people outside of my narrow social circle."

"Make sure you behave like a lady; you are too friendly at times and that may appear to be encouragement to them."

"Sir, are you accusing me of being a flirt?"

"I think you look too kindly on the young men who surround you and that may be interpreted as flirting."

"I think you are too severe. You behave as if you were my guardian. You have outdated ideas about how a young woman should behave in society. I would not want to be your daughter if you are so strict."

Dreda looked as if he could be struck down with a feather. The dance finishing, he asked her if she would go for a walk with him.

"I need to talk with you alone," he said taking her arm firmly in his grasp and leading her into the gardens and down to the lake. It was a romantic scene, the swans gliding by and the moonlight beams lighting up the shore. She said, "I think we should go back, Officer. If we are seen, it may be thought you are compromising me."

He put his hand on her bare shoulder and with the other lifted her face to his. "I wonder if that would be so bad," he said, leaning towards her. She pulled away from him and said firmly, "I will not be your Mistress, Sir!"

The moment was lost. He could not tell her how he truly felt. She was still under his protection and under his roof. He took her arm in his and said, "Your reputation is safe with me. I am not a deflowerer of innocents, but I do not see you as a daughter and you should not see me as a father figure.

'Be more careful who you go to the gardens with in future. You are too naive, and some men will exploit your innocence." He drew her back into the ballroom where she sought sanctuary with his aunt. He went out to the gardens again and stood pensively looking there.

It was time he told Felea her options. The Emperor was back the next day and the equerry had summoned her for a meeting with him in four days to discuss her future. Since talking with her that morning he had examined his feelings for Felea in his cautious and careful way. He was certain now of his feelings toward her and would have to tell her his position.

His aunt scolded her for going to the garden with him. "If you were seen by mischief-makers you could have been thought to have been compromised and Dreda would have been forced to marry you out of honour.''

Felea remembered his words and wondered if she had misunderstood him when she thought he had wanted her as his mistress.

''Dreda rarely dances with debutantes. Keep him at a distance my dear. He is too experienced for you. You do not know what you are getting into if you become involved with him.''

''I told him I will not be his Mistress Ma'am.''

''Did he offer you a carte blanche?'' asked his aunt, shocked.

''No! I thought he meant that when he said he wondered if it would be so bad if he had been thought to have compromised me.''

His aunt changed the conversation but thought things were coming to a head between her nephew and her charge.

CHAPTER ELEVEN

Three days later Dreda asked for a private interview with Felea. Nervous, as she still did not know her fate she waited silently in front of him hands clasped in front of her. The troops had identified the jewellery her father had taken with him and she still had her house and a country estate, so she was not penniless, but her father was in a house for the mentally ill.

He explained her position carefully. "Ma'am, you have been a ward of court for over three months. You have Denham to thank for this. The Emperor is responsible for your safety for the next year. The Emperor has arranged for this house to be yours for that time and will pay the bills and grant you an allowance until new trustees have been appointed to settle your affairs satisfactorily.

'He has pardoned you for any help you gave to the rebels but if I were you I would keep my head out of politics for a long while.

'Like most wards of courts, you will have some freedom but must ask permission to leave the country for periods and of course permission if you wish to marry. He will pay for the care of your father until his death. Here are the relevant documents if you wish to peruse them."

She breathed a sigh of relief feeling safe at last. "I am very grateful for your help Officer Dreda. I thought wrongly you were my enemy at first, but you were acting in my best interests. I should not have doubted you."

"No, you were right to doubt me at first. I was only interested in state security and I was acting mischievously when you challenged me. I rarely find a woman who ignores or disobeys my will."

"Well it worked out well in the end."

"Indeed."

She turned to go but he shut the door again and stood in front of it. As if pondering when to break the news to her he said cautiously, "But there may be one contingency we need to discuss. Already the Emperor has had five requests for your hand in marriage and is considering them. He wants an interview with you about them tomorrow."

She was maddened but unsurprised. She had been mistress of her own fortunes with a father who left her to her own devices and then nearly forcibly married. Now the Emperor could choose her future husband from five men and she would have her life mapped out for her. She nearly choked at the thought of being married to the weasel or one of those immature boys. Dreda was amused, watching the conflicting emotions pass over her expressive face.

"You may find not all the suitors are weasels or immature boys."

"I am pleased to hear it."

Well, she must steel herself for the meeting. She would dread having her life organized for her, but it was better than execution or exile. Perhaps the Emperor would find a kind gentle man who had her interests at heart and would let her read and ride her horses and live in peace. And a small voice in her ear said, "And you will be bored in a month." She shrugged it away and held her head up.

"Will you take me there and stay with me?"

"I would be honoured if you want me there, but I will be there anyway."

She left while she could still control her emotions. He had not explained who the suitors were although he knew the names. How would she react to them? He knew she would not open up to him and asked his aunt to talk to her. She found her in the bower and opened the difficult conversation with Felea.

"My parents let me choose my fiancé but he died of scarlet fever and they did not force me to marry.

'Is there any man you have a preference for? My nephew could put a word in for him if he thought him suitable."

"I don't know the names of the suitors who have asked for my hand."

"Danitz will know. I will ask him."

She searched for her nephew and found him in his study. "The poor girl doesn't know who she might end up with. Name them!" He named four; the weasel, one of the sons of the trustees, the young nobleman who had pestered her and a professor.

"Who is the fifth? You?"

"Guilty as charged." He made her a mocking bow.

"I am pleased. It is the best thing you could do with your life instead of wasting your time with your bits of fluff and harlots. Why didn't you tell her?"

Dreda ignored her pointed references to his usual style of ladies and concentrated on the matter at hand. He frowned and pursed his lips. He admitted, "Perhaps I am worried that she might prefer one of the others and the Emperor would have to force her to marry me. I could not cope with the indignity of that."

"Compared with you, the others don't stand a chance. Trust me, she is head over heels in love with you but just doesn't show it. For once trust your judgement in love as you do in other things. Go to her!"

His aunt was rarely wrong. In fact, she was the wisest female he knew. He went to the bower where Felea was waiting for his aunt to return.

It was only a few minutes but to Felea it had felt like hours. She had no illusions about her precarious position. If she was lucky the Emperor might allow her to choose from the five suitors. If not, she would be parcelled off to the highest bidder or sacrificed to the man who had the most illustrious title.

As a young and single woman, she was regarded as merely a pawn in the politics of statehood. The Emperor was as capricious as he was autocratic, thinking only of what would enhance the status of his country. A woman with wealth and estates she was a useful weapon in the Emperor's armoury, able to be traded in an alliance that could cement and solidify the prickly relations between his and other city states.

She had commented dryly to Denman once she was treated like a brood mare. One man had stated in her hearing, her hips were too narrow for good childbearing. The men would inspect her teeth next!

She thought Dreda would try to help her. He was not without influence at court being the man who exercised the most influence over the Emperor. To what extent would he endanger his own position of favourite with the Emperor by pleading her cause? She suspected not far.

She had overheard conversations at court which indicated Dreda was his own man, a lone wolf, only looking after his own interests and the interests of the state. He rarely put himself out for anyone according to gossip and was ruthlessly selfish.

She was pulling the petals off a flower when Dreda found her. "What has that poor flower done to you?" he asked teasing.

She was astonished. Rarely did he use a gentle tone of voice to her. Usually it was serious, warning her or admonishing her. Never one to beat about the bush he got straight to the point.

"I know the names of the five suitors. Do you want to know them?" She nodded.

"The bookies are taking bets already I am afraid. The Weasel, Professor Mati, Trustee Harrati's son and the immature boy I roughed up at the party and one other. Don't look so horrified. There is one other."

"Who is the fifth."

"Yours truly. I am afraid I must go through the same procedure as the others. I was too ill to make up my mind before we set you up as ward of court."

He thought her silence was a rejection. ''I can of course withdraw if the idea is repugnant to you. I thought we could protect you in this way.'' She just shook her head and ran to her bed-chamber.

His aunt came in. Her perplexed nephew explained what he had said. His aunt gave him a stern telling off.

''You could not have said a worse thing. She thought you were marrying her because it was the honourable thing to do and not because you love her. She knows you are the favourite of the Emperor and he would grant you almost anything and you would obey his wishes.''

'Go and make her open her door and tell her the truth.''

He knocked on the door and when she told him to go away he asked her to come down.

''Thank you but no, Sir.'' After coaxing her for five minutes he lost his patience.

''If you don't open the door I will kick the damn thing in!'' She ignored him hoping he would leave and go downstairs.

True to his word he kicked the door in and entered in a rare temper. He was embarrassed to walk into this innocent young girl's chamber, especially when she was in her nightrail, but he wasn't stopping now he had plucked up the confidence. He was determined to persuade her to marry him.

He stood as close to her as was decently possible, trying to ignore her low-necked peignoir and her hair tumbling down her neck. How often had he wanted to take her into his arms when she was arguing with him and kiss her objections away? His aunt's presence and his education as a gentleman had not let him take advantage of her vulnerable position but he had been strongly tempted and that frustration had come out as anger and criticism. Only when he was injured, and she had nursed him had he really let his guard down and he had nearly kissed her.

On this occasion, there was no reason why he could not tell her his feelings. Seeing the determined look in his eyes she tried to back away but this time he would not let her. He swept her into his arms and kissed her passionately. There was no way she could mistake his feelings after that kiss. When they surfaced for air he asked, ''Now do you know why I want to marry you?''

''I thought you wanted to please the Emperor and save my honour.''

''I can do that as well but that is secondary. I want to marry you because I love you and want you to share my life. And if you say no I will spend the rest of my life trying to persuade you to change your mind.''

"I would hate you to waste your life, so I will say yes," she replied her eyes dancing.

"Come, we must tell my aunt."

They raced down the stairs forgetting she was barely dressed. His aunt thought what a difference love made to two typically cautious, intense people. Now they had not a care in the world.

The next morning was different. They went in their best clothes to the Emperor's Palace. Felea was naturally nervous despite Dreda's assurances that she would impress the Emperor and he would hold no grudges against her.

They sat in the waiting room until the personal envoy nodded to Dreda that they could go in. The Emperor started to ask Felea some personal questions which she answered with assurance.

"I remember your mother, a beautiful woman and talented. I nearly married her myself, but your father got there first. I remember she used to give very good tutorials at the university in history as a volunteer."

"She was extremely clever."

"Like her Daughter, seven languages!

"I have had five requests for your hand in marriage Your father has no longer the capacity to make any decisions for you. I have been looking at these requests. I am not impressed by the request by your former trustee for me to consider his son. Good job he is no longer in charge of you.

'The professors are not your equal in status or in property. The young man is a fool and needs to mature. That leaves you Dreda. What is your interest? You have been looking after this young woman and you assure me she is no longer a danger to the security of the state and was misled by her father."

"My interest is personal sir. I love this lady and want to marry her for that reason alone."

"She is wealthy, now we have recovered her valuables and there are country properties we have discovered."

"I have my own fortune and I will inherit more from my parents and grandparents. I need none of hers."

"Still, it is a large fortune that could join two powerful families together."

"I have no need of power."

"I was not thinking of you but of the future of this state."

Felea began to feel sick again. "Sir, if I may be bold, I would prefer Officer Dreda to any of the other suitors. "

"Unfortunately, the decision is not yours to make alone. We

must consider wider issues. Your mother came from one of the oldest families in this city. A marriage between you and another great family from one of the other city states could seal the future of this area and create the peace we have been looking for. Only this morning an equerry of a city state, our enemy, suggested the Duke may be interested in you.

'Leave it with me and I will think it over.'' He dismissed her with a nod.

''Dreda, stay please.'' He stood there in silence waiting for the Emperor to continue.

''Dreda, I am still not convinced of this girl's loyalty.''

''Then I am the best man to keep an eye on her.''

''She duped you several times. A man in love doesn't have the sharpest eyes or ears. He ignores signs.''

''Not this time! Her loyalty is now to me not her father. I am sure of that.''

''You are a fool, taken in like your father was.''

Dreda took a sharp intake of breath. Only iron self-control stopped him from throttling the Emperor.

''She would be better exiled to a foreign country to cement an alliance.

'I have thought of another beauty for you. Aranna Duchess of the Allannitz house, wealthy, intelligent and her father the General is very loyal to the state. Think about it; it would be good for your career.''

''No thank you! I know who I want as my wife.''

''I said think about it,'' repeated the Emperor very carefully. ''You can have a month to think about it. I am out of the country for a visit and will be away until then.'' Nodding a dismissal, he turned to his papers again.

Dreda left, barely containing his anger. Years of loyalty to an often capricious, temperamental leader had been rewarded with what? A marriage to a beautiful, spoilt featherhead who was more interested in clothes and his fortune than himself. He knew this beauty and would be bored living with her within a week.

''Well. What did he say?''

''He doesn't trust you and wants you to make an alliance with a noble outside of this state. I am to marry to cement a military alliance with one of his generals. A marriage of convenience with a beautiful featherhead!'' He nearly spat it out.

Taking his arm, she led him out. She had seen him angry but never like this. A violent anger was barely contained, and he held her arm so tight she had to tell him to stop hurting her. In the carriage drive home, he brooded and went to his study as soon as he got to the villa.

He was in a quandary the next day. His aunt was not surprised when hearing of the decision. "You have always had a better opinion of the Emperor than I, Danitz."

"He has had always to think of the state first and I think many of the decisions have been right, if not easy ones."

"What do you intend to do? If your estates are confiscated and you have no career you cannot support Felea and she will have no income or property."

"I could soldier again, be a mercenary." He discarded that idea, he had tired of that life years ago.

"He has given me a month. I go back to work tomorrow, and I will have to tell my father and mother what the Emperor has proposed before they get to hear of it."

"Go and talk to Felea. She must be feeling so miserable and you left her alone last evening."

Dreda felt miserable himself. Being honourable had got him nowhere. He had been better to have seduced her as he had wanted to on many occasions. He had hoped for a quick wedding, but his hopes were now dashed.

He found her in the garden pruning roses. He stood quietly looking at the peaceful pretty picture she presented. He put his hands gently on her shoulders and turned her around and looked into those deep smouldering eyes. She in turn put her hands around his waist and rested her head on his shoulder.

"We will work something out. He will be persuaded. I know his weaknesses and will manipulate him!"

"You can, if anyone can." She was sure of that. For now, she wanted him to relax and kissed him, guessing it was the best way to distract him. He was easily distracted by her and acquiesced, folding her in his arms although his pulse raced when he held her, and she was nearly breathless.

Denman found them and was about to creep away when a soldier's instinct told Dreda he was there, and he called him to come over to them. Felea quickly smoothed her hair and tidied her fichu. She was blushing but regained her composure quickly.

"I came from the Palace. I heard a rumour. Has he refused your offer?"

"I am to marry to cement an alliance between my family and the army to give the Emperor more military support and Felea is to marry into a family in another city state to try to create a permanent peace. Very laudable objectives but our feelings are not to be considered.''

Denman looked shocked. ''You will of course look for a way out.''

''Of course, I am not marrying that brainless featherhead.''

Denman knew that look on his friend's face, pure stubbornness. He would clash with the Emperor if it were necessary. He had set his mind on marriage to Felea and nothing would change it and from the look on her face she was equally as determined not to give in. There was a rocky road ahead of them. The Emperor left the next day and would not grant Dreda an audience before he left.

They visited his father and mother at their country villa. His mother was clearly the bored flame haired court beauty with a sharp capricious personality, quick to anger and take offence but sensitive and caring despite her fiery temperament. Wasted in her bleak wintry marriage she avoided the marital home and spent more time at court whilst his father made political alliances abroad, pleasing the Emperor and gaining more esteem and estates. Dreda was the physical image of his father, the diplomat who was calm, cool and detached. His father neither cared about the fate of others nor was interested in them unless they served his aims.

Felea had never seen Dreda nervous but he was clearly uneasy when he met his parents. His relationship with them was very formal. He was attached to his mother but there was no bond between him and his father. He blamed his father for his mother leaving them. Felea began to realize how Dreda had become so cold, withdrawn and self-reliant after meeting his father and experiencing the icy atmosphere in the house. It felt more like a mausoleum than a family home.

Dreda explained his situation and his father immediately said, ''You must marry the Duchess. It will be good for the state and the family and please the Emperor.''

''Sorry, but I am not.''

His mother intervened, recognizing the battle beginning to commence between father and son. ''Is there no other way out?''

''No, the Emperor refused to give me an audience. I give him my answer when he comes back in a month's time.''

''What about the girl?'' his father asked pointing to Felea making her bristle. He didn't even refer to her by name! She bit her tongue and let Dreda handle this obnoxious man who saw her as a chattel to be traded for the best price.

''He is to find a suitor from one of the city states to cement a peace alliance.''

"We are going back tomorrow. We thought you should know if there are repercussions. I may lose my estates and position."

"What will you do if you are penniless?"

"I have no idea at the moment."

"You should think again and use your heads," said his father. "You will gain nothing by being led by your emotions. Marriage is a business arrangement for persons of our class."

"Then we will make an exception to the rule Sir. We came to deliver the news in person. We didn't want you to hear rumours at court.'"

He got up. "I will keep you informed of our decision Sir, Ma'am. 'He kissed his mother and ignored his father's bad humour. Used to being obeyed without question this defiance by his older son was clearly unacceptable. The older man left the room without another word making his displeasure clear. His mother just shrugged her shoulders and hugged the affianced couple giving them her blessing.

Disheartened, but with nothing more to say they travelled back to the city. Dreda's presence was demanded by the Emperor's son at a ball the next day. Felea wore a mauve gown that suited her so well, but her hair was now swept up in a sophisticated style and her neckline was much lower as befitted a girl who had now been presented to the court.

Dreda's eyes nearly fell out of their sockets when he saw the neckline. He became very protective of her toward other men and prudish about her dress. He would have scowled the whole of the evening but had to represent his department at this state affair as his head officer was with the Emperor and he had to accept with good grace she was not 'his' this evening. He barely had a dance with her, but she saved the last waltz for him. More men had put in applications to marry her. He was becoming aware of the competition and his chances of being the favoured suitor diminishing. Perhaps one of these men would attract her.

When they got home he went to his study and sat there in the gloom. Felea knew he was upset and was remembering his mother's infidelities. She put her arms around his neck and kissed him.

"Why do I need to stray when I have you? You always keep me out of trouble," she teased. Hating being jealous, Dreda took her into his arms. Despite his good intentions, he warned, "If you go to another man I will kill him, I promise you." She believed him. She remembered the look on his face when he attacked Gavantz. It was not wise to cross Dreda.

His aunt suggested he moved back into his own lodgings and reluctantly he agreed. From then on men flowed in every day to the villa presenting flowers and other gifts. Emissaries of other states appeared with portraits of men who would marry her. The flattery would have turned another girl's head but Felea had made up her mind. She wanted Dreda, 'walts and all'. Under that cold detached personality was a kind, caring man who would care and protect her even if he did try to dominate her. She could deal with that.

Dreda and Felea discussed their options if the Emperor insisted on her marrying another. ''We can move to another state if he threatens us with exile or the loss of our estates. No income would mean I would have to find a position, probably as a soldier. You would be on a very limited income my love.''

''I care not Francis,'' said Felea. ''All I want is to marry and be with you.''

''There is another alternative. We could present the Emperor with a fait accompli. I could seduce you and then tell him you are spoilt goods. He could let us wed or confiscate our lands. It is a high-risk strategy.''

''I think we should wait a little Francis and try to persuade him. You could tell him I can help you in the bureau decoding and translating. He might see I have more use helping you fight spies than cementing an alliance which is likely to break down. He knows these alliances rarely stand the test of time.''

''You are right my love. We will wait a short while, but I am desperate to marry you.''

He took her in his arms and kissing her passionately he carried on initiating her into the process of love-making. Tracing delicate kisses down her neck to her bust-line he stopped but his hand cupped her breast and rubbed it making her gasp and moan.

''Sweet Jesus, Francis!'' She had never sensed anything like this before.

''Just letting you know what you may look forward to on our wedding night my love.''

Felea thought if this was what the wedding night would be like she needed to marry him as quickly as possible. He knew her sensitive areas behind her ears, down her neck and on her breasts, manipulating her until she shivered with desire when he took her home in his carriage.

CHAPTER TWELVE

Felea was frequently bored at court, no longer decoding messages or translating works. She was regarded merely as a pretty companion to Dreda, a marionette whose strings were pulled this and that way; tolerated when she said the right things to the right people. Sometimes, she wished herself back to the days when her mother was alive, and she lived a less complicated life.

Dreda noted her boredom. Felea's intelligence and natural curiosity would lead her into danger and her candidness could be construed as criticism of the Emperor's policies. Her confidence grew as she took her place in court life. She felt safer and was less reserved, speaking her mind in public more often to Dreda's dismay. Once married he would ask the Emperor to let her work for the Bureau decoding or translating but for now he merely wanted to keep his sometimes outspoken, impetuous lady out of trouble.

Felea had heard a few enlightened ladies were organizing fund-raising events to raise money for the victims of the civil war. She tackled Dreda one evening when they were relaxing by the fire.

"Francis, I have heard that some ladies have raised monies for the families of the rebels. Hannah visited a camp and said the conditions were inhumane, the children suffering malnutrition and starvation."

Dreda looked up, wary she might be showing an interest in politics again. She was still in a dangerous position being the daughter of a spy even if her father was incarcerated in a home for the mentally incapacitated. No-one other than Denman and his sources knew about the monies that had gone to purchase arms or her connections with the schools for the rebels.

She had stopped teaching the foundlings after Dreda had said her flight from the country had made others think she was guilty of aiding the rebels. Only his proposal of marriage and the patronage of the Emperor kept the knives of other courtiers at bay. Some still wanted her to be tried for allegedly helping her father aid the Emperor's enemies.

He thought charity work might engage her supple mind. "My love. Would you be interested in organizing charity events to raise money to help the wives and families of the rebels who have lost their homes and incomes?"

She would not be using her own money as she did before and would be supporting a charity recognized by the Empress herself. Dreda had at last persuaded the Emperor that burning the villages down was creating more resistance to his policies. The ruler now did not want the rebels' wives and children to suffer for the faults of their husbands and partners.

It had now become fashionable for noblewomen in 'polite society' to raise money for the families. He knew some wise older women like his aunt who would take her under their wing and use her organizational skills. If she just raised the monies and left the distribution of the goods to others she should not come unstuck.

"Yes, Francis. I think I would, but I need to visit one of those camps myself to see the hardship first hand."

"War always brings hardship Felea. These women knew when their men supported the rebel cause they were flirting with danger. Villages burned, the harvest and grain stores destroyed, men made examples of; they were always aware of these repercussions."

"But they didn't always make the decisions, Francis. Perhaps, there wasn't any real choice for these women. They merely supported their husbands and fathers. Loyalty to their families comes before loyalty to the state when the life of their men is at stake."

She pursed her lips and bit nervously on her under lip thinking about the past. "Until one's back is against the wall one cannot understand all the implications Francis. I know that myself. I would visit the camps and see for myself what the families are suffering."

"I will accompany you then Felea. Without me it might look black, as if you are sympathizing with the rebels."

"You don't trust me to go alone Francis?"

"I trust you wholeheartedly Felea but there are others who do not trust you still and will want to make something out of nothing. You are not entirely safe until my ring is on your finger and possibly until you have born me an heir. You must not only be loyal to the Emperor, but you must also be seen to show your loyalty to him."

"Sometimes I wonder if this is all worthwhile, if my life would have been better I had not become involved in this wretched civil war."

"We can't turn the clock back as much as we might wish Felea and if you hadn't helped your father we would never have met."

He came over and took her in his arms. "That would have been a tragedy! I don't know what I would do without you Felea, now I have lived with you almost as man and wife! You are my soulmate, my conscience. I will take you to the camp and we will assess the situation together."

"Have you been to one of these camps, Francis?"

"Yes, but I only delivered some women and left within the hour. I saw little of their conditions."

He had only seen his role as an escort for the raggedly dressed women with little baggage walking to their new temporary home. Once there he had turned around as quickly as possible, showing no inclination to find out how they managed with little shelter or sustenance. They had merely been inconveniences stopping him doing his job of routing the rebels.

"I will make arrangements for us to visit a camp, my love."

Two days later they rode into the camp heaving with bedraggled dirty bodies fighting for space under the blankets hoisted between the trees for temporary shelter. The few tents had been taken quickly by the more dominant and stronger women who ran the camps by stealth and intimidation like those in the prisons.

The stench from the filthy latrines filled Felea's nostrils and made her retch. Covering her nose with a perfumed handkerchief she asked one of the officers who commanded the camp if there was fever there.

"Yes, Ma'am, stomach problems and sickness."

"It is hardly a wonder when the latrines are filthy and the women only have the river to wash in. Hygiene needs to be a priority here, Francis."

"It is unlikely to be a priority of the Emperor when his own troops have the same conditions when they have to fight."

"If the fever spreads these people will drop like flies. Look at those children. They are so starved their skin looks as if it is falling off them. They could not fight a fever. If conditions are not improved the death of these families will be on the consciences of the officers in charge here and the Emperor."

Dreda looked around him and for the first time he saw the conditions as they really were. He frowned as he saw the children barefooted, up to their ankles in mud, shivering with fever, their flesh barely hanging on their bones, their stomachs distended, and their eyes sunk into their heads.

Their mothers looked tired and old before their times, haggard! Small undernourished babes were at their mother's breasts, crying because the mothers who being ill-fed themselves were unable to give them enough food to stay their hunger. Many of these babes would not last the week unless their mothers could give them the nourishment they needed.

"Felea we are getting away from here now," he said guiding her to her horse. "You can raise money for them back in the city, but you are not getting near those women or children. Disease is already rife. Who knows what you might catch from them."

"Oh, it will look good, a senior officer from the Bureau, the

Emperor's favourite, bringing his Wife to be here and then both of us disappearing as soon as they fear a fever is abroad.'' She pulled away from him. ''I think not Francis. I will risk the fever.''

She walked over to a group of women who were sheltering under the trees nursing their babes. Dreda cursed her fluently. The damned woman didn't know how quickly fever could spread in these camps. It was typical of Felea thinking of others before her own health. He loved her, but she would be the death of him. He was always worrying about her. Her headstrong ways would lead her into trouble one day and he would not be able to rescue her in time.

He worried about her all the time. He had made many enemies and now they knew his weakness, his vulnerability where she was concerned; they might use her to get at him. Her enemies waited for her to trip herself up, to meet the wrong people who were once in favour but now enemies of the state, to say something inauspicious; to hang herself with her own words. More than once he had warned off men and women who had grown too close to her, enticing her with words of friendship; weaving silken webs of deceit designed to distort her innocent words and twist them until she could not prove her loyalty to the state.

He was clothing her with his fidelity to the Emperor, making her appear as loyal as himself but recently his own judgement and therefore his loyalty had been called into question. Even the Emperor had called him 'a blind lovesick fool'. The Emperor was becoming more autocratic and neurotic every day looking for enemies everywhere, even amongst his most loyal supporters in his Cabinet. He openly questioned Dreda's ability to make clear judgements any longer and suggested his loyalties were now divided if he wanted to marry a rebel supporter's daughter.

His secure position in the Cabinet was now under threat as his rivals sought to undermine him. It was a slippery slope. He had clawed his way to the top ruthlessly and efficiently destroying the power base of his rivals, but new men were climbing the hierarchy, willing to form coalitions with his enemies and to undermine and usurp him. He must tread carefully giving no man or woman opportunity to slander him or Felea. Once married to him she should be safe, and he could relax. He would have to find some more stimulating work for her in the Bureau to concentrate that fine brain of hers.

He followed her and watched quietly while she picked up a babe and rocked it gently in her arms. She turned to the woman and asked, ''What do you need to look after your families appropriately? Tell me and I may able to help.'' One woman sneered and asked, ''Why do you care about us? That man Dreda burnt our villages two years ago and killed some of our men and sons and you are with him. Whose side are you on?''

Taken back by this assault on her integrity Felea explained; ''I am Lady Felea Whelani, daughter of Professor Whelani who was arrested for helping the rebels. This is Officer Dreda, but he is my fiancé. He has killed rebels and burnt villages but this time he is here to help you. He has influence with the Emperor and can make your life easier if you are truthful to him and tell him your needs.''

Dreda saw the woman look at Felea and then him carefully assessing them. ''Ma'am, what Lady Felea says is true. I am absolutely loyal to the Emperor, but I will get you provisions if you tell me what you need. The Emperor would not see innocent children starve or die of fever.''

''We want nothing from you!'' spat a woman in his face. ''You are a murderer. You may kill in the name of the Emperor, but you are still a murderer of young boys barely britched who fight your beloved ruler to get a fair share of the harvest and a reduction of taxes.''

Dreda wiped the spit from his face but refused to retaliate. ''Come Felea. We are not doing any good here,'' he said grasping her arm and pulling her with him. As he left he said, ''Tell the Commanding Officer what you want and if you will accept the provisions I will ensure they are supplied. If you choose to refuse our help your children's deaths will be on your consciences, not on mine.''

A woman threw after him spitefully, ''He is only helping us to impress his fiancée, to make her think he is a human being instead of a monster!''

Felea answered quietly, ''You wrong him Ma'am. He came voluntarily to see the conditions here and organize help.'' Dreda impatient now, threw Felea up on to her horse and gave the horse a slap on its rear. It moved and Felea fulminated beside him. ''I can make my own mind when to leave the camp Francis.''

''We were not doing any good there. My presence has put their back up. It is better to retreat and let others persuade them. The Commanding Officer will negotiate with their priest on our behalf. Make a list of what you think they need and the officer can decide the quantities.''

''Who will pay?''

''I will organize that, but you can organize some balls and other charitable functions to raise money for the next delivery which will be needed soon in the future.''

Felea's mind was whirring. ''And education and training for the children and widows might encourage them to work lawfully instead of working for the rebels.''

"Don't get too ahead of yourself. The concept is good but getting them to accept anything from us will be an up-head struggle. Let us start with the food and blankets and tents first.''

Felea sighed. ''I didn't know we were hated so much Francis.''

''Not you my love. Just me!'' he said softly but regretfully. ''It is expected after my career in the army and the Emperor's tendency to use my militia officers to break up rebellions when they rise in the city.''

Felea felt sick. A vision was coming. She could see a tall slim man heading a troop of armed soldiers, but the vision paled into nothingness. Her head spun. Then there were men crying and screams as rifles were emptied into a crowd. She almost fell off her horse and Dreda pulled her onto his in front of him.

''What is it?'' he demanded.

''A vision of a man like you with a troop of soldiers.'' She told him what had penetrated her mind.

''I don't know what that refers to Felea. I wish you could tell me. Fore-armed is fore-warned.''

He snuggled her against him, his cloak wrapped around them both. ''Rest Felea. We will discuss this when we get back to the city. At least we are now away from that deathly hell-hole. I thought you might catch something and I might lose you!''

Felea's visions always exhausted her and she fell asleep in his arms while Dreda set his mind to resolving some of the problems of the camp. His eyes had been opened to the misery of the families there and his practical nature was searching for solutions. The church would have to intervene. His name was black as was most of the other well-known officers in the militia and army. He would help but remain anonymous.

Felea dozed fitfully but waking she could not rid her mind of that image. She also remembered the words of that last woman. Was Dreda still insecure about her love? Was he helping the rebels' families merely to impress her or had his heart been touched by their plight? She felt cold inside. Was she marrying a man without a conscience or had he begun to change?

Dreda cursed the women. He had Felea now and would not give her up. He would ensure the families of the rebels gained the provisions they needed and Felea now had a cause she could support. Dreda introduced her to the right women who also had a social conscience and an advocate who would create a trust for the organization. Felea enthusiastically engaged in the process of creating the trust and raising funds. Her mind engaged, she was happy and fulfilled again for a while.

What Dreda didn't know was she made several journeys to the camp again to assure herself what was needed. He would have wanted to throttle her for taking the risk but what he didn't know wouldn't harm him. When he married her, he would have to loosen the reins a little. She would not be an obedient wife if she didn't agree with him.

CHAPTER THIRTEEN

There were rumours of another rebellion. A new decree raising taxes was causing great poverty and Dreda and Denman were asked to help again. They thought the Emperor had brought this upon himself by being too greedy, but they couldn't refuse. The situation was grave. This time the rebels were very well trained and had more popular support.

Dreda and Denman worked together as usual. Dreda was the plotter and strategist, Denman the implementer. Within days Dreda's informers had ensured the capture of many of the leaders and the rebel alliance began to fall apart. This had been Dreda's plan, to avoid bloodshed where possible.

One main pocket of resistance held out and the men lead some troops to sort the rebels out once and for all. They were holding out in a fort near to the city boundaries. The Emperor was just over the boundaries trying to forge a peace alliance with the ruling Duke. He had not come back when promised because he had been warned it was too dangerous to return. Dreda had not supported his decision to go on this tour thinking it was too dangerous but the Emperor would have his way.

A siege was the best way to avoid bloodshed but was slow and cruel. He decided to first siege the fort then when the occupants were weakened he would send his men in. Three weeks he had waited. It was now early July and the hills were covered in a white haze from the suffocating heat.

In the fort, the occupants were running out of water but Dreda's men drunk from the river each day. His men camped out in the hills under the trees, but cover was sparse, and they became hot, bored and argumentative. He found out the best way to enter the fort was by water tunnels designed to bring water in and effluent out. They had blocked the ones which took water in but now opened them and climbed in up to their waists in water, rats swimming around them.

The tunnels lead to a cellar and lifting the grid they peered up surprised no one had guarded this. Silent like mice, they climbed the stairs and found an empty room. They peered around the window and guessed the chamber opposite was where the leaders were discussing strategy. Maps were on the wall and they appeared to be perusing these.

Like rats caught in a trap, thought Dreda.

He signalled two men to guard this entrance and then with the rest he followed the corridor round until he came to the door. He could have grenaded the lot but that would have been too easy and unnecessary. He needed them for information. Who was financing this

116

plot? Which states were supporting it?

Instead, he waited until their attention was on the man giving a briefing and then his men entered the room pistols and swords ready. Dreda, fighting his way to the leader caught him by his throat with his sword and then a pistol to his head and suggested the rebels put their guns down; they surrendered. A fierce battle commenced between the troops and the rest in the fort, but they were soon overcome after weeks of short rations and rampant disease.

It took another month before the rebels were routed. The two men continually led sorties into rebel territory and rounded them up. Finally, they started the journey home. They were intercepted by an officer delivering a note from an informer warning them the Emperor was in danger of being assassinated.

Dreda turned his horse in the direction of the next state and they arrived at the city gates the next day. He warned the Emperor he could be assassinated if he attended a state occasion the next evening.

"I can't show I am afraid of the rebels and you are sure most of the leaders are captured."

"Sir, there are many break away groups who have little leadership and may try to attack you."

"I am going but you can come with me to protect me," Dreda felt they were walking in to a trap but reluctantly agreed.

The next evening the Emperor was seated in a gilded carriage lent to him by the Duke. Dreda and six other officers were on horseback protecting him, riding by the carriage side. The streets were thronged with crowds. It was difficult to prevent anyone coming up to the carriage.

"We can only hope to watch carefully and identify who is behaving suspiciously and intervene before they do any damage," explained Dreda.

As they trotted toward the main staircase to the Palace he saw a movement in the crowd that was sudden. His sixth sense told him this was unusual. A black cloak vanished into the crowd and he signalled to one of his men in the crowd to follow that person. He or she could also be a decoy.

He rode closer to the window of the carriage where the Emperor was leaning out and waving to the crowd. Steadily they progressed, and safety was near when someone jumped out in front of the carriage and threw something. Immediately the troops moved toward him and circled him, disabling him.

It was only the start. Several others jumped on to the carriage and started rocking it, trying to open the doors and to turn it over. Dreda dispatched two of these with a sharp slice of his sword but behind him came a woman who slid open the door and threw a small grenade in. Dreda pulled her away and tried to get into the carriage to get the grenade but it exploded, and the impact blew him into the air. He landed badly and was unconscious. The carriage was a ball of flames. The Emperor was killed instantly.

Ten days it took for Dreda to recover and he had no scars, but he had lost his memory. The doctors said it would probably come back in its own time. In the meantime, peace and quiet were necessary. Denman laughed at this. He had never known Dreda to be idle, he was always working, playing sport or up to mischief. They went back to the city where a new Emperor had been proclaimed and had to be crowned.

CHAPTER FOURTEEN

Felea met their horses when they arrived at the villa. Her heart in her mouth, she knew something dreadful had happened. She had seen an image of a ball of flames and men lying on the ground. Dreda bowed and just walked past her. She went to follow him, but Denman grabbed hold of her arm and shook his head and took her into the garden.

"Physically he is the same man but emotionally and mentally he has changed. He has lost his memory of anything that happened before the assassination. He did not even know his own name or where he had come from."

"Will he recover his memory?" she asked.

"The doctors cannot be positive but think most of it will come back in time. They cannot put a time limit though on his recovery. We must be patient even if it is so damn frustrating for us and him."

"Does he know I am his fiancée?"

"No, and the doctors think it is better not to remind him at first. They believe making him try to recall events too quickly could cause him to lose his memory for good. They hope he will recognize familiar items and people and it will jog his memory."

"I will just tell him he knew me in his capacity as a militia officer and then protected me on the orders of the Emperor."

"It will not be forever. Someone will eventually spill the beans and by then he may have recalled his feelings again. He is like an automaton, just going about his daily life without any sense of direction or aim."

She followed Dreda into the villa. He was sitting in the salon resting his hands over his eyes. He looked tired and in pain. She wanted to go to him and hold him tight, to rub his shoulders and rid him of his tenseness as she was used to doing. His eyes flickered and opened but he stared blankly at her, no recognition in them.

He stood up and bowed and asked, "Do I know you Ma'am?" in a voice that made her shiver. He was so aloof, detached, the embodiment of the severe stranger she had met when he had searched her house. "Forgive me, but I cannot remember much before my accident and recognize even less!" These last words were uttered with exasperation. He was clearly impatient to regain all his faculties.

"I am Lady Felea Whelani, Officer Dreda. The Emperor ordered me to rest here under your protection. Your aunt is acting as chaperone until the Emperor decides what shall happen to me."

She took a deep breath ready to explain her situation. "My father was a rebel supporter Officer. He was found later to be senile and no threat to the state. I was arrested for helping decode messages but later pardoned by the Emperor. Your Bureau thought the rebels might regard me as a turncoat and I was safer here than anywhere else.''

"It is my pleasure to meet you Lady Felea. I cannot remember you, but my memory is returning slowly but for the damned headache which incapacitates me. You have my word I will guard your safety if the Emperor has given me that duty.''

He bent over her hand and kissed it lightly as a stranger would. ''I must rest now Ma'am but will meet you at dinner later.'' Dismissed, despondently she left his study. She had missed their evenings by the fire, playing music or reading books; his acerbic witty comments and teasing. She missed being in his arms, his caresses that had seemed to bring her closer to him.

This stranger looked through her as if she were invisible. His eyes that cold slate blue, saw through her, assessed her and seemed to find her wanting. He treated her like a young featherhead, a nuisance whom he wanted rid of. She was nothing to him! Denman was right. To remind him of his obligations to her would push him further away. She would keep her emotions tight inside her, locked away until he declared his love for her again.

Dreda stayed at the villa as his aunt wanted to keep an eye on him. He didn't even recognize her. He was having two months leave from work to give his memory time to come back. Denman took his job over but did ask for advice and Dreda seemed to still have his instincts for the job although he could not remember the procedures or forms. He did not leave the villa for a month, the headache disabling him. He needed tranquillity. City life was too noisy and intrusive to a man whose brain was a kaleidoscope of conflicting colours and notions competing for his attention. Felea took him horse riding and Denman later took him horse racing. He enjoyed this girl's company and found her very attractive, but they had not told him the whole story yet about the potential engagement.

More offers had been made for her hand. She was now in a difficult position because she was not sure if this new Dreda would want to marry her and she would not force his hand. He seemed to like her but had no desire for her. The new Emperor was more liberal than his father. He had been so impressed by Dreda's actions trying to save his father that he was to make him Commander of the militia when Dreda recovered his memory and grant his wish to marry Felea. She felt like hitting Dreda over the head herself to bring his memory back with a shock.

He seemed quite happy when other men brought her flowers

and took her out on jaunts into the countryside. This new unjealous Dreda was quite boring. She attended balls without him and heard in the retiring room a woman discussing him with another. She was tall, blond, and beautiful with a grand bosom, a very low-necked dress and great self-assurance.

"Now he has lost his memory he has lost all interest in the little girl. She was a mere infatuation. He was overwhelmed by her gratitude for him saving her and her father you know. He came and saw me last night and we are going to set up house again."

Felea was devastated. He had gone out that night and she did not know where. She was jealous for the first time in her life. She decided Denman was the only honest man she knew who would tell her the truth. She caught his arm and took him to a quiet room.

"Tell me the truth. Is she his mistress?" she demanded.

"She was but when he became engaged to you he gave her up and I have no reason to suspect they are back together again. He did go out on his own last night after drinking with his friends, but I don't know where."

"He didn't come home last night."

"He may have gambled. A lot of men do."

"He is not a great gambler."

"The new Dreda may be," he warned, "but don't ask him yet. I can find out and he may resent you keeping an eye on him. He has changed."

Dreda continued to go out most nights and treated her with polite interest. Denman found out that he had visited his ex-mistress but had stayed the night with a male friend. He breathed a sigh of relief. He had not wanted to rat on his friend but Felea deserved to know where she stood. Her future was at stake.

He talked to his friend. "Felea has had more requests for her hand in marriage."

"Indeed." He didn't seem interested. "Has she decided who she will marry?"

"I think she decided that long ago but she is waiting for him to set the date. He hasn't made up his mind yet."

"He had better be quick. With her looks she could trap any man."

"I heard the Countess Remaintz is on the loose again. She is bored with her latest beau."

"I saw her last evening. She was having a soiree at her villa and invited me and a few others."

"You remembered her then."

"She talked to me at a ball and I remembered a few details. Did I have an affair with her?"

"She was your mistress for twelve months."

"I didn't know I had such good taste."

Denman couldn't agree. He had never liked her and thought her looks were the only things that were attractive about her, but she had held Dreda's attention longer than any of the other women he had known. She must have something to have attracted him.

Denman decided to be brave and blunt. "There is a rumour that you are going to set up house with her soon."

"She suggested it, but I didn't say yes or no. What is it to you?"

"Only interested my friend, I thought her a bit too old for you, you know. Look at that young thing over there, much prettier and a better figure. I might have a try at her myself." He walked over to the 'young thing' to show conviction in what he said.

At the next ball Dreda danced only with Felea once out of politeness. She was becoming disheartened and was prepared to clear the air with him. Denman took her out to the gardens where she could curse Dreda and she did so violently.

Over the gardens in the shadows they saw a pair of people enter the summer house. They were talking animatedly. It was Dreda and his former mistress. The woman put her hands around his neck and pulled his face toward her giving him a passionate kiss. Felea gasped and ran into the house, not staying long enough to see Dreda lift his head, take the woman's hands from his neck and push her gently away. After a few words with her he re-entered the house.

"God! The cats among the pigeons now," said Denman. He followed Felea, but she had excused herself saying she had the headache and had gone home. Denman thought he would not like to be in Dreda's shoes, memory loss or not. He sought out his friend who was lounging against the wall watching the beauties dance.

"Saw you in the summer house with the Countess."

"You saw the end of a beautiful friendship. She was trying to force me to move into her villa on a permanent basis and I was not ready for that yet. We are finished."

"I think we had better have a talk," said Denman. "Will you join me?" Dreda raised his eyebrows in surprise but followed his friend. It was unlike him to be serious about many things.

Denman explained the situation between Dreda and Felea, watching his friend take everything in. Dreda frowned and said, "I can't remember anything of this. I am at a loss what to think. I will marry her of course if I have promised and make the best of it.

"I don't think she will want that. She only wants genuine affection. Talk to her and find out what she wants."

Dreda saw Felea in a new light now the situation had been explained to him. He respected the fact she had not tried to force him into marriage earlier, but he felt now he was caged and would be forced to marry her. Denman explained to her what had happened in the summerhouse, but she was not convinced Dreda was interested in her more than in the other woman.

"He knows the whole story now. It is up to him. He said he would keep his word and marry you."

Her heart sank. He was not enthusiastic and only interested in being honourable. When Dreda got to her home he was met by a cold aloof creature. He stood quietly in front of her, assessing her. He had thought about their position during the ride back to the villa and intended to clear the air in his usual decisive manner. He saw the hurt in her eyes and would try to make her accept his hand. It was not of his choosing, but he could not humiliate such a charming young woman. Spiteful women whose beauty and eminence in court were fading were already tormenting her.

Her father was a rebel and had aided spies! An intellectual she had not the same superficial interests as them. She did not fit in and was informed her manners were not that of a lady at court. She was an outsider with few friends to support her, needled by poisonous barbs aimed at her each day, undermining her, demeaning her. If it was thought he had jilted her she would be mincemeat once the knives were out in court.

"We can have a slightly longer engagement until my memory comes back and we become used to each other again!"

Felea felt as if she had been punched in the stomach. The Dreda she had known before the explosion had wanted the shortest engagement possible, to get her in his bed. He was the one who had been impatient. This man was trying to defer the wedding, wanting a way out! She understood his position. He was at heart a gentleman trying to act honourably. She decided to let this cold and indifferent stranger off the hook.

"You now know the whole situation. I shall go to the Emperor and look at the list of suitors he has for me. Then I shall see who suits me best. You are under no obligation to marry me."

She then went to her chamber and cried her eyes out. She felt sick. Then she shivered, freezing cold; a coldness from within, her fingers frostbitten as if ice ran in her veins. It was if a cold hand had seized her and trapped her in its grip, numbing her feelings; she no longer able to feel pain. She had winter in her soul! If she cut herself off from her feelings she could no longer be hurt by any man.

She had too much pride to demand Dreda marry her. If she took the risk and married him he might never regain his feelings for her and resent her for being locked into a loveless marriage on his side. She could visualize a polite Dreda becoming more distant, coming home less each day, mounting a mistress after the heirs had been created. She had no illusions. Unless Dreda loved a woman deeply as he had loved her he would not feel loyalty to her nor want to spend his time with her.

She wanted the Dreda who could melt her heart merely by looking at her with those intense blue eyes. She wanted him to take her into his arms. She remembered him running his finger across the nape of her neck and her shivering as a shock travelled down her spine. The old Dreda pretended to the outside world he was cold and unfeeling, but she knew he was wicked, mischievous, and sensual and had enjoyed tempting her to give herself further and further to him each evening.

Very few people knew the private man under that soulless mask but Felea had slowly begun to reveal his finer qualities and earn his trust. Sadly, he now no longer wanted her. He preferred the shallow ladies of the court, the superficiality of women who only wanted finery but needed nothing more from him. He would take affection but give nothing in return.

Dreda felt he had betrayed her but he didn't want to give her a loveless marriage. She was too lovely for that. He enjoyed having her around, but he felt no affection for her. He wanted no permanent entanglement with any woman. Since the explosion, he had felt cold inside, wanting to shut himself away from any emotional involvement with anyone. Peace and solitude were what he needed and rest from tension. He was gradually involving himself in his work, reading reports in his lodgings and clubs but still his head ached, and flashes appeared from nowhere disabling him for hours.

The situation carried on. Felea told the Emperor what she wanted, and he agreed but suggested she waited as Dreda was gradually getting his memory back and had gone back to his work. His aunt noted his presence there at the villa was causing Felea some distress and had asked him to move back to his lodgings. They rarely saw him except at society events or when he had to sort out some business for Felea. The Emperor insisted he should continue to look after her financial interests as he was regaining all his faculties again.

He was enjoying his job again but missed being back at the villa. His work occupied him during the day but as he regained his memory and the flashes receded the welcome solicitude turned to loneliness. His lodgings felt cold like a church, lacking something. He remembered warm relaxed evenings by the fire, gentle music and laughter. Something niggled in his memory and a face appeared in his dreams at night. Felea!

That damned girl was infiltrating his mind without trying. Not that she was trying to get him back, far from it. She was polite but distant, when possible avoiding him as if he had the plague. Telling himself he needed some female distraction and companionship to take his mind off her he established himself with a new mistress and Felea saw the lady draped around him at the opera. He seemed intrigued by her.

Felea had hidden her despondency well but she was losing hope he would revert to the Dreda who loved her. She still could not find a man who would match his qualities and was despairing. Denman was thoroughly disgusted with his friend for letting the love of his life slip from his grip.

CHAPTER FIFTEEN

Dreda sat with Denman in his club reading the latest journal. Two more months had passed, and he had almost re-established his life again, but he was blue-devilled and restless, not knowing what was wrong with him. Denman noticed his black mood and tried to shake him out of it.

"Want a game of cards? Best of three?"

"Yes, I can't seem to concentrate on the news today."

"Headache, old fellow?" asked his friend sympathetically.

"No, I don't know what the matter is with me. When I get back to the Bureau full time the restlessness will probably pass." Denman had his own idea what was blue-devilling his friend but failed to pass comment.

"Going to the villa soon?"

"Yes, I must pass some financial information on to Felea. The Emperor still expects me to act as her protector despite our history and the fact I don't live there now. He ignores how embarrassing it is for both of us."

"I thought you were rubbing along quite well."

"We are but all I get is sanctimonious and reproving comments about our splitting up." He frowned. "Not from Felea. She is polite but formal. You should hear the servants! It is a shame about Lady Felea, she is such a nice young lady. She runs this house like a true mistress. She is so kind to everyone!"

"She is very popular with the Bureau men."

"You would think she is a bloody saint the way they put her up on a pedestal," snapped Dreda. "She is only a pretty mannered young wench and a stroppy, managing one at that!"

"Well you know what I think. If she hadn't been doe-eyed over you I would have tried for her myself. Intelligence, spirit and beauty all in the same package. They rarely come together!"

"You said she was too strong meat for you!" Dreda remembered the conversation at the wedding and those dances with a suspicious and defensive Felea who disliked him intensely.

"That was before I saw her sweet side. She melted your cold heart, my friend. Are you reconsidering your position?"

"Not at all. I just wish everyone didn't treat me like a cur for not being keen about the idea of marrying her. I have offered for her three times recently and have been rejected. For a girl in love she treats me like a discarded shoe."

"She is hurt. She won't marry you unless you love her. She has too much pride.''

"So, she will sell herself to the highest bidder, title and all. Hardly a girl of principles!''

"She is trying to get as far away from you as is possible, you addlepated fool. She loves you but why I don't know, for you are the coldest, most detached creature I have met.'' He rose, exasperated. "I am going to join the faro table. Join me later if you feel like it.''

Dreda stayed in his place, surprised at the strength of his friend's feelings. Felea seemed to bring out the best and worst in people and made them want to protect her. He was beginning to understand why so many people liked her; her sweetness, her kindness; then at other times she was the most irritating, provoking girl he had met, arguing with him, defying him and challenging him. What on earth had made him propose to such an energetic, resourceful woman? If he married he would want a quiet, gentle woman who made his life and home tranquil, not a petite tornado who turned his life upside down and created turbulence in his orderly life.

She was beautiful, that was for certain. He had watched her at balls moving gracefully, swaying her tight derriere in a way that would entice most men. She was the most tempting piece of ass he had ever seen but she had a hands-off label unless one intended to offer for her. One didn't offer a carte blanche to one like her. He intended to remain polite but distant from her in the manner of a good friend.

They met at a ball; he was representing the militia again. She was dancing with a younger man, a Duke from another state. The bookies were betting on this one being the one and for once she was close to agreeing. He was charming, resourceful and well-educated. He was also rich and well connected or he would not have been contemplated. She smiled at him and he waved. The Duke took her into his arms and danced very well. She remembered the dances with Dreda and wished she could banish them from her head.

The man leant down toward her and whispered something in her ear. Dreda watched her laugh at something he had said. She was so relaxed, at ease with this new man. For some reason, he felt uncomfortable when this man touched her shoulder or put his hand on her waist.

He was perplexed. He had made it clear to her he was not romantically interested in her. He could only offer her a marriage of convenience and yet he didn't want this man to paw her. He told himself he had no right to dictate to her who she could dance with and yet he wanted her to dance with him instead. He must be going soft in the head.

The dance finished and for once Dreda came and asked for the next dance. She was wary but agreed.

"You dance wonderfully."

"You are excellent as well."

"Did we dance together a lot?"

"No, just a few times."

"It is coming back." A waltz was about to be played and she moved away but he pulled her back and said, "Let us try this one together."

"What about your Countess?"

"I have danced with her all evening."

"She doesn't look very happy."

"She doesn't control me," he said tartly. Felea filed that in her memory for the future.

He swung her about the floor and held her close, resting her head against his chest, but she couldn't bear being so physically close to him when he was so emotionally detached from her. Everyone was watching them as they made a handsome couple. The busy bodies were rumour-mongering again. How long would it be before they were back together? Felea couldn't stand it. She had waited long enough for him.

As soon as the dance was over she made for the retiring room. His Mistress was standing there and uttered bitterly, "He was only taking pity on you. He feels sorry for you having rejected you."

Felea walked out refusing to argue with this sad woman. She went to the Duke who had been watching and smiled at him encouragingly. He made an offer for her hand to the Emperor and a day later she accepted his proposal. The Emperor arranged that the wedding would be in four months' time in the Duke's home city.

Dreda was unaware of this as he had left the city. He had spent a month in Vina with Denman routing a new group of rebels. He had had a devil of a job thinking straight when cannons were firing around his head. The Emperor had sent him back into the battle before he was ready, and he felt exhausted and drained.

The excitement of warfare had worn thin and he resented being drawn into battle whenever the Emperor needed the militia to reinforce his regular army. Coming back thirsty and tired he looked forward to his own hearth and tranquillity. A seasoned warhorse, this time he had seen things that had chilled his blood and questioned his loyalties to the Emperor.

When informed of the prospective nuptials he gave the bride to be his congratulations. He showed no regret she was choosing another man. The reality of the situation had not hit him yet. Felea accepted his congratulations gracefully but her words of thanks tasted like ashes in her throat. Denman had told her she was making a mistake, but she had ignored him. She couldn't wait forever. The day of her leaving came closer. She wished herself away to the other state her misery growing every day. She had to get away from this man before she gave herself away and showed her real feelings to him

Dreda was engaged in a swordfight at the fencing school with his friends. He was trying to get fit again for his job. He slid and hit his head against the stone terrace. A flash appeared in his eyes and he saw stars. He was unconscious for a few hours but then waking with a severe headache he went home to sleep it off. In his dreams, he saw himself and a young girl dancing, she agitated, he enjoying teasing her. He then dreamt of him rescuing a girl from being violated by a soldier and a battle happening.

The next morning, he had images pushing though his mind. He felt dizzy as more exploded into his consciousness. By the end of the week his memory was almost fully recovered. He was confused. He had a beautiful mistress but felt nothing for her anymore and had told her this honestly. She had left his house with a generous payment of jewels as befitted her status.

He went to the villa and saw Felea's final preparations being made. For the first time, this hit home. She was truly leaving! An invisible hand squeezed his heart. Air couldn't pass into his lungs. Panic stifled him. He could not explain it to himself, but he had to stop her leaving and marrying this other man.

He did not want her to marry for convenience into a strange family and country. He had to try to stop her making a dreadful mistake. He surprised her in her bower, taking her hand in his.

"I would have words with you Ma'am."

"What can I do for you officer?" she asked pulling her hand away. "I hear you were successful in your last campaign for the Emperor." His face turned dark. "We are not here to discuss my role Ma'am but thank you for your congratulations." He turned the subject quickly as if he wished to rid his mind of it.

Carefully he broached the sensitive subject that was on his mind. Denman had as good as said Felea was marrying on the rebound and would regret it later. He could not have that on his conscience.

"Lady Felea I think you make a mistake with this marriage. Please reconsider my offer."

"Thank you but no Sir. I think we would not suit."

"To marry a stranger so quickly could be injudicious," he said carefully. "Be sure you are making the right choice for the right reasons

Ma'am.'' She pulled her head away, not wanting him to read her expression on her face, her sadness in her eyes. He had not said anything about his feelings for her.

''What other reasons can there be Officer? I please the Emperor, we make a political alliance that will ensure peace and I have a groom that can offer me a safe and comfortable life.''

He frowned still surprised and piqued she had refused his offer again. He took her chin in his hand and made her look at him, to read the truth in her eyes. If eyes were the window to the soul, he could read her emotions there.

''Why not for affection Ma'am, when a short time ago you professed to love me?''

She pulled her head away again. He was offering a duty marriage. The nerve of the man! Throwing the memory of her love back at her. This man fought dirtily. She rounded on him, eyes flashing, flaying him. Most other men would have shrivelled under that regard. Dreda accepted silently the onslaught she hurled against him. He knew he deserved every insult and complaint.

''What would you know about love? You are cold and harsh and have no heart! Perhaps, my feelings have cooled Officer. Love can cool over a time when it is neglected. It withers and dies.''

Dreda smiled wryly. She was paying him back with his own coin after he had turned away from her. A seasoned strategist he now knew he had lost her. Nothing he said would convince her to change her mind. Felea was stubborn and had made her mind up. For now, he must retreat but an experienced campaigner, he would come back fighting later.

''Very well Ma'am, as your mind is made up. If I can be of service do not hesitate to call me.''

''Thank you, Officer,'' she said coolly. ''How are your headaches?''

''They are almost gone, and my memory is returned bar for a few unimportant things.''

Her eyes widened. Did that mean he remembered their love affair? She dashed that hope immediately. He had not mentioned loving her, just affection and her love for him.

''I hope you continue to improve Officer. A blank memory must be so inconvenient,'' she snapped, the words sounding like insults.

''Oh, I can remember enough now.'' His eyes pierced her, assessing her; pinning her there like a butterfly fluttering, secured to a card. She was unable to take her eyes off him. He could still send shivers down her spine when he looked at her like that. Drat the man!

When would she stop reacting to him like this? He was too handsome and self-assured for his own good.

Dreda saw a woman in front of him who was still attracted to him, but she had grown up in the last few months. She was a cool woman who knew her destiny and had accepted it. They watched the bags being packed.

"Who is taking you to your Groom's city?"

"Denman has offered to guard the carriage with a few friends."

"You will be in good hands then."

"Yes, he is a good soldier and friend."

He took her hand and kissed it. "I want you to be happy." She tugged her hand away as if she had been bitten.

"I am sure I will be," she snapped and dismissed herself.

He sat on the terrace. Realization hit him! When living with her he had been truly happy for the first time in his life. It was she who had made him content and at peace. He wished the images would fall into place. Everything was confused and moving about in his head. He had suffered the headache for months and had felt flat and devoid of emotions.

He went to Denman and told him how far his memory had returned. His friend was pleased but worried about the latest head knock. Then came the bad bit! He had to admit to Denman that he was having second thoughts about the proposal to Felea. He didn't want her to leave. He wasn't entirely sure about his feelings for her, but they were deeper than he had realized. His memory loss had disguised them.

Denman snapped at him, "It is a bit too late. She is leaving tomorrow." Dreda's natural stubbornness reared its head. He would not allow Felea to sacrifice herself in an unhappy marriage. He owed her more than that. He would act as her bodyguard and wear down her resistance at the Archduke's court; persuade her to jilt her fiancé and come back to Taylia. He would persuade the Emperor to give her more time and more choices. She deserved better than this loveless marriage forced on her by his coldness and her loneliness at court.

"You can help me. This is what you can do," he plotted with his friend.

The next morning the bags packed, Felea waited. Five men on horses came up the drive and she noticed Dreda was leading them. He bowed and took her arm ready to help her into the carriage.

"Good Morning, Officer Dreda. Where is Officer Denman?" she asked suspiciously.

"Ill, I am afraid. I am here in his place."

This was just about the worst thing that could happen to her.

She was already feeling raw and travelling for days in his company would tear her nerves to shreds. She couldn't think of a way to get out of it and with poor grace she sat in the carriage.

What the devil was that dratted man up to? She had no doubt he had manipulated Denman's sickness to take her place. But for what purpose? Dreda was not the type of man who would want to suffer willingly the humiliation of his former fiancée marrying another; to listen to the gossips discussing them and tearing their past relations and reputations to shreds. Dreda smiled at her reluctance. He was beginning to remember the wrangles they had and his enjoyment when battling his wits against her. This could be an interesting journey.

They drove fifty leagues that day and rested in a very small inn. She asked to be excused and to have food in her room. Dreda knew that this was a ruse. She wanted to avoid him. Strangely he felt piqued. This was the girl who was supposed to have fallen head over heels in love with him.

The next day was more arduous and slow; they had to follow mountain tracks just wide enough to take the carriage and Dreda was aware it was bandit country. He was glad he had taken this role to ensure her safety. He knew these mountains inside out having fought here as a mercenary. Denman knew them less well.

There was a ridge over the mountain where ambushes frequently took place, but he was ready for that eventuality. As they passed over the ridge four men came riding out and tried to take the reins of the horses. The groom resisted and Dreda and the other officers, swords at the ready, slashed the throat of one and pushed another over the cliff. They knocked two others off their horses and ran them over, their horses' hooves smashing their foes' skulls. Felea was grateful he was there; knowing he was a skilled fighter or she could have been killed or violated by these men.

He slapped the horses on their rears. "We can't wait for their friends to catch us up." He pulled the carriage down the mountain as fast as he could, steadying it as it went over ruts and hillocks until the safety of the valley was reached. He then looked in the window to see if she was well. She was knocked about and shocked but safe.

They all sat beside the river and caught their breath. The men had cuts and bruises and she got out her balm and salved their wounds. She was much quicker cleaning Dreda's wounds than the rest; close proximity to him was not what she wanted at all. She felt much too aware of him when he came too close to her.

They moved quickly on again resting that night at a villa her family knew of. She could bathe properly and sleep in a comfortable bed. She could not avoid Dreda at all. They dined with the family and Dreda the diplomat's son kept up a string of civilized conversations throughout the evening.

Her forthcoming nuptials were discussed. Dreda noticed she was lively but he knew her well enough to know she was not looking forward to the wedding. She said she knew her groom very well now; he was kind, handsome and well educated. They both spoke many languages and would deal well together. Dreda had recently acquainted himself deliberately with the groom and thought he was intelligent but as dry as dust. He would bore her in weeks and she would try to ride rough shod over him. If he were a man sparks would fly.

She slept badly, being woken up by nightmares. Her new husband was holding her but Dreda was trying to make him let her go, to take her back to the villa. When would this man release his hold on her? To let her live-in peace! Felea was confused; he was sending out mixed messages, showing extra concern for her, even flirting with her at the table but not showing any signs of commitment to her. She wished he would leave her alone.

Dreda slept well, more dreams driving his imagination. He now remembered his past feelings for Felea. His respect deepened when he remembered she had risked her life for her father and had saved his own life. He wanted her to avoid this marriage. He remembered enough to know this couple would not suit and it would be a miserable marriage like that of his parents. She deserved better than this.

The next six days were much safer both physically and emotionally for her. Long days travelling left them tired and they retired early for the night rising at dawn to make good progress. They arrived at the Palace safely.

The Duke was not pleased to see Dreda. He would rather he had stayed at home, particularly as he could see Dreda had regained his health and was regaining his memory. A wily man, he knew the officer had been engaged to Felea and wondered if he had an ulterior motive in offering to bodyguard her. He could not be anything other than polite to Dreda given his family status and his political proximity to the Emperor. He invited him to dine at their table but clearly, he wanted to expedite his exit.

He wasn't pleased when he was told that Dreda would talk with his father on matters of state business and extend his stay. He couldn't easily object. It was in the interest of both countries to join their intelligence forces together if this alliance was to stay stable. They could back up each other if there was a potential threat and if they had common enemies. Dreda appeared to talk like a concerned politician and the Duke arranged for an audience with his father as soon as was convenient.

The next day a ball was held in Felea's honour. As usual she outshone the other ladies there in looks and personality. She was presented to the Archduke who was pleased to see her portrait was an accurate representation of herself. The Duke kept her apart from Dreda who observed he looked like a cornered cat trying to keep his toy from a stronger predator. Felea stayed close to her fiancé wishing the papers for the marriage could be signed and the ceremony over. She remembered what Dreda had said about killing any man she married. If he fully regained his memory in the future how would he react?

In fact, by the night of the ball Dreda could remember everything and had made his mind up. This marriage would not take place if he could prevent it. She was not going to sacrifice herself because of the explosion. Taking her in his arms he threw her up in the air during a fast country dance. He led her energetically round the floor making her breathless and excited until they stopped and collapsed on chairs.

"You look a bit dizzy," she said.

"No, it is only the occasional headache making me feel like this. I get them, but they are going very slowly." She was concerned he had travelled in blazing heat to keep her safe, suffering with headaches and had not complained at all.

"I will ensure the Duke's doctor sees you in the morning." She touched his forehead and it felt very hot. She worried it might be a fever again. "Your aunt says you are getting too old to suffer any more beatings. You should stop fighting," she scolded.

"My aunt interferes too much. I could fight for many years," but he winced, still remembering the burns and bruises that hurt him every so often. He did feel old today, particularly near to this fresh young woman.

He also liked her scolding and caring for him. He felt wanted, something he had never felt with his immediate family. He realized when he was protecting her he had felt needed, but nobody had ever loved and nurtured him. His aunt had been kind but sharp and was not a substitute for a real mother.

"You need someone to look after you. You are hopeless, getting into trouble all the time." He laughed, he had accused her of that so often in the past, but the tables were now turned.

The Duke came to separate them again. "You seem to be on very good terms with that man again."

"He saved my life but doesn't look after himself enough. Can he see your doctor tomorrow?''

"Certainly, but I would prefer you didn't associate with him again before the ceremony. People are commenting that you are too close.''

She agreed but he had put her back up. A little voice niggled her, asking if it was going to be like this when she was married. She resented being told how to behave and reminded she hadn't been given the usual upbringing of a noblewoman. He had implied that in the past her upbringing had been very loose. Now he was in his own domain he was changing; becoming more critical of her, domineering and insisting she respect the conventions of his court.

She couldn't help comparing him with Dreda in her mind. Dreda had scolded her when she endangered herself but after they had been become engaged he had relaxed a little. He had been very liberal in his expectation of her modes and manners except for when she wore 'that dress' and he was jealous of other men. He had hated the restrictions of the court himself which was why he chose the army and later the militia when he could have been a diplomat like his father.

Dreda saw her frown and was delighted. He wanted her to leave this relationship of her own free will and the Emperor would sanction it if the grounds were good. He had had misgivings about the alliance between the two city states. He had heard rumours that this state had backed the rebels and gave them monies, accommodation and ammunition until they were losing and then turned about face evicting them. He hated turncoats and he had disliked the Duke on sight. He remembered what he had told Felea about killing any man she went to from him. He had said that in the heat of the moment, but he had killed Gavantz and knew he had to restrain himself.

The next morning the doctor pronounced him fit, but he had a small fever brought on by exhaustion. He had to rest for a week before travelling. Dreda was delighted, an excuse to stay on. He spoke to the Archduke, playing him along, finding out who else he was allying with. Felea didn't like the Archduke herself. He was too interested in talking about her wealth and he had plump hands which travelled too keenly down her back under the pretence of making her seat comfortable.

Dreda noticed her discomfort. Even more reason to remove her from this odious place. He wanted her back and to marry her. He had been a fool, an ill fool but a fool nevertheless and he would have to admit it and make it up with her. There was no time for pride here. His feelings were growing deeper every day as the memories returned and he hated the fat Archduke 'pawing' his future wife.

He remembered 'that dress' and his reaction to other men

looking at her. Quite irrational for him, the cool detached son of a diplomat. He realized he didn't like the person he had become before he met Felea. He had grown like his father, but she had begun humanizing him.

Felea felt more uncomfortable every day. The ladies of the court had more experience of court life and showed they found her lacking. Her dress sense, her choice of music and books were démodé they said, picking her up on every little thing. Felea knew her dresses were ā la mode, having been ordered from Paris, her bridal dress from Worth himself!

Her bridal dress was cream; a dreamy concoction of panelled lace, revealing a tantalizing slip of skin, designed to make any bridegroom want his bride on his bridal night but she couldn't summon any enthusiasm to look at it or try it on. She remembered Dreda threatening to defy the Emperor and get a Special Licence.

She imagined herself in that dress and the way that Dreda would have unwrapped her lovingly as if she were a special gift. He had suggested a small private ceremony with just a few friends and relatives. Wistfully, she fingered the lace of her gown and thought she would have worn a sack if she and Dreda could have married in that informal way with a few friends in a small chapel.

Sadly, he was not the man for her, playing the diplomatic role for his Emperor to a nicety, humouring the Archduke. *He seemed to be pleased the nuptials were progressing,* she thought despondently. She gave herself a mental shake. She must grow up and stop thinking of him and not think with distaste of the oncoming bridal night and ducal bed.

A knock came on the door and her abigail said with surprise and disapproval, "It is Officer Dreda, Lady Felea."

Felea was confused. Single men did not pay visits to a single lady's boudoir when she was unaccompanied by a chaperone. Her chaperone had been escorted home by the soldiers who had accompanied them. Dreda would not come to lady's sanctuary unless it was urgent! He might take more liberties in private, but he presented himself in public as a gentleman and would not willingly ruin a young lady's reputation.

"Let him in but stay Rimi! Leave the door open," she ordered the woman who pursed her lips. She was a new maid, a country girl, who had recently been chosen by the Duke's housekeeper to dress her.

Sweet Jesus! The people in this Palace are even more staid and judgemental than in my own city if that can be believed! Even the servants looked down their long noses at her as if she was not good enough for their Duke. How she would tolerate their condemnation she did not know!

Dreda walked in and stood in the doorway waiting for the woman to leave.

"I think it is inappropriate for a gentleman to visit an unwed lady on her own in her bed-chamber, Officer," Felea reprimanded him.

"I think your groom would excuse this one occasion once he knows what I am going to say."

"Very well but please be quick," she said dismissing the girl who swept out her nose in the air as if she had smelt a bad smell. "If we are alone too long people will gossip."

"I want you down in the servants" quarter. No eavesdropping or you will regret it," threatened Dreda. The woman looking at his stern face knew he meant it and scuttled down the stairs. He felt safe. He could hear anyone approaching the bedchambers.

"You must make it clear to that woman if she breathes a word about this she will be dismissed."

"I have no power over that woman. She was appointed by my groom's agent."

"I will deal with her. A word from me and she will toe the line if she knows what is good for her!" Felea believed him. Even here in an unfamiliar city his reputation was known to the court and he was to be feared.

"What can I do for you?"

"I just came to warn you that I heard some disquieting rumours in the Palace that makes me worry that the Duke is not a suitable groom. He seems to have been forced into this marriage and is rather idiosyncratic."

"By which you mean?"

"I would rather not explain to you but if it is true you might wish to break the engagement.' Dreda looked a trifle embarrassed. She waited for him to expand. He sighed. "He may be less manly than he appears, or you would want. Does that suffice?"

She went bright red, but it would explain the Duke's possessiveness but unwillingness to kiss her. She had thought him over gentlemanly but now she guessed the unpalatable truth. In truth now, she knew him better her skin crawled when his clammy fingers had moved over her, but she couldn't admit to Dreda she had made a mistake. Her pride would not let her.

"I am sure the rumours have been set about by some foul-minded person with ill intent toward the Duke. What evidence do you have?"

"None, yet. I merely know that the Duke has had only a few

alliances with females which for a man of his age seems rather untypical and he seems to have had alliances with his own sex!''

"Not every man is a rake Officer! One should not judge other men by oneself,'' she retorted damningly.

"What are you inferring by that?''

"A lady may like a man who behaves the gentleman and doesn't try to persuade her to bed him.''

He mocked her. "You seemed not to mind an experienced man who introduced you to love-making. I did not hear any complaints!''

She flushed bright red. For a moment, she was hopeful he now remembered enjoying the more pleasant aspects of their relationship but then she pushed that hope away. There was no point in tormenting herself. He had given no reason for her to believe he desired her still.

She ignored his accusation that she had encouraged his desire to become more intimate with her. She said negligently, "Make of my comment what you will. Not all women want their grooms to be overtly sexual in advance of the wedding. Some want discretion until the wedding night!''

"Not you Felea. You are of much sterner stuff, passionate and warm and overt! You two will not suit but you must make up your own mind.''

"Lady Felea to you,'' she retorted sharply. "My mind is made up Sir. I have no other gentleman waiting for me nor have I any interest in any other man.''

"I think the lady protests too much. Time will tell!''

"Don't talk in riddles! You are like talking with an eel.''

She turned to open the door and dismiss him. In doing so she put down her wedding dress which had laid across her arms whilst she was talking with him.

Dreda looked at the garment and crossed the room fingering the lace panels. A spur of jealousy stabbed through him. His gut wrenched! Macho to the core; all he could think of was that feeble pervert eying her creamy flesh through that fine lace, lusting after her, taking her!

If a man wanted another man as well as women, he did not care. He had turned a blind eye to many illicit relationships between men in the army, but it was different where Felea was concerned. Whatever his sexual peculiarities involved the Duke was not man enough for her. He would disappoint her and make her unhappy.

Dreda knew her well enough to know she needed a true man who wanted her and only her and would pleasure her and make her cry his name out for him. This duke only needed her to keep his father happy and would discard her once an heir was born. She would be trapped in a cocoon of loneliness, a prey to the vipers of the court who would enjoy poisoning her with their venom when they realized her neglectful husband would no longer protect her.

"If you change your mind I am ready to rid you of this place."

"What would happen to me in that circumstance?"

"I would get you out so quickly one would not see your backside for dust!"

"Would that not cause a rift in diplomatic relations? I would have thought the Emperor would want to exile me for that. At the least he would give me to the first man who offered for me however old or peculiar he might be. I would be in a worse position than I am now. At least here I will have a title and status."

"I never thought status and title meant so much to you Felea." He regarded her in his cold assessing way. She felt as if she were an insect under a microscope waiting to be dissected by a much stronger creature.

"A title may make up for other things lacking."

"The girl I knew would not sell herself for status and title. She had too much self-respect."

She tossed her head as if indifferent to her fate. "I have grown up Officer. I am not the young girl who you knew before. I am accepting of my fate!"

"I think that girl is still there waiting for the right man to come along," he replied approaching her. "This is not a wedding dress suitable for a marriage of convenience. You had this designed for quite another occasion, didn't you?"

She looked up aghast. He had worked out the truth.

"This was a dress made for a woman who loved her fiancé wasn't it my Lady? Would your groom be pleased to know his bride chose him on the rebound and even wore a wedding dress made for another groom?"

She could not deny the dress had been designed for their marriage and only the explosion had stopped her using it, it only arriving a sennight later. They had finally decided before the explosion that if the former Emperor had tried to coerce Felea into marrying for convenience they would marry against his wishes and face the consequences.

"A lady often designs a bridal dress pattern before she chooses the groom. You are presumptuous Officer!"

He picked the dress up and held it up against her. "This dress was designed to entice a man, to make him want to touch that skin under that fine lace; to feel his lover tremble under his touch and then for her to invite him to her bed!''

She pulled away from him, but he held her firmly by the shoulders. His eyes impaled hers. ''You are fooling yourself if you marry the Duke in that dress Felea Whelani. You will regret doing it every day of your life!'' She stared at him, fixated, like a rabbit caught under the stare of a stronger prey unable to move for fear of being caught.

''You have too high an opinion of yourself, Officer. One groom is as good as another if the title and wealth are sufficient. I repeat, I am not the same woman you asked to marry. My priorities have changed now I have observed 'polite society' and know its workings.''

Looking at her keenly, he tried to read her mind. Her eyes were as cold as pebbles by the lake. No warmth shone in them. She looked at him as if she despised him. This was not the Felea he had known. Yet he knew she was not totally indifferent to him. Her skin had trembled under his fingers and he could see her breasts rising and falling as her heart beat rose.

Her voice had dropped, now deep and husky. Her voice had always changed when she had wanted him to kiss her. He resisted the temptation! Now was not the time to pursue this line of argument while she was embarrassed and defensive. He wanted to embrace her but like most good army strategists he would wait until the time was right and then pounce.

He finally let her go. She rubbed her shoulders where he had held her so tight he had bruised her. ''If you change your mind let me know. I will sort something out with the Emperor. All may not be as it seems in this Palace anyway,'' he said mysteriously but left the room before she could ask him to elaborate. He sent Rimi up the stairs.

She called her abigail in. ''It appears that my father is ill and unlikely to last very long. I will tell the Duke, but I need not leave as he could have passed away by the time I got back. Officer Dreda was kind enough to break the news personally to me.'' The woman pursed her lips but accepted Felea's reason for his visit.

Felea prepared herself for the evening's entertainment in her honour. Smiling all evening, she felt as if she had been turned inside out and gutted. Dreda had gained some malicious satisfaction breaking the news about her fiancé to her. He was a dog in the manger, not wanting her but unwilling to let another man have her!

At the banquet Felea wore an amber dress with rubies in her hair and ears. A ruby droplet necklace adorned her neck making it look slim and swanlike. The dress brought out the colour of her smoky green gold eyes. She danced as if she had not a care in the world knowing

Dreda's eyes were on her the whole time.

Moving to the retiring room, she smiled at a woman there whom she recognized as one of the Archduke's courtesans. The older man seemed to be very virile in his autumn years. The blond woman seemed at least thirty years younger than her protector and very self-assured.

"You must be finding this situation very difficult," said the blond.

"Why so," asked Felea, deliberately feigning ignorance.

"Why marrying a man who has no interest in you and has another he has eyes for!"

"This is not a love match," said Felea.

"T'is bad when the competition is not of the usual sex," hinted the vixen. "It is a lonely life when the heirs are produced, and the Groom no longer needs the marital bed."

"I hear women then may take lovers if they are discrete," retorted Felea although the woman's blunt words made her feel ice cold. It was one thing to know these things but quite another for them to be thrust down one's throat in that callous manner.

"This is quite an old-fashioned court. Adultery by a duchess would not be tolerated."

"Perhaps a duchess would not tolerate her husband having male lovers. That is for the married couple to decide, not for others who wish to interfere."

"Of course, the Duke also has female companions. He shares them with his father who has first pick. The Archduke was looking at you but says your manners and dress sense need improving before you meet his requirements."

"Well that is all to the good. I don't want to bed an old man," retorted Felea and left the room cursing to herself.

She was at the mercy of the women of the court all night. Why did she a young virgin not wear white or pink or another suitable colour? Why did she not wear her hair short with curls drifting down her neck as was the fashion? Her necklines were too low for modesty and made her look a harlot. Nothing she wore or did met their approval. Felea ignored the women's catty remarks, refusing to bite back but she felt alone. The only familiar face was Dreda and she tried to keep a distance from him.

That damned man haunted her dreams and she kept getting images and a feeling of being discomforted. An image of fire and smoke entered her mind and she had a feeling of anticipation. Something was going to happen in the next few days! Her images always preceded an event, some good some bad. Something made her believe Dreda was linked to the future events. She wished he would go and leave her to her fate.

He was still the most enigmatic and handsome man she had met, and she burned to have him hold her tightly in his arms. He had spoken the truth in her bed-chamber. Despite her still being a virgin, Dreda the experienced rake had begun to introduce her to love-making, slowly, gently, making his shy young fiancée desperate for his kisses and caresses until she wanted him as much as he wanted her.

She hadn't understood when her few married friends had told her how difficult it had been to restrain themselves and their fiancés during impassioned sessions of love-making but now she understood clearly having struggled with Dreda for self-control during the long stops in the carriage by the river on their way home from trips to the opera or the theatre.

Dreda had been a gentleman but impatient to make her his own. She had only dissuaded him with difficulty so was he desperate for her in his bed. He had been prepared to risk the wrath of the Emperor even if they could not marry. The cold dispassionate Dreda, cautious in most areas had been behaving recklessly and irrationally like any man deeply in love.

She had feared the vengeance of the Emperor if she disobeyed him and bore Dreda's child. The Emperor had been looking for scapegoats and could easily have punished Dreda by death. Her fortune would be confiscated. Left with an illegitimate child, she would be thrown on the mercy of the charity of the nuns in the convent. It was not to be contemplated. She could not bring an illegitimate child into such a condemning world.

Now she had only to look forward to her bridegroom, an intelligent but fussy man whose idea of passion was to bury himself in a study with his latest lecture notes or books. Even if she ignored the salacious rumours about him he had little to recommend him. He rarely took exercise and she could not help comparing the two men; the one who coughed and spluttered when he had to run up a flight of stairs and the other who was always active, whose muscles rippled when he groomed his horse or danced an energetic dance. One was a bookworm and an indoor man; the other a man of action as well as an intellectual; a man always looking for new adventure; a man a woman could look up to and respect.

CHAPTER SIXTEEN

It was two weeks until the wedding but Felea felt uneasy. The night before she had been cornered by three of the ladies of the court. Looking disdainfully down their noses at her, they began to question her about her former life at the Emperor's court.

One of the ladies turned limpid blue eyes on her and noted in what could be construed as a concerned manner, "Officer Dreda. He seems to be very careful of your safety. He looks after you very carefully. What does he think could happen to you here?"

Felea's antennae twitched. On guard, she suspected the woman's concerned manner hid a more devious meaning. Wide eyes open she looked the picture of innocence. Felea directed an equally innocent gaze at her tormentor.

"Why Madam, he was commanded to guard me by the Emperor. He takes all his duties very seriously!"

"But of course, he has a greater interest bearing in mind your recent engagement to him," pursued the woman.

Felea said as casually as she could, "I think he would be as careful with any young innocent woman." A carefully raised eyebrow showed the woman's scepticism.

"The Duke thought he was unduly familiar with you when he danced with you at the ball last night." Felea now felt in dangerous territory, the innocent questions turning into an inquisition about her supposed intimacy with Dreda.

"A very experienced man, not to say a rake or libertine. A dangerous man to have around if one doesn't intend being affianced to him!"

"Officer Dreda has always behaved gentlemanly to me. Now we are not engaged he treats me like any other woman he must guard."

"And yet he danced very close to you like a lover would! Perhaps he regrets your estrangement and would want to continue his affair with you once you are married!"

"Madam," said Felea pretending to be shocked although she had known all along what the woman was hinting at. "You do both of us an injustice. I would not cuckold my husband and Officer Dreda would not take another man's wife!"

"Sometimes one cannot help one's emotions," insinuated the other woman "and cannot but help but take the dishonourable route. And it would not be the first-time Officer Dreda has liaised with the wife of a complacent husband."

Felea decided to change the conversation to a neutral subject before she lost control. She was no saint and could easily wish these harpies to the devil. It was no longer none of her business what Dreda did with other men's wives, but she didn't want to hear about his bedroom adventures even if they were in the past.

"I hear the Archduke is considering building new schools and hospitals. The people will be grateful! Where are they to be situated?"

"Oh here and there," said the other woman not wishing to be deviated from her topic of gossip. "We hear there was need of help in your Vina region. The casualties were appalling."

Felea had heard of the battle in her state between the Imperial and rebel army. Why this woman had brought the subject up baffled her. A very feminine and elegant lady she did not seem to be the type of woman interested in battles, a subject that largely interested men!

"I know little about that battle."

"There will be many women who resent the officer in charge after their men were slaughtered," explained the woman. "It was a bloody massacre I hear!"

Felea's eyes widened. There was much more to come she feared. The woman carried on. "I hear the men offered to surrender but their white flag was ignored and most of the men were run down after they had laid down their arms."

"Those poor women," said Felea. "Is anyone helping them and their children?"

The woman retorted, "The officer in charge had a guilty conscience and paid himself for blankets, grain and tents. The Emperor rewarded him well for putting down the rebellion, so it was a drop in the ocean for him."

"Was the incident not investigated?" asked Felea. Dreda had intimated the army and militia were cleaning up their act and there were less renegade officers creating mayhem.

"Why would the incident be investigated when the officer in charge was the Emperor's favourite? He could do no wrong and found some of the widows acquiescent in offering their favours when he wanted his bed warming."

The words, 'the Emperor's favourite' ran warning bells in Felea's head. She felt sick for a moment her head buzzing with the words. Was this merely the random gossip of a bored woman or were these words spiteful barbs designed to destroy her faith in Dreda?

She asked the words she dreaded to utter. "Who was this officer in charge?" The smug smirk on the woman's face confirmed her fears. "Why your Officer Dreda of course! Didn't you hear about his exploits with his friend Officer Denman?"

Felea stepped back and said, "I was not |Officer Dreda's fiancée at that time. We had agreed we no longer suited and I knew not his business!"

"Well he was certainly busy and his friend also in between routing the rebels. Some widows will be expecting petit paquets quite soon."

Felea was less worried about his sexual adventures than the fact Dreda had massacred the men. She knew most noblemen had sired illegitimate children through their mistresses and although Dreda and Denman had never intimated they had any she was not so naïve to believe they had not sired any issue. Like most women of her time she had not delved into the romantic life of her fiancé before she had met him; it would have been both unwise and bad ton but she knew he must have had many lovers before her,

She suddenly remembered her vision; a vision of a tall slim man giving an order to fire on soldiers. She shivered remembering the cries and screams. She now knew the circumstances were so similar it must have been a vision of the massacre at Vina. Had Dreda given the order to massacre the men?

She would ask Dreda about the massacre when they had a quiet moment. He had never talked about his work and she knew he was totally ruthless but from the battle she had witnessed at the fort she believed he always tried to avoid any bloodshed from either side. This description of his behaviour did not match the man she knew.

She went to bed feeling despondent. If the woman's inferences were true the man she had loved was an alleged womanizer, a mass murderer and had covered up his behaviour by his sycophantic smarming of the Emperor. She could no longer respect the man and wished him to the devil.

Dreda had driven her and the Duke mad over the past two days. She had tried to avoid him, treating him coldly but he seemed always to be there, holding her chair, asking for a dance, everywhere! The Duke had argued with her because he believed she encouraged him and she realized her fiancé would be a possessive and jealous husband and dictatorial, another Gavantz.

She also believed Dreda was being deliberately mischievous, goading the Duke into arguments with her. After one such heated argument she had sought Dreda and demanded he meet her in the garden. When they got there, she had attacked him straight away.

"Why are you trying to cause mischief between the Duke and myself? Are you trying to stop the marriage?"

Dreda had managed to get a message by pigeon to the Emperor

warning him that the alliance was not all it seemed. He had learnt enough talking to other Ambassadors who had come for the wedding. He was waiting for an answer and if it was the right one he would remove Felea from this Palace in all haste whether she liked it or not. The Emperor would want this as it meant hostilities would be started again between the city states. Her leaving would only be the catalyst for this. This had been on the cards for a long time and her wedding had been organized to try to postpone hostilities for a while.

He could not tell her the truth, not having received the message back yet. ''No, I was only trying to be helpful and friendly as I am stuck here, and I treated you shamefully in the past.''

''Well, leave me alone. The Duke thinks there is something between us.''

''Which of course there is not?'' he said but with a questioning look in his eyes.

''No! Of course not! You are too attentive to me. You are behaving like a fiancé yourself.''

''You seemed very lonely. You have no friends at court yet.''

She would not admit it, but she did feel very alone and friendless. The female courtiers seemed intent on tripping her up which they did frequently as she had little experience of court life, especially foreign court life. She was frequently embarrassed and only intelligence and pride got her through the days. She looked so sad that he forgot himself and held her hand to comfort her. She tried to pull it away.

''I remember the flower you tried to dismember. Do you?''

''No,'' she lied, pretending not to remember that day when she had been so unhappy and then so full of joy after his second proposal.

''I think you lie, Ma'am,'' he said turning her slowly to him.

She knew what was coming and for self-preservation she tried to slap him. It did not deter him; he merely caught her wrist and held it tight. He bent his head and kissed her gently and when she tried to resist he twisted her to him and immobilized her.

After a minute, he lifted his head and then she snapped, ''You said you would never bed an unwilling woman, but you kiss a woman who doesn't want you.'' He immediately let her go and walked off retorting, ''I have never kissed you when you didn't want it, nor will I bed you until you wish it.'' He was smiling as he walked off to the card room whistling to himself.

She was beside herself with anger. How dare he insult her so? She had not encouraged him in any way. She had merely treated him with kindness as she would an old friend. She chose to ignore his comments about taking her a willing party to bed but that night she dreamed of herself in his arms making love to him.

The message came two days later. She was to be brought back. Other information showed the Archduke was not to be trusted. He breathed a sigh of relief. He had served his purpose. He arranged for his men to leave the city with him that day and then he would creep back to collect Felea and take her home. He would have to make a diversion to give them time to escape.

He had put round a rumour that a bomb plot against the Archduke was plotted. He had also bribed some servants and found a way out through tunnels under the city gates. He made his goodbyes to the Archduke and Duchess. Felea was there and he bowed and kissed her hand. She looked so doleful but put on a brave face.

She dined that evening with the Duke laughing and joking with him. He relaxed now Dreda had gone and became more familiar with her. She was glad to go to bed. She fell asleep but woke feeling someone had entered the room.

She was striking a match for the candles when a hand covered her mouth and she was carried to the window. The intruder pulled a rope hanging from the curtain hook and lifting her with him he slid out over the ledge. He let them down until he reached the bottom terrace.

He pulled her along with him. She knew it was Dreda. She recognized the firm grip and that muscular chest and his lithe leopard like run. She resisted him, wanting to find out what was happening. He heard a noise and thinking they could be discovered if they argued he hit her swiftly on the chin, knocking her out.

He then carried her through a manhole down a tunnel until they were outside the city gates. He whistled, and a horse and rider arrived with a spare horse. He threw her up on to the animal in front of him and they sped away. They rode seventy leagues without a break. He was used to riding leagues and leagues while campaigning in the past.

In the Palace, a bomb slowly smoked in a dressing room until the chemical cocktail was ignited and a flame shot through the clothes. For ten hours, the flames worsened until the whole room was alight and smoke was seen under the door. When the door was opened, an inferno fired the whole corridor and torched the dry timber which took the water men two days to get under control. In the mess, no-one noticed Felea had left until lunchtime when she hadn't appeared.

Dreda's man separated from them. Two lots of tracks were more difficult for their enemies to follow. Felea and Dreda didn't take the normal route home. They took the steepest paths which only a few people like he was familiar with. It was slow but safe and cut three hundred leagues off the road network.

She recovered consciousness and her jaw hurt like hell but on inspection Dreda said, "I haven't cracked it." From the malicious look in the patient's eyes he might as well have done. Green gold eyes smouldered angrily at him. She went on the attack! "I suppose I should be grateful you did not hit harder then?" Eliciting no answer, she continued furious with him, provoking him. "So, if you want to terminate an argument with a woman you choose to hit her."

"Oh no, I can think of a better way to shut you up," he said, pulling her to him. His eyes sparkled mischievously. He was happier than he had felt in ages. Felea had escaped her farce of a marriage and he now had his woman in his arms; for keeps this time he promised himself. He enjoyed sparking a reaction from her, matching his wits with her. An angry but passionate Felea was an improvement on the 'frostpiece' he had faced over the last few months.

"Spanking you would be much more interesting but this will do," he said covering her mouth with his and making it impossible for her to speak. She pushed him away when she was able. She might love the man but hated his presumption she would walk back docilely into his arms.

"You are odious and insufferably arrogant. I might have wanted to stay there! "

"I couldn't watch you becoming more miserable every day my love. The Emperor instructed me to bring you back. The Archduke is not to be trusted and your marriage contract is to remain unsigned." She thought it was more likely that Dreda had persuaded the Emperor to change his mind. What he wanted he usually got.

He put her on his horse again. She was so exhausted by the nights of interrupted sleep and the long day's riding she lay back her head against his chest arguing no longer. He remembered another time she had ridden in front of him, grateful for being rescued and he enjoyed the warmth of her soft body resting next to him. Her soft breasts nudged his arms with each step of the horse. When she moved, her sleepy body close to him, her tight derriere hugging him, he could barely contain his need for her. He thought, *this journey had better be over soon,*

They slept rough that night cuddled together under a blanket. Dreda pulled her to him, his arms tightly around her keeping her warm. With Dreda's arms around her, even fully clothed, Felea knew she wanted him! She had missed his kisses and his caresses. But he had to make a commitment. She would not be his mistress! He seemed interested in her again, becoming like the old Dreda again, domineering and manipulative but still had not mentioned love or marriage again.

They had four days' ride ahead of them but Felea didn't feel comfortable. She had a feeling of foreboding. Danger was ahead! An image of a tall slim person floated in her mind. Felea could feel the malevolence emanating from the image; anger and vindictiveness eating up that person's soul. That anger seemed directed at them! She shivered and wished she had more control over her visions. They were reliable when predicting or warning something would happen but not accurate enough to help her contain or ward off trouble.

"I saw a vision Officer. Someone is near us who wishes us ill." Dreda appeared unusually worried. He didn't mock Felea when she spoke of her visions. He had been with her enough time to know she was not imagining them.

"Describe the vision."

"A tall, slim, very dark-haired person who seems to hate us. That is all but this person is coming closer!"

Dreda's breath tightened in his chest. He had seen something shining up the mountain behind them. Someone was following them! He thought he had shaken off the Ducal troops, so this must be a new danger. Whoever was following them seemed to be taking their time as if they wanted to be sure and capture their prey easily.

They sped on his horse, now mature but still fleet of foot and ready for a race. Felea knew something was very wrong and when they stopped to give the poor animal a break she touched Dreda's arm and confronted him. Dreda was not a man who communicated his problems easily with people; by necessity self-reliant he had always brooded rather than trusting others.

"Are we being followed?" she asked. He smiled. He should have known he could not keep much from this girl, intelligent and wise beyond her years. He had not wanted to frighten her!

"Yes, but I don't think it is the Duke's men. They are not trying to catch us up quickly and return us to the Palace. They seem too content to follow us. Perhaps, they want to ambush us somewhere."

"Do you know this territory well?"

"Very well. I was a mercenary around here when I left the state. Boney's men had captured the city and the Emperor was a puppet leader so I fought independently here, and later Denman joined me. We fought with the English later in the Peninsula."

"Who might know you and wish to capture us?"

"I can think of three groups. I have a price on my head if they took me to the rebel camp. Only one person has a real grudge against me in this area."

He broke off and Felea felt uncomfortable again. There was

something in his past he was hiding from her again. She felt like slapping him! He had kissed her but would not trust her.

"Who is this person? Why does he hold a grudge against you?"

"We had better get moving again. I wish I had another horse. Fire needs a rest, don't you old boy?" he said avoiding answering her and rubbing the horse as it nuzzled him. "Like me you are not in your dotage but you find this pace hard!"

The horse whinnied but started galloping again. Felea was pleased he did not kick at her so often and had nuzzled her neck when she fed him that morning. Like his master, he was slow to trust but gave true affection if he loved someone. Felea gave up pumping Dreda. He was a closed book and would tell her when he was ready.

Dreda pushed Fire on until the horse ran out of steam. He stopped. "We will walk the rest." He covered their animals' hooves with cloths.

"Try to avoid leaving prints if you can." He wore a frown and Felea felt his anxiety.

"Where are we going?"

"There is a cave behind a waterfall where we may hide for the night. Pray our pursuers do not find our tracks. They have followed us for leagues now down the steepest tracks. We clearly are their prey!" He was no longer cared about scaring her. She needed to be ready to defend herself if they were attacked.

"Who is this enemy?" she asked, this time determined to get an answer from him. "How do you know of him?"

He grimaced at her persistence. She was like a terrier refusing to let go. *Damn the girl!* The things he liked most about her irritated him as well. Strong-willed, determined and persistent, Felea could drive him mad when she got the bit between her teeth. He wished she could work for him. He had watched her decoding some maths puzzles for pleasure and acknowledged her brilliant, analytical, problem solving mind. He might be able to use her in the Bureau if he could get them both back in one piece.

"Felea, it could be one of two people after us. Both served with me in the army against Napoléon's men when we made sorties into the city and attacked the forts. One holds a grudge against me but the other might just want the bounty on my head. Let's hope it is the latter. Recently the two have acted as bandits preying on vulnerable travellers."

"How do you know they specifically want us?"

"They are fifty leagues away from their normal patch and have followed us for at least four hours. Normal travellers would have taken the shallower routes. They know these trails like the back of their hand or I would have lost them by now.''

"Do they know the waterfall?''

"I never went anywhere near it when I was with them, so my fingers are crossed they don't know it.''

The climb grew steeper and harder. Dreda admired Felea's tenacity. Her breathing had become shorter and harsher as she slipped and slid on the now wet moss. He was tired and much fitter than she who like most young woman only had the opportunity to dance and walk or ride to maintain her stamina.

At last he saw the overhang of rock partially hidden behind the vines and branches. The waterfall ran down the side of this track but there was a cave behind the vines. It would be a good hiding place or an inconvenient trap. He pulled Felea up the last part of the steep track and pushed her quickly into the cave. He had tied the horse behind some trees a short distance away. He went down and brushed their footprints away as best as he could and then swiftly ran into the cave.

"No hot food tonight Lady Felea. I cannot risk a shot.'' He had some berries and some cold bits of rabbit from the animal he had shot and cooked over a camp fire the night before.

"Fill yourself up with water. It will assuage your hunger.'' They were in dire straits. If the foe numbered only a few men he could pick them off but if more than that they might pin the two of them there for days. If they had to hold up for more than a few days, they would be weak from hunger.

He was not willing even to risk lighting a fire and wrapped his greatcoat around the pair of them and then the blankets. Felea rested back against his chest and sank into a deep sleep while he watched over them both. He was used to little sleep and rest, his stamina developed over the years.

Even he nodded off for a few moments and woke up suddenly after hearing a noise in his sleep. It was a scuffling noise as if someone had slipped and was trying to maintain his grip on the slippery surface. Dreda immediately lay Felea down and grabbed his pistols and rifle. Felea stirred and he covered her mouth with his hand stifling her.

"Hush,'' he whispered. Felea grabbed a pistol herself. They sat silent, Felea's heart in her mouth and Dreda watching the entrance stoically, eyes intent on noticing any movement outside.

Footsteps grew nearer, easily heard by now. Their pursuers were no longer trying to hide themselves, their confidence growing all the time. Felea looked at Dreda. He looked as if he expected the worst.

The colour had drained from his face.

The footsteps halted outside. There were two pairs, one lighter than the other, *a man and boy,* thought Felea. *Good! A boy might be easier to overpower.*

"Dreda," cried a loud masculine voice. "We know you are there. We know you have little food and are cold. We can wait until hunger drives you to us or you can surrender now."

Dreda said nothing, trying to think his way out of this mess. He could not have picked a better place the mountain having few caves and trees for shelter. He decided to light the fire he had readied. Lighted branches could enable him to fight his way through the entrance. Dreda put some oily rags on the branches and set them alight. The man outside was growing impatient and would smell the fire burning soon.

"Dreda, are you surrendering or are we coming for you? It will be the worst for your wench if she is caught up in the firing."

"Come in for me Toni," yelled Dreda. Or are you a coward?" Felea's eyes widened at this insult. Dreda's methods were usually to try to appease the enemy rather than goading him. *What was on his mind?*

"When they come in use the flame on them. Light their clothes and aim also at their faces," he whispered. "You may have only one chance so make it work. Then use your pistols or sword." He hugged her. "You can do it!"

They watched the curtain of vines move and three men pushed in. Dreda waited until the men were in the cave and then moved like lightning signalling Felea to follow his lead. The branches in one hand firstly, he doused the men's hair and then a branch in each hand he directed the flames to the men's flimsiest and most flammable garments which would shrivel and light most easily when oil dripped down their torsos.

The branches then rose in an arc and lit two men's hair. He then stabbed their faces causing them to scream hellishly and fall back through the cave entrance, their faces red and inflamed. On fire, the men ran to the waterfall still crying out. They did not reach it before being consumed by the flames.

He now used his sword and pistols on two other men who followed, slicing one in two and putting a bullet through the forehead of the other. More men came forward and forcing him to one side with swords they entered the cave and two headed for Felea. She was the weakest point in their defence. She used the branches, but they were no good against pistols and she dropped them, raising her pistols and shooting each of them, dropping them.

She had no chance to hurt the third, a tall darkly clothed fellow with his face hidden by a hat. He stamped over the dead men and pushed her hard against the wall, the breath knocked out of her, his hands now at her throat. She coughed and spluttered trying to breath.

"We have your wench now Dreda," said the man Dreda called Toni. "Surrender or I will hurt her badly!"

Filthy bastard, thought Dreda but put his sword and pistols down. He could not endanger Felea's life and there were more men waiting to take him on. His hands in the air he walked back into the cave.

"Let her go Toni. She is an innocent party in all this," he demanded. "This is between us not you and her!"

"No," said a voice at the cave entrance behind him. He swung round. "This is between you and me Danitz! She will be a good bargaining weapon I think."

The flickering flames of the fire enabled Felea to just make out a tall but slender figure with long ebony hair and piercing blue eyes; a lithe but muscular figure but feminine to the core. Her only defect was a long thin scar stretching from under one eye down to the bottom of a cheek. Even scarred she was still stunningly beautiful!

The woman dressed in a man's clothes stopped in front of her. "Hands off her," she commanded, and the brute released his victim. Felea stood up straight trying to control her gasping and breathing. This woman was clearly a person of authority and knew Dreda well enough to challenge him.

Coming to Felea she took Felea's chin in her hand and looked at her keenly. "So, this is the little spy who captured your interest Dreda. A beauty!"

Felea wrested her head away from the woman objecting to being manhandled like a pet. She leant back against the wall looking at her eye to eye, giving her back stare for stare.

"Feisty too! I can see how you snared him my dear," said the woman in a patronizing tone.

"I didn't snare him," retorted Felea. "One snares an animal. A man loves a woman by choice!"

Well done Felea! thought Dreda. This is why he adored this wench. Even in serious trouble she failed to bow to another's will; she was indomitable. Her ancestors would have gone to the stake rather than giving in to their tormentors and she was made of the same steel.

Unfortunately, this was the wrong tactic with this woman. Lucia was looking for conflict and confrontation. Dreda needed to defuse the situation before the woman lashed out at Felea. He knew her temper and vindictiveness and the scores she had to settle with him. His blood ran cold at the thought of what she would do to Felea if she thought it would hurt him indirectly. Two men had gripped him by the shoulders forcing his hands behind his back, but he violently shrugged them off and approached the two women. The dark haired one turned around.

"She is a feisty wench," said Dreda "and I thought I was in love with her, but one can only have so much spirit. I was beginning to tire of her before my head injury. Luckily, when I recovered consciousness I realized it had been merely infatuation and Felea behaving gentlewomanly for once released me from my engagement. I have no strong feelings any longer for this young woman!"

Felea gasped and exclaimed, "You Bastard! I was glad to get rid of you myself. You were a condescending fossil, a crusty bachelor, jealous and complaining about my flirting and necklines. It was the best thing that happened when you hurt your head!"

He came over and took her chin in his hand knowing his every movement was being watched by the woman who hated him. "I couldn't even marry you off to the Duke. He found you irritating and the bloody Emperor insisted on my bringing you back. I can't get rid of you!"

He turned to the woman and said, "She was supposed to seal a peace alliance between the two countries, but the Emperor found the Duke and his father were conniving behind our backs and ordered us back. It was a good job. She had already put his back up by her uppity ways! Who would want a mouthy, stroppy brat like her?" He pushed Felea's head away roughly and stepped back.

Facing the woman, he said, "And what do you want of us or me specifically Lucie? Something must be important for you to channel so many men and so much time and energy into racing after us!"

The woman had watched the interaction between the former loving couple. She had been amazed a woman had snared Dreda at last after so many ingenious and inventive females had failed and such an innocent at that! She knew Dreda's predilection for mature women in his bed, who knew what aroused him and would service him in exactly the ways he demanded. She had been such a woman, younger than his average, but passionate and eager to learn his desires. She wondered what extra this wench had offered him in bed. There now seemed little love lost between them as the girl stood snarling at him and he gave her that detached, disinterested look that characterized him so well.

"We will make camp tonight and eat and then move back home tomorrow. Dreda, you will find out what I want from you at my leisure. I am not here to please you." She motioned to her men.

She went over to Dreda and stood close to him. He stood back not wanting any intimacy with her. She undid his jacket buttons slowly and then those of his waistcoat and shirt. Her nails were blood red in contrast to her black hair and her lips were painted ruby. Revealing the fine fair hair which traced his musculature down to his breeches she raked her fingers down his skin leaving deep scratches and making him wince although he tried to hide the grimace.

Felea had quickly understood the status of this woman in Dreda's life. A former mistress who clearly knew every part of his body intimately, she was showing to Felea she now possessed and controlled this man and he was hers to do with what she wished. Felea saw the look of disgust on Dreda's face. Relieved, she also felt his helplessness and humiliation as the woman traced the scratches with her lips and tongue down his abdomen, branding him.

With inhuman self-control Dreda moved not a muscle until the woman, a look of disappointment in her face, moved away and said, "You used to be a more passionate man Dreda. Maybe a boring desk job and age has uneuched you!'

He just shrugged, refusing to rise to her bait, feeling beyond embarrassment that Felea had had to witness this exhibition. Felea felt vomit rise in her throat. The thought of Dreda in this woman's bed, his hands caressing her made her shrink from the pair of them. How had he become snared by her! How could she, Felea, want to touch him again after this creature had abused him?

"Tie them up and give them more blankets and feed them. I want them alive and well!''

With one more triumphant look at Felea Lucie left them to look at the horses and talk with her brother while food was being prepared. Dreda sat by Felea who didn't want to look at him.

"At least we will get a good meal tonight," whispered Dreda, trying to open a conversation.''

"The sacrifice is usually fed before the slaughter,'' said Felea.

"I have no intention of us being sacrifices, Felea. We now can start planning our escape.''

He seemed uncaring and unaffected by the woman's actions. Felea turned angrily to him. "What was that woman to you Francis and how did she ensnare you? What attracted you to her? She is vile, a monster!''

"Believe it or not she was quite normal, a pleasant, pretty girl when I first met her.'' Felea raised her eyebrows and he took her face in his hands and said, ''It is true! She is a skilled fighter and fought alongside me when I left the Emperor's army. Her name is Lucia

155

Remenaz and the brother is Antoni of the same name.

'She was my lover for a year but then she was taken by the enemy and brutalized and scarred, kept as a prisoner for two months. She never recovered, her temperament changing. She wanted me still and I think I could have forgotten the violation of her, but she became vindictive and each time we caught enemy prisoners she wanted to beat and torture them and send them back as a warning.

She called it reprisals for the loss of our men, but it was random revenge for the assault on her. I began to withdraw from her and she accused me of being ashamed of her. Our relations never recovered, and I never went back to her bed. I went to fight with the English and later joined the Bureau. She has never forgiven me and wants revenge on me for my apparent desertion of her.''

He saw the cold detached look on Felea's face. ''You must believe me Felea, I have no feelings for her and have had none for years. She is warped and sad and my only desire is for us to get out of her reach.

'You must pretend you dislike me and me you or she will hurt us both and use our hurt as weapons against each other. She is a clever, intuitive woman, more intelligent than you can believe, just much damaged.''

''I do believe you Francis, but that woman has touched you intimately and you her. It just disgusts me! I need some time to come to terms with this!''

''Watch out, they are coming in again,'' said Dreda. ''Abuse me! Make it look as if you hate me!''

''That won't be difficult. If you had not been so weak we would not be in this position now,'' she snapped. ''Any woman could see what sort of harpy she is.''

''I repeat she has changed for the worse. Don't let your jealousy blind you to the truth, Woman!''

''Jealousy! I am supposed to be jealous of that strumpet. Huh, you wish. You are conceited and arrogant.''

She slapped him as hard as she could as the men and Lucie entered the cave again bringing food. He moved so close to her she backed against the wall. He stared menacingly at her. ''If my hands weren't tied you would feel the back of them against your pretty face my girl. Wait until I am free. You will regret slapping me again. I warned you before about hitting me!''

''You Bastard! You are just a lecher, a womanizer who would bed anything, so desperate are you!''

Lucie watched this interchange with interest. She noted the

sparks flying from Felea's eyes. This was not the young girl who idolized her older fiancé as described to her by her spies. This was a virago who challenged her intimidating ex-lover, returning his threats with insults of her own.

"Move them to opposite sides of the cave. We want some sleep. I will deal with them in the morning."

Turning to her brother she asked, "Do you have any preferences as to their fate Toni?"

"I want the bounty and that is more if he is alive than if he were dead but other than that I don't care. It is you who has the vendetta against him Lucie. He did not wrong me even if he left our group."

She nodded and let him get his sleep while brooding over what she could enjoy doing to Dreda and his pretty little friend. *Alive did not mean unhurt,* she thought!

CHAPTER SEVENTEEN

Dreda spent part of the night thinking of an escape route. He had no illusions that if he stayed and Lucie had her revenge he would be missing body parts or left unable to use them. Lucie had personally gelded some of the unfortunate soldiers she had caught. He had been sickened by the pain and terror on the men's faces before they had been thrown still bleeding over their horses to be taken and released outside of the city gates at night. He had vowed that from then on that none of his own troops would ever mistreat the enemy without just cause.

He slept heavily the last few hours of the night until he was rudely shaken awake to find some bread and oatmeal thrust in front of him. "Nearly as bad as your broth," he taunted Felea.

"I hope it chokes you," retorted Felea, eating hers with a gusto, thinking it might be her last meal. Even if she was going to her death she was not going to starve herself. She thought once Dreda had given enough information she would be put to death.

He would give the information. She was sure of that after he had surrendered so quickly when he thought they might hurt her. That reaction was interesting, showing his feelings for her were more entrenched than he showed publicly. He was like an orange. The more one peeled the more enjoyment and taste there was to find.

Dreda knew Lucie was still infatuated with him and he could use that sexual desire against her if he could remain alone with her. He had to convince her she still had a chance with him or at least tempt her to one last passionate tryst with him. The latter was more likely to succeed after his dispassionate coldness to her.

Lucie approached Felea and asked Dreda, "How much will you tell to avoid me hurting her Danitz?" To illustrate her conviction, she pulled Felea's hair back as hard as she could, making Felea gasp.

"As much as you need to know Lucie; enough to get you the bounty your brother wants. Let me talk with you, preferably away from here while the others clear camp."

"You say she is a nuisance, but you want to save her from harm Danitz. What means she to you?"

"She is a favourite of the Emperor and I don't want to risk his wrath. I do not want her in my life but having been her protector I have a certain affection for her as if she were my own child. She is immature but will make a man a good wife if he can be patient and tame her. I am not that man. You know I have little patience to teach innocents the ways men like in bed. I prefer mature experienced women."

Lucie licked her lips thinking of his experience in the bedroom and how he had imparted this to her, a young innocent girl. She had fallen in love with the handsome and rakish Dreda; a man much wilder in his younger days, who had enjoyed women like most army men did. When she had been returned from her capture she had seen the shock on his face at her scarred countenance.

He had never bedded her since and she had vowed she would pay him back for that insult. She felt self-disgust for she still wanted him; no needed him in her bed and the news of his engagement had sickened her. With her virginity lost and her scarred face she had nothing left to offer any discerning man! Her stomach had turned over until she had heard his engagement had been broken.

She was delighted when she heard he had bodyguarded Felea to the Palace and then was surprised again to find him bringing her back to the city. This had been her opportunity to revenge herself on him and that girl. She imagined his hands and lips over herself. One last time in his bed would not hurt her and even if the wench did not love him she was woman enough to resent her kissing and making love to her former fiancé.

"I think I could give you a little private time," she said pulling him up and escorting him by the arms through the entrance to the cave.

"Disgusting," he heard Felea say to herself as he left.

Keep it up Felea, he thought. He was going to have a lot of explaining to do after this, but he thought he would enjoy making her listen the same way as he had yesterday morning.

"I cannot touch you with my arms bound," he said.

"I can do all the touching," she replied.

"Damn, was she going to mount him?" That would not get him anywhere excepting a short excitement and sexual rush that any man would get from being taken by an attractive woman and then self-disgust. He allowed her to draw him to a sheltered spot and lay down where she directed.

She was enjoying being the mistress of this situation and he had a desire to throw her down and take her; the domineering macho male inside him taking over the sophisticated militia man. Lying him on his back, she undid his shirt and breeches and drawers pulling them down. He looked up and her ample breasts spilled out now she had opened her shirt to her waist.

"I can't reach them easily," he complained, eying the aureole of her nipples. "I'll have to be a contortionist to do the job properly," he added wryly. "I forgot just how beautiful your breasts are Lucie." In truth Dreda was physically as aroused as any man could be by a woman hanging over him with breasts ready for sucking.

Mentally, he was turned off by her wantonness. He was a man who would normally dominate a woman not the other way around! If he had his choice, he would bring her back untouched to the city to be tried for kidnapping and theft, but he was stuck here with an aroused woman ripe for seducing.

After one unsuccessful attempt at caressing her breast with his mouth Lucie said, "Turn on your back and I will release your hands."

Thank God, thought Dreda reading the lust in her eyes. *They had a chance now!* He still had to incapacitate this woman without her alerting her brother. They were only a few yards away from the cave entrance.

Feeling disgust, he set to sucking her nipple making her gasp. She relaxed at last as he smiled and said, "I have missed this Lucie." Her eyes closed with contentment as he began to caress her lower down and then he struck. His hand covered her neck, finding just that spot where if pressure was applied she would lose consciousness. She collapsed and then he cracked her with his fist on the jaw.

He pulled himself off her body, pocketing her pistols and carried her and lay her under a tree tying her hands and gagging her. He could not believe she had acquiesced so easily and unbound him, but he had seen the madness in her eyes and the uncontrolled lust for him. It had swayed her better judgement. He cursed the soldiers who by abusing her had warped and destroyed her.

Moving quietly, he went to the entrance of the cave. Out of the men who had come with Lucie and Toni four were left. Not good odds when he had no weapon, but he had faced worst. Felea was there with her hands unbound. Good! She had fought well yesterday. Now, how to distract the men!

Felea had not been fooled by Dreda. She knew it was a pretence when he said he would make a tryst with Lucie. He was a master actor when his skin was at risk. Felea knew when he was aroused. He had held her close enough during their dances and carriage rides.

His eyes had always turned a moody blue when he lusted after her. In contrast, with Lucie his eyes had remained a cold blue grey, as cold as a fish on a costermonger's slab. He was foxing that harpy, pretending he lusted after her. She had heard a few gasps and moans and guessed Dreda was making love to Lucie, to what purpose she did not know but he was clever and ruthless enough to seduce her and execute her if need be. She had no illusions as to what kind of man Dreda was.

The moans had stopped, and she heard someone outside the cave. The four men were in cabinet discussing their next move and which trail to take. None of them wore weapons and she was near a sword and two pistols. She had seen one man prepare his pistol and a rifle. If that was Dreda outside where was the woman? All the gasps had stopped so she thought the woman must be incapacitated. That left only four to deal with. If she killed two Dreda could deal with the other men. If she could hear Dreda he could probably see and hear her.

She got up and stretched. "Please may I go and stretch my legs? I need a call of nature." One man said, "Wait a minute while we finish our meeting and I will take you." As if impatient, she walked around the room settling even nearer the pistols which she edged near to and covered with her skirts, the men's backs to her.

The man who offered to take her outside came over. She got up gracefully, gathering the pistols in her skirts, praying she would not drop them; swaying her hips deliberately, making the man keep his eyes on her petite derriere instead of on her front. He let her go in front of him saying to his mate, "What a flaming piece of ass! I wonder if Toni will let us have a go at her before he returns her to the city."

"Unlikely," said his associate. "She is too valuable to the Emperor. Money and a title! It would be a different story if Lucie gets her way. She will throw that girl to us as vengeance!"

Lucie was still in the copse, now regaining consciousness, realizing blearily she had been had. She could not call for help but she could get up, her wrists only tied in front of her, when her head stopped spinning. She saw Dreda at the entrance of the cave but could not warn her associates when Felea came out and threw one pistol hard at Dreda. Turning around he shot her unfortunate guard in his stomach. One down!

Dreda pushed her aside and through the vines he shot two more men. He pulled back as one more shot back at him. He told Felea to get out of harm's way. "Get the horses ready while I deal with this last one. Go! You are in the way if I have to worry about you. Keep an eye on Lucie over there."

Acknowledging the authority in his voice Felea moved toward Lucie but she was no longer there. She had managed to get up! Where was she? She looked around her and finding no-one she called, "Watch out for Lucie! She has escaped Francis!" She went to the horses and readied three in case Lucie had to come with them. Going back, she heard a crack. A pistol shot!

Sweet Jesus. Who was getting hurt now? Reaching the cave, she saw Dreda pull Toni out of the cave by the scruff of his neck. Blood was pouring from the man's arm and Dreda pushed him against a tree and manacled his wrists behind him then secured a bandage around his wound letting the man fall to the ground in a deep faint.

"He will be secure there. Have you found Lucie?" he asked.

"No!"

"She should have been out for hours the crack I gave her. Damn the woman, where is she? Ready another horse for her brother please Felea while I search for her. The rest of the men are dead, but she is the most dangerous, a loose cannon!"

He went to collect their belongings and the weapons and Felea turned down the track, but she heard something. A tall slim figure was looking through the vines at Dreda and slipped in the cave, silently behind him.

"Sweet Jesus, it is she!" exclaimed Felea. She rushed up the track to the cave entrance checking the carriages in her pistols. Looking through the vines she saw Dreda facing his ex-mistress who had her pistol aimed at him.

"You always were a liar and deceiver Dreda. You said you loved me and then betrayed me, ashamed of me."

"I never said I loved you Lucie. It was only an infatuation on both of our parts and I was only ashamed of you when you tortured and gelded those soldiers, not of your scars."

"A gelding Dreda. How that would suit you. I haven't got a knife, but this pistol will do. A well-aimed bullet between the legs and the job will be done just as satisfactorily. You will not be able to satisfy that young bitch, will you? You do love her, don't you?"

"My feelings for Felea are none of your business Lucie. Keep her out of this," he snapped. "She is young and innocent unlike us and deserves our protection."

"You must be head over heels to react like that Dreda. I would never have believed a chit of a girl could entrance you so much. What has she got that others don't have?" asked Lucie sadly.

"Honour, a caring for others before her own needs. She makes her servants love her as well as her friends. She is gracious and kind and doesn't realize how beautiful she is."

"She sounds like a saint," spat out Lucie, green with jealousy.

"No, she has faults like anyone else. She is stubborn like a mule, passionate and thinks too quickly for her own good. She is too loyal to others and endangers herself and she likes animals too much, even a bloody, mangy cat! She makes me want to throttle her and spank her nearly every day. She has many faults Lucie, but they make her human and loved by others."

"It is a shame you chose her over me for neither of you are of any use to me now. Toni wanted the bounty, but the money means nothing to me. I just want you and the girl dead. I was going to throw the girl to our men to experience what happened to me, so you would realize how I suffered but her death will suffice.''

She held her pistol up to get a direct shot. ''You first Dreda and then I will be at peace!''

''Not a chance you evil witch,'' muttered Felea. Lucie swung round and would have shot her but Felea closing her eyes pulled the trigger and sent the woman flying against the wall. She opened her eyes and asked, ''Is she dead?''

''No, but she is losing a lot of blood. I will stem her wound and bandage her and we will take her back to the Bureau.''

She looked a bit faint and he asked wryly, ''Why did you take so long to get to me? I thought I would lose my vital parts.''

''As usual you are gracious in your thanks. You should be grateful you can still make children instead of abusing me.'' She had heard only the part of the conversation where he had criticized her, the waterfall drowning out some of the words.

''I have many faults and you want to throttle me and spank me. Saddle your own damned horse. I am looking after my own.'' She turned away swishing her skirts, angry but tired, exhaustion overcoming her now the tension of the day was released.

Dreda followed her smiling. Trust her to have the last word. He would have to rid of her of that bad habit or he would never win an argument again. He tied the woman and her brother over their horses, this time so tight they could barely move. ''They can bloody suffocate for all I care,'' he explained. ''They have terrorized innocent travellers for years.''

''She would have encouraged those men to violate me,'' said Felea. ''She hated me before meeting me. I hope she gets what she deserves at her trial.''

He knew she was deeply upset by his behaviour with Lucia. Despite being one of the most rational women he had met Felea was woman enough to be jealous of his former lover when she was still unsure of his feelings for her. He kept forgetting how young she was, and he remembered how he had ignored her after his accident, in effect rejecting her.

He took her hands in his. ''Felea, I had to caress that woman, or we would have died. She would have turned you over to her men if she had had the chance. She was a virgin when I took her, but her mind was turned by her abuse by those soldiers.

'She tortured and gelded some soldiers. I rejected her because of her cruelty but she thought it was because of her scar and her rape.

That sort of rejection hurts a woman badly. Her touch revolted me Felea, but I had to pretend I enjoyed it.''

She pulled her hands away. ''Why are you telling me this? It doesn't concern me.''

''I think it concerns you very much. I am healthy you see!''

She coloured, and he changed the subject. He had had to reassure her he didn't carry the pox. Felea was gratified he had told her the truth.

Even a young virgin could see in the Palace women and men whose loose and careless lives were being cut short by that malady. The blindness and sores were hidden most of the time by the sufferers who were incarcerated in their bed-chambers, but rumours leaked out and they presented a warning to others.

He knew she had seen one poor woman confined to her bed. She had taken potions and some poultices to her, but these had barely helped the woman's suffering. An innocent victim of her husband's liaisons with harlots she was dying slowly and painfully.

It had made Felea think she would select her husband carefully subject to the Emperor's interference. She now felt reassured, but she still could not get the image of Dreda caressing that moaning woman out of her head. She hoped the image would fade with time.

She was now in two minds about her relations with him. She had told him the truth when she had said she was a different woman from the young girl he had proposed to. Without his authoritarian presence guiding her she had made more of her own decisions, developing more confidence and self-esteem.

His aunt was there to help her navigate through society avoiding the pitfalls an innocent virgin could easily fall into. Living in the Palace with the Duke and his father had made her realize she wanted more independence and to be her own mistress. Dreda seemed to want to dominate her, master her and bend her to his will.

She still loved him but disliked the way he had manipulated her and mistrusted her. He mocked her continuously, kissing her when she protested at her behaviour; an experienced man using her own passion to gain his own way. He was as dominant as ever ignoring her wishes. He could not see her as an equal and must be master. She had begun to feel suffocated by him.

Wounded deeply by his former rejection of her she had raised her barriers against him. She could not trust him again. If he could be inconstant before could he reject her again? She had suffered the humiliation of being put aside once by him and the sniggers behind her back, his former mistresses claiming she had just been a lovely distraction; too immature to hold the attention of such a sophisticated and mature man.

Dreda watched her carefully. She was unusually quiet, pensive, something was on her mind. Secretive, a product of her difficult background she did not trust easily. During their short time of intimacy together Dreda had gradually encouraged her to open to him. Since he had rejected her she had turned inwards again and was as tight as a clam her feelings hidden.

He realized she was still hurting badly and he did not know how to reach her. He cursed their situation and himself for handling her insensitively. The trust and friendship that had characterized their relationship had been ruptured and he had to rebuild their relations again. The thought he had hurt this lovely girl he idolized made him feel a bastard. Felea was brave and intelligent but she was still a sensitive young woman, not an army recruit. He would have to woo her and offer for her yet again with the Emperor's permission.

He lifted her on to her horse and led it knowing she no longer wanted him to touch her. She started to fall asleep in her saddle and he climbed behind her holding her against him. Fire was following, no burden on him this time. He deserved his rest.

Later they stopped, and he made a fire. Awake, she sat bleary eyed watching the prisoners who were tied up against some trees. He gutted and cooked some rabbits he had shot. He talked while he stirred the stew knowing what he said that night could determine their future relations.

He surprised her by talking about the incident in the cave again. He usually shut disturbing incidents away in the back of his mind and refused to discuss them. "I was proud of you back there Felea. You fought as well as any man there and treated Lucie with the disdain she deserved. I could not have asked for anything better from you.

"I don't think I am made for this life of spying and intrigue," she said wryly.

"You are right. You could do this work, but I think you would not enjoy it. Leave the sordid work to me and my men. We are better suited to it."

She nodded. She could easily enjoy the investigative side of the Bureau's work and carry it out competently, but she did not have the mentality to kill and torture like his men or Lucie. She would stick to her codes.

"You are too honest," he said. "You need a devious mind to serve the spies the same dish they serve you."

"And yourself," she said accusing him with her eyes; those

eyes that had bewitched him. She made him feel he must justify himself. In the past, he had undertaken his role without a thought of any injury to the people who stood in his way. His objectives had to be achieved by any means! If innocents were caught up in the mess so be it! There were always innocent casualties in war and his country was divided by civil war.

Since he had met Felea he now saw things were not so clearly cut, not black and white. People were pulled in different directions, their loyalties not so clearly defined. Once he would have commanded his men to herd the women and children of the captured rebels into camps and then left without another thought for them. Now the faces of children emaciated and hollow eyed, struggling to the grain wagons on rickety legs haunted him. He had personally put some of his own fortune aside for the purchase of grain and warm blankets and tents. More importantly, he had now tried to persuade the new Emperor to change his policies, to provide schools and doctors for the rebels' families; to win them over by mercy rather than by brute force.

He didn't want her to know of his generosity. It was something he had to do for himself, perhaps to prove to himself he was changing due to meeting Felea. He did not like the man he had become, an automaton without feelings, stamping over people who were vulnerable; carrying out blindly the policies of a spoilt autocratic ruler who had never suffered.

The execution of the family whose only crime was to provide food for a rebel's starving family had pricked his conscience. A man of his class he still supported the Emperor's inalienable right to rule. He was wary of the move to universal suffrage many intellectuals supported in Europe but recently he had questioned the policies of this Emperor, seeing the human costs of his dicta. He had been torn, wanting to resign but had instead felt he could influence the Emperor more as a member of his advisors than as a critic outside the Cabinet Office.

He stopped stirring the stew and twirled a ringlet of her hair around his finger, pulling her closer to him. "I am afraid I enjoy the intrigue. I like being one step ahead of my foe. It keeps my brain sharp."

Despite telling himself to move slowly and treat her tenderly he could not resist dropping a kiss on her hair and he put his arm around her. "That is why I adore you Felea. Your gentleness and tenderness. Stick to your linguistics and codes and office work. I will ask the Emperor to let you solve some problems for me at the Bureau."

She agreed. She would enjoy solving puzzles for the Bureau,

but she was still confused about him. She loved him, but did she like him enough to spend the rest of her life with him? The more she knew about him the more complex she found him and there was a dark side she was finding more about each day. She still hadn't asked him about the massacre, for once scared of hearing the truth. If Dreda had given the order to massacre those men Felea couldn't live with him no matter how he might profess his love for her.

The rebel men had trusted his word and put down their arms expecting mercy. The man who gave that command was merciless, ordering his men to run down unarmed men, cutting them to pieces. That man could ignore how his behaviour could affect the families left behind, the innocents. That she could not live with. That coldness and detachment was inhuman.

For the moment, she relaxed in his arms enjoying the moments of intimacy with him, trying to forget what else he was. He then surprised her again. "This new Emperor is making changes to the infrastructure and providing more funds for schools and hospitals. He is negotiating with the rebels. There may be less need for bloodshed and rebellion if the poor particularly in the hinterland are treated more fairly."

She was astonished. She had always thought he was a firm supporter of the former Emperor's policies, acting with contempt when others dared to criticize the Imperial decrees.

"Father always said more grain and jobs would have encouraged the young rural men to stay in the hinterland rather than joining the rebel army."

"Some months ago, I had to execute a family who I had known from childhood who were aiding the rebels with money and shelter. These were not fanatics Felea but merely people who cared about the peasants on their lands who were starving."

"How did you remain in your role?" she demanded.

"With difficulty!" he answered regretfully.

"Of course, you can detach yourself from your emotion, compartmentalize yourself! You don't empathize with others, do you?" she accused.

"Don't Felea!' 'he said. "For the first time, I was torn between loyalty to the Emperor and between gaining justice for these innocents caught up in the politics and intrigue when they merely wanted to help their people."

He sighed. "I decided to remain in my post because there were others equally as ruthless as me who had the ear of the Emperor. They were sycophants! They would agree with him just for the sake of pleasing him. The poor would have been worse off if I had resigned my position.

'The explosion changed everything. The present Emperor is more open to new ideas. I can influence him a little and I am pleased he let me lead the Bureau. No more unnecessary patronage or torture for the sake of it and men now recruited for their competence. I am making small changes.''

''And what about competent women?''

''At the moment, no real movement there. Some work as advisors but no full-time professional permanent jobs. Change is slow in our state Felea!''

He turned her so he could look in her eyes and said, ''I am not a total amoral bastard Felea and the reason I have changed is because of you. You have made me see there is good in people and I need someone like you in my life; your goodness and caring attitude toward people and even that bloody mangy animal you love so much.

'It was you who drew my attention to the plight of the orphans and widows. You who offered to raise funds for them. I would not have thought of them without you. I am a better man for knowing you.''

She touched his cheek tenderly; this severe, callous man who was opening his heart to her. ''If the goodness had not been inside you I could not have changed you. It was just hidden deep!''

''Trust me Felea,'' he said and kissed her passionately, holding her tight to him. She put her doubts aside for that moment and kissed him back until he wrapped them both in his coat. She would ask him about the massacre when she got back to the city. He held her tightly. They slept fitfully until dawn and then they set off again.

After three days, they met some Imperial dragoons who took the prisoners off their hands. They travelled swiftly now they were on roads again and got home safely in record time. Dreda carried her half-asleep to her bed-chamber ignoring her protests. He laid her gently on the bed, her abigail hovering, like a mother hen to his disgust.

''My Lady is not ill, she is merely tired. Give me five minutes with her alone, please!'' He stood over her and then sat on her bed holding her hand.

''You should not be here,'' protested Felea.

''You are right. For both our sakes I had better leave. My self-control will last only so long!'' Looking suggestively at the big bed he said, ''Soon you will be in my bed my love and that is a promise!'' Leaving her gasping at his arrogant certainty he would have her he left for his lodgings to get a change of clothes.

CHAPTER EIGHTEEN

Dreda's Aunt was sick so Felea went to a soiree on her own, determined to show her independence from Dreda. He had another think coming if he believed he could click his fingers and she would come running like a pet. She intended to renew the acquaintance of the few friends she had made at court before she had left for the Archduke's Palace.

When he had been her fiancé Dreda had always told her to be circumspect and let him vet her friends. She thought him over cautious but had agreed not wanting to incur his wrath. He had often seemed on edge in court, beside her all the time, as if some harm might befall her; over-possessive she thought and too guarded, but she had tolerated his interference. He was older, wiser and understood the ways of 'polite society', guiding her so she did not put her foot wrong in this hypocritical two-faced world.

She took a drink from the lackey and moved toward a group of intellectuals she knew well. Her father's friends, they had always taken pity on the little girl who had asked inquiring questions wanting stimulation.

"Lady Felea," said one, a smile lighting up his face. "We thought you had left the state, but you are back."

She curtseyed smiling. "Von Retz. I am afraid the engagement didn't work out. The Archduke was plotting behind the Emperor's back, so I am here again." The man bent and kissed her hand. "That is good fortune for us gentlemen at court then my Lady." She coloured charmingly but then noticed a rather quiet man appear at her side.

She had seen this man before. He was sallow in skin and had dark hooded eyes set in a thin face. He was dressed all in black, with a snowy white cravat making his skin look even darker. He was broader and more heavily set than Dreda, but he wore that same air of assurance and even arrogance; a man used to getting his way.

"May I present Count von Herzen," said her friend. He appeared a little uneasy.

Von Herzen bent over her hand and kissed it a little too long, in a rather too familiar way. She took a step back feeling rather overwhelmed by this powerful looking man, his saturnine face assessing her in a measuring way. She dropped a curtesy and smiled, "Have we met Sir, I think I know your face?"

"We have passed each other at Court," he said, "but I have never had the opportunity of making your acquaintance before, something I wanted to rectify."

"I was away for a while," she said, "but I am back for good now I hope."

"Dreda brought you back then," said von Herzen. "He couldn't stand being separated from you for very long."

Felea looked askance at him, at his boldness. It was if he was trying to make her say something out of place. *Sweet Jesus, did others think she was still Dreda's woman?*

"I think he was acting on the Emperor's instructions Sir."

"Oh, you cannot fox society Lady Felea. Dreda deliberately manipulated the political situation in his masterful way to ensure the Emperor brought you back. A little longer and a peace treaty might have been signed."

The man looked at her cynically. "Possession of a woman was more important than his duty to the state," he replied categorically, shocking her. In this state dominated by intrigue and suspicion to accuse Dreda of putting the state second was almost tantamount to calling him a traitor in anyone's eyes.

"I think Officer Dreda would put loyalty to the state before any loyalty to a woman. His first loyalty is to the Emperor," she said, trying to think of a way she could evade this man. She shivered, and a dark cloud appeared before her eyes and her head felt as if a band was tightening around it. A vision was coming, and she could not prevent it.

She felt faint. She said to her father's friend, "A seat please Sir, I have the headache and I feel somewhat faint." The man took her to the seats situated around the outside of the room, but her tormentor followed. Why had he picked on her that evening and what did his words mean? Was Dreda being accused of acting against the interests of the state by helping her? Had she inadvertently caused him to be out of the Emperor's favour?

Her vision lasted only a few seconds this time. She saw a dark haired saturnine man and a tall blond slim man arguing until the blond man bowed sharply and turned on his heel, the other angrily calling after him, "You will be seen to be a traitor you know. You cannot hide forever." She now recognized the two men arguing as von Herzen and Dreda. Her instincts had been correct this time. Von Herzen was her enemy, a trouble-maker.

A movement to her side made her look up sharply. Dreda stood there with the most contemptuous look she had ever seen on his face. He took her hand in his and asked, "Lady Felea what is the matter?" He was relieved and yet angry he had found her with this man, who was so obviously, his enemy. She explained, "I was talking with Count von Herzen and then I came over faint." Dreda recognized a vision taking over her body but knew she did not want these broadcasted to the outside world for fear of her being defamed as a witch.

He turned to von Herzen. In the coldest voice she had ever heard, he said so softly, but with menace in his voice, "Thank you for caring for Lady Felea von Herzen but I am here now to give her aid."

Von Herzen understood the warning and possessive tone in his voice. "Oh, I know you wish to protect your own Dreda!"

"I am still her protector under the Emperor's direction until she marries," explained Dreda quietly, although he wanted to grab this man by the throat and throttle him for his impertinence in even approaching Felea. When he saw the man's lustful eyes run over Felea, he held himself back, only by iron self-control. All who knew them knew von Herzen was his sworn enemy in the Cabinet and in Court.

Von Herzen could only have had one of two reasons for making Felea's acquaintance; one to poison her mind against him or worse to try to charm her for himself and make her his lover; to destroy the relations he was building again with Felea. Either way, he was a snake who wished them both ill.

Von Herzen would never marry Felea. He would set her up as his courtesan to use as his will. When he married, he would marry for status and patronage only; one of the ladies from the neighbouring royal families, a marriage designed to increase his power.

He had laughed in Dreda's face when Dreda had admitted he was marrying for love. "A love-sick fool, really Dreda. Marrying a traitor's daughter. How can the Emperor trust you now?" Dreda had walked off but had found out later he was the one who was blackening his reputation.

"I will take Lady Felea home to rest," said Dreda dismissively.

"Your Servant, Lady Felea," retorted von Herzen. "Until I have the opportunity of making your enchanting acquaintance again."

He lingered over her hand again making Dreda grit his teeth. How he wished he could smash that man's teeth down his throat and ruin his pretty features. The loathsome creature left their presence looking back once to see how they were affected by his leaving.

Dreda helped Felea up and guided her to her carriage smiling and explaining to her few well-wishers she felt slightly faint in the hot salon. Holding on to his temper by a hair's breadth he reached the carriage. Once inside he exploded, anxiety warring with tolerance and patience. She may be young, but she had failed to heed his warning once again. That man was dangerous and could hold a noose to both their necks. He had to be harsh with her for both their sakes.

"I warned you not to come to any social events on your own.

What did von Herzen want with you?'' he demanded of her.

''He was horrible. He inferred that you had acted as a traitor, deliberately destroying the chance of my marriage and thus stopping the signing of a peace treaty between our two nations. He accused you of acting selfishly, putting wanting me before the interests of your country.''

The Bastard. It was what he had expected. Luckily in his cautious way he had tied all the loose ends. There were Ambassadors from several states there for the wedding and they had witnessed the shadowy negotiations between the Archduke's advisors. Taylia's own Ambassador had warned him of the Archduke's duplicity.

Von Herzen had picked the wrong poisonous words this time to try to destroy him. His back was covered sufficiently and the episode at Vina had gained him the Emperor's gratitude although it had incurred Felea's wrath. He was safe for a while and intended to consolidate his support in the Cabinet although his name was black in 'polite society'. He had never been popular but now he was regarded as the devil himself.

''What was your vision?'' he asked curtly, still furious with her.

''Two men resembling you and von Herzen arguing and then you walked off.''

''That happened well before we left for the Archduke. He called me a love-sick fool for wanting to marry you. I told him my loyalty was still to the Emperor not the rebels, but he has been trying to persuade the Emperor I have divided loyalties.'' He took her hand and said, ''Felea you must be careful who you speak with. Von Herzen is my sworn enemy and would take you for himself just to spite me. He is waiting to trip you up.''

''He kissed my hand rather too intimately,'' agreed Felea. She recognized Dreda had been right. She was too naïve and unaware of the dangers that lay before her. She needed guidance while others were out to destroy them.

''Until I have spoken to the Emperor I will go into society only with your aunt or you.''

''Very well,'' he said. He lay his head back against the squabs and tried to forget the episode although it kept entering his mind. Von Herzen had reminded him of how tenuous their positions were in this toxic, venomous court. He must go to the Emperor and secure her future before the vipers at Court dragged her reputation through the mud.

Felea and Dreda attended a ball at the Emperor's Palace the next evening. Dreda thought it politic to show their faces. He also wanted the Emperor to show he still approved of his ward. Scurrilous rumours were being put about concerning his behaviour with Felea. Her virtue was being impugned. Their names were being banded together but someone had put it about that he would offer her a carte blanche as she was no longer virtuous.

When he and Felea entered the ballroom with his aunt the conversations stopped, and all eyes were directed at them. A few minutes later talk started again but Felea was given dark looks by the patroness and the men ran their eyes over her, inspecting her as if she was on a slab in a meat market. Dreda burned with anger, his fists clenching and murder in his eyes. He felt like reminding the men she was no 'light skirt' they could give the eye to, but he had no right to defend her honour.

He cared not for his reputation but could not ignore the influence of the patronesses of society who could ruin her with one word or the careless turn of a shoulder away from her. He cursed fluently beneath his breath. He had made one of the first serious mistakes of his life, escorting her home alone without other soldiers or a chaperone. He had given the gossips ammunition and they were firing it for all they were worth.

As soon as the Emperor gave them permission to marry he would put his ring back on her finger and get a Special Licence before anything could separate them again. He took Felea out on the dance floor for a waltz, but she felt uncomfortable still being the object of attention.

"Don't worry. Once the audience with the Emperor is over we can concentrate on our normal life again. Just ignore the tittle tattle Felea."

"I have not heard what they are saying Francis," she said looking perplexed. What had she done to warrant the approbation of the patronesses?

"Nothing that should worry you," he reassured her. When he had finished mingling with the crowd he would have scuppered some of the rumours. A word in the right ears would stop the tattle-mongering; a threat that certain daughters would be removed from the lists of the Emperor's balls or certain debts could be called in and financially embarrass some fathers.

Dreda would use every bit of influence he had to protect Felea and more; crossing the line of moral turpitude if necessary and using blackmail and bribery. Felea could not be allowed to be devoured by the vicious vixens in society who waited for any slip by a debutante before they tore her to pieces.

He left her in the hands of his redoubtable aunt and went to mingle and start his campaign in defence of her. She crossed to Denman who was joking with a lady under his protection who danced on the edge of morality in society. Now her staid husband had died she was her own mistress but had run through most of his money. She had found rich protectors who would finance her expensive lifestyle in return for satisfying them in bed.

Felea did not sit in judgement on such women having been stigmatized as immoral herself in the Archduke's court. It was difficult for women to remain virtuous when they relied on men for their money and wellbeing in this judgemental society. She cursed her own position; being forced to remain at the mercy of the Emperor and unable to choose her own lifestyle.

"Ah you are back Lady Felea," said his lady.

"Yes, I found my groom was not the man we thought he was. He was planning to aid the enemies of our state and intended to set a force to take our borders again. I was merely there to act as a decoy and make the Emperor drop his guard."

"Officer Dreda looked after you well though!" opined the woman her fine brows arching. "Of course, he had an interest in doing so." It was more of a statement than a question and the innuendo dripped off her tongue.

"Why so?" asked Felea carelessly, not waiting to give this harpy any ammunition. *Where did Denman find these women?* she wondered? Could he not see the bitterness and callousness behind their smiling masks?

"Why we all know he wants you for himself, but he doesn't have to pretend any longer," she said from behind her fan, as if she was using it to protect herself from any barbs Felea might send her way.

"Pretend about what?" asked Felea raising her guard, ready to make a quick exit out of this woman's circle. Other women were hovering, listening and waiting for Felea to react. She would not give them the pleasure of seeing her shrivel under this woman's words.

"That he has to offer you marriage when now you will accept something less," said the woman getting to the point at last. A lady gasped at her words and Felea's face lost all colour.

"I don't know what you mean, Ma'am," replied Felea very softly. "I have no intention of accepting a carte blanche from any man."

"Now, now!" said Denman sternly, embarrassed at his Mistress's spiteful digs. "That is enough!"

Felea moved away while she could contain her anger. She felt like choking but plastered a smile on her face trying to hide her distress.

Is that what Dreda meant about being in his bed? Was she naïve and had misunderstood his meaning although she had not lost her virtue to him?

Cordelia turned her shoulder, sulking at Denman's rebuke. He never showed the serious side of himself to her and often mocked members of 'polite society'. She didn't know he was so close to Felea and would defend her as if she were his sister. "I am only saying what everyone who is anyone is saying. Everyone knows she lost her virtue to him and has nothing to trade when he is as rich as Croesus. You mark my words, she will be in his bed as soon as fly."

As she went to move away a deep voice said firmly, "You are right Ma'am. Lady Felea will be in my bed but as my lawful wife," said Dreda, "something you aspired to many years ago, but failed in your aspirations. You were satisfactory in bed but lack the elegance and charm to grace my table as my spouse."

"Danitz," said the woman, shocked he had overheard her barbs. "How pleased I am to see you back safely," she said, trying to remove the sting from her words. He turned steel blue grey eyes on her. There was no kindness in his eyes now; just malice and a desire for revenge

He hurt as much as Felea when someone upset her. She was his woman and he wanted, no needed to protect her. He would destroy anyone who harmed her whether they be male or female.

"You will apologize to Felea tomorrow quietly and create no fuss. I will make sure you are not welcome at any of the balls of the Emperor or any of the haut ton from now on. Cordelia von Ravanitz will not exist on the lists of 'polite society'. No longer will you find rich protectors in the city to finance your extravagances Ma'am."

"I didn't mean to upset Lady Felea," said Cordelia back-peddling but could see it was too late. Dreda was implacable, having made up his mind to destroy her, a warning and deterrent to any other mischief makers.

"Tomorrow you would be wise to leave for the country as you will find doors shut to you Ma'am."

Dreda bowed and left the pair to look for Felea. Felea had not heard him defend her or mention marrying her. She did not want to appear to have been driven from the ball by that woman's vicious words and looked for some of the Bureau men who would ask her to dance.

Denman disgusted by his Mistress, merely said, "You may use my carriage to go home Ma'am. I will inform the driver. I suggest you avail yourself of it soon. Your house will be vacated within the month please. My agent will negotiate our terms on my behalf." He bowed and noticed Felea before Dreda could find her.

Taking her arm, he asked her for a dance, holding her gently in his arms in a waltz. She was grateful as usual for his smooth manner.

"That is right, hold your head up," he said. "When you vanished Dreda came back and destroyed Cordelia. He has cut her out of all the balls mounted by polite society and she will apologize to you tomorrow. Her future and chances of getting a rich protector are destroyed."

"Does Francis have so much influence?" She knew he was powerful but had no idea how much power he could wield when necessary.

"Even more," said Denman. "He is the most powerful man in this state after the Emperor. He will protect your reputation."

"It is too late. I have already been cut by several of the patronesses," said Felea, remembering the humiliation of elegant shoulders being turned to her when she spoke to some women after leaving Cordelia and Denman. She had thought these women were her friends, but they were fair weather friends, their honey covered words hiding spite.

One group had allowed her to join them. Relieved and grateful she had relaxed too quickly. "Dreda should be careful these days," uttered one woman with sharp green eyes, watching for her reaction. Felea shrugged her shoulders; she didn't understand the woman.

"He will have few allies left soon. His reputation is shredded after the massacre at Vina." She stopped for affect, wanting to see if her poisonous words penetrated Felea's barriers. Only a widening of her pupils showed Felea had even heard the words.

"If he offends the Emperor he will lose all influence. His influence is waning and those who he protects will be at the mercy of his enemies soon. There is already a list being prepared of those traitors who were not prosecuted by him when they had conspired against the Emperor."

"Perhaps a spell was put upon him!" suggested another. "He was always such a loyal and level-headed man in the past."

"Even the coolest headed patriot can have his head turned by those who practise the dark arts," whispered another, just loud enough for Felea to hear. "There are sanctions still for those who use sorcery to conspire against the interests of the state."

A chill had passed through Felea, freezing her very marrow. Dreda's aunt had talked with disgust about stirrers who were appealing for sanctions to be taken against those who had worked against the interests of the former brutal Emperor. She had warned Felea that even Dreda's loyalty to the Emperor had been disputed by his enemies because he had become engaged to her; a daughter of a spy. He had walked a tightrope during their engagement.

If Felea's enemies dug deep enough she could be hanging from a noose if Dreda wasn't there to protect her. Or worse! When she was a girl, a woman accused of conspiring to kill the Emperor by using witchcraft was sentenced to being burnt at the stake. She had only been saved by a plea to the Emperor himself and had been hung instead.

Felea said, "Then he had better please the Emperor. He is very good at doing that." She reassured herself she would be right. Dreda was a master politician. He would fight carefully but dirtily to save his position, destroying all opposition that stood in his way. She was sure he would come out the victor.

She had been relieved when Denman had rescued her from these evil witches. One had gone so far as to use the words, 'a harlot dirtying our presence,' as she left them. Felea was woman enough to wish them to Hades under her breath and hope they suffered badly when they reached that hot and fiery place.

"Here is Danitz," he said leaving Dreda to take the next dance. No one could mistake Dreda's intentions toward her. Possessively, he put his arm around her and held her as closely as decorum would allow an un-affianced couple.

"Cordelia will not harm your reputation nor will others anymore Felea. She was jealous having been an ex-mistress of mine. She wanted to be my wife years ago but could not fit the criteria."

"What were the criteria?" asked Felea unable to contain her curiosity. "She is witty and beautiful and had a dowry. She attracted a wealthy and powerful man in her first husband."

"She lacks a heart. She is as cold as ice and uncaring about others.

'The criteria to be my wife." He paused as if he gave it great thought as Felea held her breath. "She must have charm, intelligence and grace but above all she must have a kind heart; be a lady and love me as much as I love her. You fitted those criteria my love, which is why I offered for you." Her heart lurched, and she glowed under his rare praise.

The dance ending, he took her hand and kissed it and led her to the carriage and took her home. No longer did she feel alone and very small. She could face her critics if Dreda was by her side.

CHAPTER NINETEEN

Felea's good humour with him was short-lived. The next day she asked him about the massacre and he brushed her aside. "Francis, I heard rumours when I was in the Palace about men being massacred in large numbers at Vina. What happened there?"

"I don't want to discuss it Felea!" he said turning from her. "It is something I wish to forget."

"Some ladies last night were slandering the officer in charge, Francis, saying he deliberately gave the order to run the rebels down after they had raised the white flag. I thought you said the Imperial Army was more careful about taking the enemy alive."

"I don't know what concern it is of yours Felea. Forget it. It was an unpleasant incident, an aberration that couldn't easily be prevented. It is not for the ears of such as you!"

She was disappointed, his curt matter telling her the conversation was at an end. His impassive face, his cold eyes as hard as steel warned her off the subject. He had hardly ever been so cold or detached from her. It was if a shutter had come down on his face disguising his emotions. He was hiding something from her.

"Very well, I will ask you no longer to explain what happened but if you were the officer in charge Francis I am disappointed! You are accused behind your back by gossip-mongers of giving the order to massacre men who had surrendered." He still said nothing, as if willing her to stop!

"Were you the officer in charge, Francis?"

"Yes," he admitted. His face was white and drawn. "But the rumours you heard are untrue.'

'I have nothing more to say Felea. Desist from interrogating me," he snapped. She bit back her own sharp retort. When he was in this mood there was no point in arguing with him. He had withdrawn behind his barriers again.

"I understand, Francis," she said quietly. "You do not trust me."

"It is not that Felea. The situation is more complicated than you understand." Dreda sighed and then said, "Look I have a meeting with the Chiefs of Staff in a few days and must prepare for that. Forget the rumours. Soon we will meet the Emperor and your future will be decided."

"I want to decide my own future."

"Sometimes that is not possible my love. We are all puppets directed in some way by others more powerful than ourselves. Few

178

people can direct their lives in the way they want. Most of us must compromise!''

"What compromises must I make, Francis?'' she demanded, fearing she would be edged into a corner by circumstances she had not designed.

"We will see Wednesday. You need not worry Felea. I will act as your protector. You will be safe while I am by your side.''

She thought Dreda still cared for her but apart from saying he wanted her in his bed he had not mentioned to her he still loved her or wanted marriage. He had used the word protector. That word often applied to a man who took a mistress.

Then 'fitted my criteria.' He had used the past tense as if the situation could be different now. If society now regarded her as a fallen woman perhaps the proud Dreda would not think her worthy of marriage and would only want to offer her a carte blanche. He kissed her hand and left her angry and with questions unanswered. Drat the man! Just when she had been liking him again after he had defended her at the ball he must treat her like a child and put her back up.

She poked around asking questions of others at court but met brick walls, shuttered impassive faces, a resistance to her questions as if she were digging up unwanted memories. Dreda's reluctance to discuss his role and his admission he was the officer-in-charge made her wonder what else he was hiding. She had found out he had used his own money to provide the first provisions for the camp women they had visited. Was he easing his conscience then? He had acted anonymously but for what reason?

The only person she thought might tell her the truth was Denman. He had always discussed their behaviour warts and all and was a much more open character than Dreda, but he had been involved. Was he also the author of the massacre? Sadly, because of his past reputation she could believe Dreda could be that ruthless but not Denman; she would ask him.

She sent a groom to Denman to meet her at a tea room. Surprised, he greeted her with a kiss on her cheek.

"Why are we here instead of at the villa Felea? Does Danitz know about our meeting?''

"No Denman. He doesn't know and mustn't know! He has told me the subject of this meeting does not concern me.''

"I hope you don't expect me to break a confidence Felea,'' warned Denman. "I won't do it.''

"I just want to know the truth about what went on in Vina, Denman.'' She looked embarrassed and blushed. "Francis has intimated he still has feelings for me, how deep I do not know but I need to know what sort of man he is."

"Of course, he has deep feelings for you. He has regained his memory and knows he loves you. He will ask you to marry him again after you have met with the Emperor."

"I thought he might have changed his mind and will offer me a carte blanche," she said reassured. "But I still cannot marry a man who murders unarmed men Denman, even if he only gave the order to kill. Blood is still on his hands!"

"Is that what all this is about?"

"You may think it is a paltry matter to give the order to massacre unarmed men, but I don't. You are of the same kidney as Francis," cried Felea in disgust.

"Whoa!" said Denman. "I have never lied to you and never will! You must not breathe a word of this and swear to that on your mother's grave, Felea. If word got out Francis could lose his neck. I can only tell you an outline of what happened without breaking my word. No names or nor positions."

"Of course," she swore. Protecting Dreda was of upmost importance regardless of their relations. She would not undermine him in any way.

"What do you want to know?"

"What happened and what was Francis's involvement? Why will he not tell me the truth?"

"Danitz did not give the order to massacre the men. He asked the Emperor to bring the perpetrator to justice, but the Emperor refused as the man was very young and under his patronage. The truth would have caused a scandal so Danitz took the blame.

'In return, he gained concessions from the Emperor, changes in the legal code, more money for education and the conversion of buildings as temporary homes for the widows and children. But Felea, he gave a promise to keep the truth a secret. If he told the truth, he could be exiled or worse. The Emperor looks after his own!"

"How could he let the perpetrator get away with his crime? Francis always talked about justice, even rough justice. He must know the reputation of the Imperial Army has been shredded beyond repair by this man's actions."

"He has negotiated a movement of the man to a position where he can't do any harm. In fact, it means the fellow has lost all chance of leadership in the army or a position in the Cabinet Office in the future. It was Danitz's price. It was the best anyone could have done in the circumstances. Others would have buried the evidence and let the perpetrator take a higher position in the army where he could have done more damage.

'Danitz was no longer engaged to you. He cared not for protecting his family reputation. He sacrificed himself. He is no coward or criminal Felea."

Felea was a little relieved but didn't understand how the perpetrator who must have been a junior officer could have given the command. He would have been too junior in rank to countermand Dreda's orders.

"How did the officer give the command?"

"Danitz had sent me to rout another rebel group. He was still suffering the headache and the noise of close cannon fire disabled him, sending him to his bed for a night and a day. The perpetrator took it on himself to take over when Danitz was asleep. He told the junior officers while I was away he was in charge.

'He mistrusted the rebel leader's words and thought he might renege on his offer to surrender. He saw one flare lit and panicked. He gave the order to shoot at the men although he was told the men were laying down their arms. A few shot back when they were fired on and he then told the soldiers to shoot and run them down.

'It was part inexperience, part callousness and part misunderstanding. When Dreda found out he couldn't pin him down. The perpetrator persuaded other officers to blame his action on the dark night and inexperience."

Felea understood now but still felt Dreda could have trusted her if Denman could explain this to her. She would have kept his confidence. "How did you find out?"

"I was in the first meeting with the Emperor and witnessed the initial negotiations between the two men. Dreda came out the winner but lost face in the eyes of the public. He said it was worth it."

He looked at Felea and said, "You can trust him Felea. Danitz is ruthless and severe but he is a fair fighter. I have never known him give the order to fire on an unarmed man. He was disgusted by the whole affair and gave his own monies for the families of the men who died."

"A guilty conscience?" asked Felea. "Perhaps the women would have wanted a trial instead!"

"In a perfect world, they would have got one, but this state is run by an Emperor, a not so benevolent dictator. No blood money Felea! Just an attempt to right the wrong done. Danitz did the best he could in the circumstances."

"What about the provisions he paid for out of his own money?

Does that suggest he has a clean conscience?''

"He gave grain, blankets and tents after he visited the camp with you Felea. He told me that visit shocked him, Felea. He is not the same man he was when he first met you. He has changed for the better and considers the human implications of his actions now. More than that Felea. A child was ill with the fever and he rode with him to a more skilled doctor in the nearby town and probably saved his life.''

Felea was relieved Dreda had had good intentions in making the gifts but she was still angry with him. "He is just the same with me Denman. He expects me just to accept his dicta without question. He doesn't consider my views and mocks me when I challenge his commands. He maddens me!''

"Yet you love him still don't you!'' It was a statement not a question. She sighed and nodded. "Yes, I still love the man, damn him! He has said he expects me in his bed very soon. I am expected to docilely walk back into his arms when he has rejected me and humiliated me. I was told by the courtiers of the Duke he had tired of me, a mere immature girl! They said he had left by-blows among the widows of the rebels.''

Denman grimaced. "They really rubbed it in your face, didn't they? No wonder you are angry and unsure of your relations with Danitz.''

He took her hands in his. "Trust him. He is the same man you became engaged to, but he told me he was terrified of losing you again. That is why he is so protective of you. You do not know the danger the two of you have been in, Felea.'' She looked perplexed.

Damn Danitz, thought Denman. *He is like a bloody clam, trusting no-one, not even Felea when their lives were in danger, insisting on bearing his burdens alone. I must explain the circumstances to her, so she could trust Danitz again.*

"Felea,'' he said, "when you became engaged to Danitz you were still under suspicion by the Emperor's spies. The reason he would not allow you to marry Danitz was he believed you could still betray the state. You might have had divided loyalties you see. Danitz clothed you with his fidelity to the Imperial Crown.

'His status and respectability became your own once you were engaged to him, but he feared your sometimes-unguarded tongue would betray you into saying something which could appear disloyal to the state. That is why he warned off some courtiers from befriending you. He thought they were faux amis Felea, wanting to you to trip up and betray yourself.

'The Court is full of vipers and Danitz has made many enemies, fighting for his position in the Cabinet. He was possibly too ruthless in destroying his enemies on the way up but there are now new powerful men just as callous as him who want his position and him destroyed.''

"He knows I will never betray him Denman.''

"He knows that, but it is easy to say something that can be distorted by those with malicious intent. You saw at the ball how some vixens were ready to tear you apart. One false move and you could betray yourself and take Danitz down with you. Marry him and keep your head down a while and you will both be safe. He will then relax and give you more freedom when he has secured you for his own.''

He frowned again. "And about those by-blows. At that time Danitz wasn't engaged to you in his mind and didn't profess to love you but he was so involved in the fighting he had no time to womanize. When he wasn't fighting or organizing his men he was flat on his back disabled by the headache.''

Relieved, she kissed him on the cheek and he led her to her carriage. "Thank you |Denman. You are a good friend to both of us. I am still not sure of what I want but you reassured me Francis is not a coward or a murderer.''

"Then I have done all I wanted to do. I hope you make the decision that brings you both happiness.''

She went back to the villa to think her situation over and to decide what to tell the Emperor at their meeting the next day.

Denman caught Dreda at his club. "I need a word with you, old fellow. You are in the shit!'' said his irreverent friend.

"What the hell have I done now?'' demanded Dreda, thinking of the past few days. "It must be Felea; that girl has been bristling like a broom since I brought her home. How have I antagonized her again?''

"Been a bit heavy handed, haven't you?'' said Denman "and haven't trusted her! She is no empty-headed featherhead or gossip. She collared me this afternoon and asked about Vina.''
"How much did you tell her?''

"The truth, which you should have done instead of keeping mum. I didn't give any indication as to the identity of the perpetrator. You are a lucky man. She now believes you did not give the order to massacre the rebels.

''You are not a martyr in her eyes though. She thought you gave the money to the widows to ease your conscience.'' She thinks you should have trusted her and resents your treating her like a child.''

"Shit!'' swore Dreda and mouthed more filthy epithets. Normally the coolest of men Felea could easily anger him. The thought of losing her could drive him to drink!

"How can I appease her?"

"The vixens of the Archduke's court said she was not mature enough for you and you left her for more experienced women. You have left by-blows among the widows as supposedly have I."

"Would that I have had the time and you were up to your eyes in blood and gore if I remember correctly?"

"I didn't get into the sack with any woman there, widow or not," said Denman. "I was glad to get back to the city. Celibacy doesn't suit me."

Dreda smiled. He had never known a time when Denman had not a lady in tow. He was always looking for his next conquest, a charmer in and out of the bedroom. Denman was also his best friend who had stuck through thick and thin with him and he respected his friend's judgement. He now had his work cut out getting Felea to marry him.

"What did Felea say at the end?"

"I had reassured her you were not a murderer, but she was still not sure what she wanted. Go easy with her. Don't dominate her so much. She is too intelligent to be treated like a featherhead."

Dreda shook his friend's hand and thanked him. He left him to think of a strategy to win Felea over. She was not the same girl he had left before the explosion. She was still young and inexperienced but was maturing fast and deserved more respect from him.

CHAPTER TWENTY

Felea dreaded the meeting with the Emperor. Since they had returned from the Archduke's Palace Dreda had in turn charmed her and then put her back up. She intended to give him the set down he needed when she next saw him. Arrogant bastard that he was, he was not going to walk over her again! She would ask the Emperor to let her have some freedom from marrying for some time. She wanted to be her own mistress. Denman had reassured her Dreda was still interested in marrying her but Dreda would have to prove he deserved her before she would agree to marry him!

He collected her in his carriage. She was cold and aloof, and he wondered how to win her over. "I hope the Emperor is in a congenial mood," he said. "He may give us what we want."

"I am sure he will give you exactly what you want," she said acidly. "You can't do anything wrong and do exactly what he desires!"

Dreda turned to her. "What precisely does that mean?"

"Why, you said the courts are full of sycophants," she replied, smiling at him. They got out the carriage before he could ask her to explain her meaning and the barely concealed insult directed at him.

He secured her arm more tightly than was necessary and whispered, "You will explain that later, my Lady."

"There is nothing to explain," she said pulling her arm from his. She walked to another courtier smiling, putting her arm in his as they walked toward the Emperor's reception room.

"Damn her," cursed Dreda. She was acting the 'frostpiece' again and he didn't know to pacify her. His palm itched. The sooner he had his ring on her finger and her in his bed the better. This uncertainty was killing him, and he knew he could placate her better in his bed than in any other place.

She had melted in his arms when he had kissed and caressed her when he was courting her; any injuries she had sustained to her self-esteem forgotten when he said he loved her. He was a tough ex-soldier, sometimes unable to use romantic words but he knew how to make this lady feel the most important person in the world when she shared his bed.

They appeared before the Emperor arm in arm, pretending that all was well between them. Taking her hands in his own the Emperor said, "You seem to have to have suffered no harm bar a bad jaw. Dreda did a good job."

"Yes, Sir."

"What do we do with you now?"

"I prefer to stay unmarried for a while Sir. I could teach at the university voluntarily like my mother did."

"I still have that list of suitors although after what happened some might consider you spoilt goods."

"I believe she is still a virgin, Sir."

"All those days alone with you! Some might not think so. A few have already withdrawn their offer!"

Felea was aghast. The Emperor was treating her like a soiled dove. "I assure you Sir, Officer Dreda didn't touch me improperly. He treated me as a lady should be treated."

The Emperor shifted uneasily, the subject rather a delicate one to discuss even in front of a girl who might have lost her virtue. "Rumours abound my dear. You cannot be too careful. One comment is enough!"

"Who commented Sir?" asked Felea wanting to know who was destroying her reputation.

"Oh, no one in particular. But word has got around that Dreda was becoming too intimate again with you in the Archduke's court. People are saying there is no smoke without fire."

Felea thought of his visit to her room, his constant attendance of her which had irritated and made the Duke suspicious. Had anyone seen him kiss her? And they had left together at night and travelled together without a chaperone. Anyone might have thought he was resuming his courtship again. She fell silent.

The Emperor considered her carefully. "You are still a pretty piece. Plus, your lands and income! We might still find someone who might be persuaded to take you on!" He looked at Dreda as he said this. His officer ignored his Emperor's tactless hint. He was in enough trouble with Felea. He didn't need any Imperial interference.

"You would be better to accept a decent offer from an honourable man than study and get too old to catch a spouse. The Imperial Household might also donate extra estates to a bridegroom who helped us out of this difficult situation.

Dreda raised one eyebrow at Felea. She glowered back at him. The Emperor noted his ward's antagonism toward his officer. "Nevertheless, I will think about what you have asked for Lady Felea and come back to you. In the meantime, Dreda will be your acting guardian and you are to answer to him." She was then dismissed.

She waited for Dreda in the carriage. Her situation was much worse than she had expected. She was not guaranteed her freedom but had been put off again. She had to wait six months before she attained her majority and then technically she could marry who she wanted but she had no control over her fortune until she was five and twenty.

She guessed who had told false tales about her, a Caroline von Kramer, one of Dreda's former ladies who was jealous and was now the mistress of the new Emperor. She was a dreamer, a self-deceiver who had hoped Dreda might marry her despite her past. She blamed Felea for her lack of success in trapping the elusive officer. Now Felea's own reputation was in shreds and this new Emperor still saw her as a pawn. He would put pressure on Dreda to marry her, to wash his hands of her and Dreda would do as he was asked. He was the Emperor's favourite.

The Emperor thought he was doing her a favour. The Emperor thought that although she was wealthy and beautiful he would need to bribe her future bridegroom with extra estates as compensation for taking on a fallen woman and for giving up his freedom. This is what Dreda had meant by compromise. He would marry her if pressure was put on him, but he would resent her in time.

A life with a distant and aloof husband, detached and dismissive as only Dreda could be, horrified her and yet she was too proud to accept the other alternative; a villa, jewels and a carte blanche from him. A governess's or schoolmistress's position might be her only solution if she had to disobey the Emperor and lose control of her fortune forever.

She sat waiting angrily for him in the carriage. She would have to pretend she no longer wanted him. Her pride would not accept a duty marriage. She ignored the little voice in her head that called her a liar and reminded her she wanted to be in Dreda's arms and in his bed.

Dreda waited to be dismissed but the Emperor thanked him; then, ''You have a debriefing with the Chief of Staff tomorrow at nine. He needs to know how likely it is the Archduke will proclaim war against us.

'Sit down. You did well getting that girl safely out of the Palace and bringing that woman and her brother back.''

''The first part was quite easy, but I didn't expect to be followed and captured by others. It was by good fortune we escaped. Lady Felea played her part in deceiving and then shooting the female.

'She is brave, and a resourceful lady and I think she could help us at the Bureau using her language and decoding skills. Her competences shouldn't be wasted. She far outshines the men I have working for me in those areas now.''

''Use her then although she can't work as a permanent officer. You know the prejudice still remains.''

He looked carefully at Dreda who sat waiting for the next question which he knew would be more personal. ''What about yourself? You rushed after the girl taking Denman's place. Are you still smitten with her or are you withdrawing your offer as well?''

''The offer still stands.''

''Out of honour?''

''No, out of love. I don't want to see her being accused of being compromised but I care not for my or for her reputation. I know the truth.''

''You may have her if she will have you. She didn't seem very impressed then.''

''She will have me. I can assure you of that. She will give you her answer tomorrow.''

''You are very sure of yourself.''

''I have fought with that girl time and time again. I know her mind.''

He went back to the villa with 'that girl' seething beside him in the carriage, a mutinous expression on her face. *Books were much safer than people and young students more trustworthy than older, cold ruthless men.* She ignored his hand when she descended from the carriage and made straight for the stairs and her room and her sanity.

He was amused and annoyed by her truculent manner. He needed to cut this tangle once and for all. He caught her wrist when she was climbing the stairs.

''Meet me in the study in ten minutes please. I want to change out of my hot uniform.'' She didn't answer him and went to her chamber. She had no intention of talking to him again that day.

He hadn't trusted her with the whole truth or asked her view on the matter of the marriage with the Duke. He hadn't defended her reputation to the Emperor except to say he thought she was still a virgin. He had almost seduced that woman and he had said she Felea had many faults. He had wanted to spank and throttle her! He could stew in the study on his own!

She undid her braids and brushed them out. She ignored a knock on the door but when it became more insistent she decided to answer it because she knew he would kick it down again. Opening the door, she saw he was fuming.

''I asked you to come down.''

''You are not my master.''

''You forget that I am your acting guardian and you should respect my wishes. I don't want to talk to you here in your chamber.'' He remembered the last time he burst in there. ''Will you come down now?''

Haughtily, she stepped downstairs and into his study. She could not fathom why he was so angry.

"What has upset you so much?" she demanded.

"I did not know I was going to be your guardian."

"I don't want it either. I was being ordered about by the Duke, now you!"

"While I am your guardian I cannot touch you!"

"That is all to the good then. Given your former dubious liaisons I would probably catch something. I will find another suitor now even if the Emperor thinks I am spoilt goods and a lost cause!"

"I hope you choose better this time," he retorted, stung by her remark.

"My next choice can't be worse than my first one. At least the next one might be constant!"

"From what the Emperor said you will have few choices," snapped Dreda. He did not mince his words. "Your reputation is in shreds. A soiled dove I think is how you are being described at court."

Felea went white, the blood rushing from her face. As quick as a flash she slapped him with the full force of her hand and stood shocked as a red mark appeared across his face. Equally as fast he retaliated, grabbing her wrist, twisting it behind her and pulling her close to him. She had raised his blood and he wanted, no needed to taste her again. He kissed her until she was breathless and then let her go. With great difficulty, he regained his self-control; she was so tempting in his arms.

He swore; "Damn you Felea! You make me act ungentlemanly when I am supposed to be your guardian!"

"Well that is all to the good because then you cannot in all honour offer for me." Dreda realized it behoved him to tread carefully. Felea was bristling and acting defensively. "You need not marry me out of duty. "And I certainly don't need the Emperor to bribe my groom to marry me. I will find someone who wants me for myself or I will become a governess.

Dreda now realized what was irking her. "I am not an object of pity Francis Danitz!" snapped Felea, poking him in the chest to emphasis her point. Exasperated and losing patience he took her hand and held it still.

"Stop arguing and let me tell you something.

'Firstly, I have told the Emperor my offer of marriage stands. Don't interrupt!" he said putting his finger gently over her lips.

"I am not marrying you because you have been compromised. I have tried to avoid that on all occasions so we both have had choices as to this engagement.

'Finally, I am marrying you because I love you. If you say no I will never give up and will carry on hounding, you until you give in. I am ruthless you know.

I know I hurt you when I rejected you and ignored you. I apologize for being an ass, but I was ill, not able to think straight nor feel any emotion. When I took that mistress it just felt wrong, but I didn't know why. I now know it was because I felt I was betraying you.''

At last she could breathe a sigh of relief. He still loved her and wanted her not as his mistress but as his future wife.

Smiling through her tears of relief she at last said, ''I thought you had completely given me up! There was no one to match you so I took the least bad alternative. I could not live in the same small city, meeting you, constantly knowing you were with another woman.''

''You need not worry about any other woman. Since Antonia, the only woman I have ever wanted to marry is you. All the others bored me silly. You entertain me and amuse me. I can argue with you about things I normally have to talk to men about. We are soul mates.''
She still looked undecided.

''Felea, I know I was harsh and dominated you, but I realized when we were in the Palace how much you meant to me. I was and am still terrified of losing you. Without you my life is empty. I cannot promise to be a liberal husband, I am too used to having my own way, but I will respect you and honour you as a husband should.

'I feared you might be betrayed by one of your enemies in court if you stepped even a little out of line and I have enemies who would have enjoyed destroying your reputation to get back at me.

'I am sorry I didn't trust you before, but I was sworn to secrecy about Vina. Denman knows only half of it. I could not even tell him! I know you thought I was the perpetrator at Vina, but I am not that type of man. I fight fairly Felea!''

She could read the truth in his eyes which had turned that moody blue, reflecting his hidden passionate nature. He was bearing his soul again to her. She knew how much this meant to him; he was such a reserved, withdrawn character. He now trusted her as he had trusted no other woman. She had to take that leap of faith and trust him to take care of her.

''I was so ashamed of my colleagues I nearly left the Bureau, but I thought I could do more good influencing the Emperor there than if I left him to his sycophants.''

He took her other hand in his and kissed her wrist, gently and tenderly. ''Now I want a different life. I want my children with you

Felea, a home-life; you beside me when I come home. Now will you marry me, you obstinate woman?''

"Oh yes."

He couldn't take her in his arms and kiss her as he was her guardian, but she had been called forward and loose being spoilt goods according to the Emperor. She put her arms around him drawing him to her and kissed him passionately. She would give her answer to the Emperor tomorrow.

CHAPTER TWENTY-ONE.

Dreda stopped his curricle outside of his villa. The staff were waiting outside to congratulate them. He picked up Felea in his arms and carried her through the doors and up the stairs, running without catching a breath.

The wedding had gone well. Over the threshold of the chamber he dropped her lightly on the bed and stood back to watch his new bride. Felea lay back against the pillows and drew back her veil. They had married by Special Licence a week after she had given the Emperor her answer.

Dreda had put his foot down saying wryly, "I am not waiting much longer. We will argue, and you will leave me if we leave it any longer. I am not taking the chance!" The Emperor had agreed, and they had an informal wedding with a few close friends and Denman as his best man.

She waited for him to close the door behind him, her maid hovering beside them. A bath of steaming bubbly water smelling of sweet herbs and flowers rested beside the bed. "I will help my Lady undress Lucia." He crossed the floor but Felea stopped him. "I think I would like a few minutes to prepare myself, Francis."

Recognizing her shyness, he said, "You may have as long as you wish, my love. But I am sure you need some help to get out of that robe." He pulled her off the bed and lay a kiss on the nape of her neck making her shiver. Melting under his caress Felea whispered shyly, "A little help would be wonderful!"

"At your service my dear," he said turning her round and undoing her dress, placing a kiss on her skin as he unhooked each hook and eye. Frissons of sensation passed down to the base of her spine as he pulled the dress down to her waist revealing her creamy breasts.

"I thought we would never get to this point." His pupils narrowed and darkened as he saw her peaked nipples aroused and waiting for his caresses.

"I thought I had lost you forever when you cracked your head. I no longer existed for you!"

"I was in my own world, a mess. Thank God for that sword fight and fall. It would not have made a difference in the long run Felea. We were destined for each other. From the moment, I first set eyes on you, I wanted you and knew you would be mine. I tried to pretend otherwise but it was a lost cause. I had to have you!"

He slid the dress down her body, inspecting her minutely as the silk pooled around her ankles. She stepped out of it revealed in all her nakedness. "I couldn't have born the Duke taking that other dress off you," he said. "I was as jealous as hell! I knew then I must marry and keep you."

"You were right although it was not gentlemanly of you to taunt me! I had chosen the design of that the dress only for you."

"Forgive me my sweet. I hated that man for having the right to touch you in that way. I was consumed by envy."

"I have never wanted another man but you Francis!"

"I will make sure you always feel that way my love."

He then turned to the task at hand, taking one nipple in his mouth and sucking it until she moaned and gasped. Felea not to be outdone pulled him to her undoing his shirt, dragging his cravat off impatiently.

For months, she had waited for this moment. She ran her hands down his chest marvelling at how firm and muscled he was. She had known he was strong when he had fenced her and had held her tight when he had kissed her, but she had only seen him half-naked when he was sick, and she had tended his wounds.

Now helping him out of his breeches and smallclothes she had lost her shyness, wanting him. She could tell he wanted her as much as she wanted him, his arousal evident as he pulled her tight against him.

"A bath for you my Lady. I want to scrub your back!" he said carrying her to the tub and gently dropping her in. *Where was the stern officer?* she thought as he tenderly caressed her shoulder through the bursting bubbles? He had lost all his cares of the world and sat relaxed on the edge of the tub gazing at her. The cold secretive man was receding as the ice around his heart was being melted by her love.

He left to give her a few minutes to relax and prepare herself. She lay back in the warm, fragrant bath thinking of her wedding day. When Dreda had first gazed on her walking up the aisle she had seen the look of awe on his face. She had chosen this wedding dress carefully knowing only a few would see it.

Not for her the pale virginal whites or creams, but a turquoise dress trimmed with marine lace. Like her previous dress the side panels were made of lace, the fine pattern revealing her creamy bare skin. The back of the dress fell from puffed sleeves from the shoulders to a deep v finishing at the waist.

It was a dress that invited the groom to inspect his bride's wares and she had felt Dreda's inward drawing of his breath. He had whispered, "You look divine my love, like a mermaid," and she had swished the long sapphire and turquoise and marine train behind her seductively. Only a sapphire and marine droplet necklace and earrings decorated her, their simplicity enhancing her long neck. Dreda had removed these when they had prevented him from kissing her in the curricle once they were out of sight of the well-wishers.

She washed her arms and breasts carefully, still feeling how sensitive her nipples were after his kiss. She had felt sensations down to below her waist and had wanted him to go further. Dreda entered quietly behind her and watched her as she washed her creamy leg, partly hidden by the suds.

He came beside her and traced the pattern of suds down her finely muscled legs and then up further to her hidden core where he caressed her making her eyes widen. She gasped, and he leant and kissed her while pleasuring her. "This is what you have been waiting for my darling."

"I can't wait much longer, Francis. It is killing me," she said as sensations overwhelmed her.

"This is just the aperitif, my love." He picked her up and dried her with the towel in his arms and carried her to the bed. Laying her in gently he got in beside her. "Now for the main course my sweet. You are so edible, my love."

She pulled him down and kissed him. "Now Husband! Show me what you have for me," she demanded.

"I always thought you were a saucy wench. Forward, are you?" he mocked, his blue eyes sparkling, teasing her. "At your pleasure, my Lady," he said and started to caress her until she could take no more. Knowing this was her first time he took it slowly making sure she was ready for him and then entering her gently, carefully. Her eyes widened as she took the whole of him inside her slowly expanding with the size of him.

He was much bigger than she had expected but oh so gentle with it. One hard thrust and she felt a sting as something tore and then he started to thrust again gently. Harder and faster he raised the pace as she dug her nails into his shoulders and back, asking him for more until they peaked, and he fell back gasping, his arm still round her shoulder, nestling her to him. They lay there for a few minutes caught up in the moment.

Dreda felt at peace at last, a gentle contentment he had thought he would never experience. "This is forever Felea!"

"Forever Francis," she repeated knowing that they would stay together now. Their different background and ages and loyalties had been overcome. Their life together was their only concern now. They made each other complete; two secretive, private, sensitive individuals who would never let anyone separate them again.

The end.

ABOUT THE AUTHOR

This author studied history and politics and then business and law. She became a law and economics lecturer in Higher Education and later left to start her own tutoring agency. She has since run a guesthouse and lives with her husband and two crazy Birman cats in a restored cottage near to a canal in Knowle in England. Many of the novels derive from the cases she read during her teaching career.

She enjoys Zumba and yoga. She loves art and illustrates her own book covers. Her current passion is making succulent and cacti bowls for her gazebo where she likes to write in the summer.

She writes romantic suspense and crime novels under the name of Toni Bolton, historical romances under the name of Alexie Bolton and books for children under the name of Dawn Bolton.

Dawn loves to connect with her readers. To be sent her newsletter please email kixley@btinternet.com **To connect in other ways please use the addresses below:**

Dawn Bolton's author page on Facebook

https://www.facebook.com/dpbolton1

https://twitter.com/dawnbolton2

Novels by Dawn.
Historical novels.

The Militia Man's Lady. Available on Amazon and Kindle. https://www.amazon.co.uk/Militia-mans-lady-Dredas-Book-ebook/dp/B079YKTJNW/ref=sr_1_1?ie=UTF8&qid=1527350094&sr=8-1&keywords=the+militia+mans+lady

Crime and romantic Suspense novels by Toni Bolton.

Escape From fear. Book one of the 'Men of Valour, Women of steel series, available on Amazon and Kindle.

Whisper Softly or You're Dead. Book 2 of the Men of valour, women of steel series, available on Amazon and Kindle.

'A blinding flash.' In the anthology, 'Hey you, I think I love you'. Cree Nations and Liberty Parker.

This will be a novel in its own right in July on Amazon and Kindle.

Innocence and deception will be published in August 2018.

Excerpts from other novels.

The Militia Man's Lady.

Helena is in prison accused of imprisoning her brother.

Denman came to see her and smiled. ''You don't look good.'

'You should see the other woman. She tried to steal my food!' she replied indignantly.
'Well has this shown to you what prison life will be like if you are lucky enough to have a death sentence commuted to life. Have you changed your mind about telling the truth?'
'I am sticking to my story.'
'Which in court will be torn to shreds.'

There was no answer. She merely stared back at him, meeting his eyes directly, arrogantly, as if she didn't have to answer to him. This time he did erupt in anger, his promise to himself to stay detached forgotten. He pushed her against the wall. He lifted her head, his hand under her chin until he had eye contact. Spearing her with his eyes, he said quietly and deliberately, 'I will not allow you to perjure yourself and be executed or rot in a place like this.'

She stared defiantly at him. 'Keep your nose out of my affairs. You are not my father.'

'If I were your father I would put you over my knee. You are a barefaced liar!' He was trying to provoke her, break down her barriers but merely inflamed her pride further. As quick as a flash she slapped him as hard as she could, but he was not a man to take that lightly. He took both of her wrists firmly and held them by her side and holding her against the wall he kissed her. All his militia training could not help him now. He was fearful of losing her and raw emotion took over. She resisted for a moment but recognising it was futile she sank into the kiss which seemed to go on forever.

Escape from fear.

Excerpt one.

The Prologue

Indonesia, June the 2nd 2013.

Kirsten felt as if a bell was ringing deep inside her head. Rough hands were shaking her awake, digging into her, bruising her whilst she tried to bury herself in the safety and security of her sleeping subconscious; the obscurity of the darkness, wanting the anonymity.

The hands were around her throat groping her, choking her. A heavy body was suffocating her, bruising her, until the blessed darkness engulfed her. Her dream not over she regained consciousness slowly coughing and spluttering, still seeing those eyes above her, emotionless flat grey pebbles staring at her while she cringed away from them.

She made an inhuman effort and pushed them back and woke up with a start, feeling sick as she fought the lethargy and sickness induced by the sleeping pill. It had only been a nightmare thank God. Her breathing slowed down as she realised she was alone in the room, but her phone was bleeping. 'Oh God, have I been found here?' she wondered, her heart in her throat. Only three people outside of Indonesia knew her existence on this small island.

She fumbled for the light switch, ice gripping her heart. All the blood had rushed out of her face. She could hardly bear to look at the mobile but peering with half-shut eyes at the number she saw that thankfully it was her Aunt Freya's number. The sweat pouring out of her froze on her icy skin.

She got out of bed to wash herself and pulled on a robe. It was 23C in Indonesia, but she was perishing cold, a reaction to the fear that had engulfed her. She made a hot chocolate, a comfort drink that helped her overcome the shadows that threatened to envelop her even in this isolated place where few people knew her and hid her in safety.

Now her pulse was no longer racing, and she was warming up she could concentrate on her aunt's phone call. Her aunt had given up ringing and finally sent a text. She had bedded down early the heat making her tired. It was only 10.30pm. In England she was a night owl and her aunt would have expected her to be up for hours. They often talked into the early hours of the morning Kirsten having worked flexi hours and staying at the office late into the evening.

She read the text. 'Kirsten Darling. I have something I would like you to check for me. A man wants to buy my house and is rather insistent I sell. He has phoned me five times and will not accept I don't want to sell to him. He now wants to meet me in person and visit the house. Michael said he will stay with me while the man comes but I want you to look into his details for me. I feel something is not quite right. The way he spoke gave me the shivers.'

She texted back. 'Send me his name and anything you know about him Aunt Freya. I have an internet connection and can follow it up.' She went back to bed to an uneasy sleep her aunt having worried her. Freya was a cool lady with good instincts.

The next morning the details were in a text. She had to teach that morning, but the early afternoon was too hot, and she had two hours free until the late afternoon lesson. Sat at her desk with laptop and mobile she put the details into the machine and pulled out what she could.

The man who was pestering her aunt to sell was a rather seedy property developer who had made money during the bubble of the eighties and early nineties. He also had connections with some investors in banking and mining, but she couldn't find out anything else because the telephone connection kept failing. She finally got a line and emailed a friend who had police connections in the USA and he wrote back stating the guy had a record.

The connection was failing again. Storms had brought the feeble lines down and the island had suffered severe storm damage. Many of the women were leaving with their families until their homes could be rebuilt by their menfolk aided by the relief agencies. It was the appropriate time for her to leave for England, a month earlier than she had agreed in her contract, but she could do little here and could follow up her leads on the man who was pestering her aunt much more efficiently in England than in Indonesia.

Devil's Creek Florida 4th June 2013.

Thick smoke enveloped the table she was leaning on. Putting a towel around her neck and mouth she coughed her way to the door and pulled the handle. It rattled but stuck.

'Stay calm Freya!' she told herself, but panic was beginning to overwhelm her as the flames grew closer, the white heat almost burning her eyebrows and lashes now. Her throat and lungs felt tight as the black smoke invaded them, clogging them. She gave one more tug and gave up and tried to force herself toward the window.

A smash at the window attracted her attention. A towelled hand smashed the broken glass away until a man could force his way through. It was Michael. He climbed through with an unexpected agility for an eighty-five-year-old man.

He pushed his way toward her through the gaps between the flaming furniture, stopping for a moment as the heat and intensity of the flames drove him back. His head was covered with a towel and he pushed his head like a bull and charged again kicking the furniture away with his heavy boots making a pathway toward her.

She in turn didn't waste time and launched herself toward him ignoring the biting heat of the inferno.

'Freya!'

'I am here Michael! 'She cried as he glimpsed her through the wall of thick black smoke. The towels were burnt off his hand and she could smell the sickening sweet smell of burning flesh, but he continued to press toward her. She made one last push forward and was in his arms. He put his arm around her and they headed toward the window. Too slow! A beam crashed and hit her on her head and shoulder and she almost collapsed to the floor.

The old man caught her as she fell and he half carrying her they pushed forward and reached the window. He pushed her out of it uncaring as she hit the hard ground. 'She was safe now,' he thought and climbed over the sill and fell choking on the paving himself. His last thoughts to himself before he lost consciousness where he would get the bastards who did this, or his name was not Michael Defoe.

London, 4th June 2013.

Kirsten took her mobile out and read the text her aunt had sent her late the night before. The urgency of the message stunned her. Her aunt was not a panicker, something must have really spooked her. She read the words again to herself trying to make some sense of the situation. 'Kirsten Darling. Someone is threatening me and searching my house. Someone is trying to get me to move out and sell the house to him. If you can get here I need your help. Text me please, Aunt Freya.'

She booked a flight that evening paying through the nose for flying at short notice, but she would economise at the other end. Her aunt's life was more important. Her aunt would not have contacted her and asked her to fly out unless she was in danger. She knew Kirsten wanted to remain anonymous and respected her privacy. Thank God she had returned from Indonesia one month earlier and her work could be done online from anywhere providing there was an internet connection.

She packed that night and went to bed early but was woken by a phone call early in the morning.

'Ma'am this is Dr Brant from Devil's Creek Hospital. You were put down as the next of kin of Ms. Freya Andersson.' Her heart lurched at his words. 'Yes Doctor, what has happened to her please?'

'She was caught in a house fire and is alive but suffering from severe smoke inhalation. If you wish to come I would advise it as soon as possible.'

'Will she survive Doctor?'

'I am afraid we are not sure at the moment.' He left the rest of his statement unsaid. Someone would be needed to sort out her personal affects and house if she died.

'I am taking a flight later today Doctor. My aunt contacted me last night and asked me to come.'

She finished the call and got up and taking her bag took a taxi to the airport. Counting the notes in her wallet she cursed her financial situation. She hoped her aunt would be awake and able to lend her some money when she arrived. Would the house be liveable in? She had little spare cash to pay for living accommodation. The flight cost had absorbed most of her spare cash. Not for the first time did she curse the man that had condemned her to her present impecunious position.

Excerpt 2

Kirsten goes to Florida to find out who tried to murder her aunt. Someone wants her out of the way. Josh Rutland neighbour's grandson wants to help her and is attracted to her. She rejects his advances and he thinks she is a tease.

'Something had changed in the way he watched her. The atmosphere in the room had become thick with sexual tension. Hours before he had behaved gentlemanly, treating her like an acquaintance but now she sensed his manner toward her had changed. There was no longer any pretence. He behaved like a man who had chosen his mate and wanted to secure her for himself.

She sat warily watching him move about the room with precise careful movements. He dried his torso quickly and tamed his wavy hair. Gloriously masculine he prowled the room picking up a fresh pair of boxers, smart pants, his shirt, jacket and tie. A quick change in the bathroom and he moved back to face her.

She drew an intake of breath, wanting to ignore him but she could not take her eyes off him as he pulled on his shirt over a muscled torso. Fully clothed he maintained a veneer of respectability over that raw masculinity he could not easily disguise.

'Like what you see?' he questioned, green eyes pinning her in place.

'I have seen other handsome men dressing before. Don't kid yourself you're something special,' she bit out. He smiled bitterly. He could see the affect he had on her. She was aroused and interested in his body. A sexual creature, she appreciated a man's torso. What had turned her from a warm passionate creature to this icy imposter inhabiting her body?

Kirsten was tired of battling him. Rutland was one of the most sexually exciting men she had encountered. She shivered when he turned those deep green eyes on her, a hidden promise in them. He was a handsome devil and before she had loved Justin she would have enjoyed flirting and possibly kissing him, but Justin had destroyed her confidence and turned her off domineering men for good.

When he called her Kirsten instead of the formal Ms. Gateman Rutland's Southern accent sounded like smooth hot chocolate almost seducing her into making the first move and kissing him. He was sex and sin on legs and he wanted her! He knew she also wanted him, but she was too frightened of taking up the challenge he presented and risking her health and sanity.

'My lovely Kirsten,' he said moving toward her having finished dressing. She moved back toward the kitchenette not wanting close proximity with him. They moved slowly as if in a dance until he trapped her against the kitchen cupboard and there was no escaping him.

Excerpt.

Whisper softly or you're dead.

'Sorry I live with my sick Mother and have to make her dinner when I get home.' 'Thank God for that excuse. She knew he was waiting for her to ask him to dinner or to bring the carry out to her place, but she ignored the unnatural brightness in his eyes and then the disappointment that replaced it. They were nearly there. Only five more minutes to drive. She should be safe at home soon and away from this creepy man. His eyes had drifted dangerously off the road every few minutes surveying her legs as her skirt had shifted a little up her thighs.

His hand strayed a little from the wheel but noticing her unease he put it back in its place until he stopped at the end of her cul de sac as she drew a sigh of relief to be back safe. He turned to her and said, 'I don't suppose you would like to go to a show or to the cinema with me or even dinner?'

'I can't get out easily. I have to plan weeks in advance to find a sitter,' she said knowing it was a feeble excuse. He frowned seeing through her deception. 'Perhaps we could have a night in then at your house if your Mother goes to bed early.' His arm had strayed around her shoulder and he pulled an escaping ringlet from across her face. 'Such pretty hair,' he said. 'Matches a pretty face.'

'Thanks awfully but my mother doesn't take to strangers easily.'

'Perhaps you should introduce me now and let her get to know me over a cup of coffee,' he said. 'God, this guy doesn't give up,' she thought. No way was he passing her threshold. She would never get rid of him. She wriggled out of the reach of his arm and made to open the door. 'Thanks, but I can't I am afraid.'

'Why not,' he said, now more insistent putting his hand on her knee making her skin crawl. She opened the door, but his hand moved across to hold it in place refusing to let her out. 'You don't have any other guy dating you at the moment, do you?' She felt horrified. He must be watching her to know her movements. She needed to lie to get out of this hole she had dug herself in taking lifts from strangers. How often had her Mum and teachers warned her about the dangers of taking lifts? 'I have a long-distance relationship with a guy from my hometown. We are going to be engaged soon but we don't see each other very soon.'

'He can't be that keen if he hardly ever comes to see you,' said Dave. 'Let me try to change your mind,' he said leaning over to steal a kiss. He didn't make the kiss. His door was pulled open and he was yanked out of the car by the scruff of his neck landing heavily and painfully on the tarmac outside.

'The Lady said she didn't want to go out with you,' said the stranger. He held hold him down prone on his front his arm folded behind his back and a foot strategically placed to stop him getting up.

'Apologise and I will let you leave unarmed. Avoid her in the future or you will be hurt very badly,' threatened the man.

'Sorry Ma'am. I didn't mean to take liberties and offend you,' said the man terrified by the look in the stranger's eyes. Let free he scrambled up and hurried into his car driving off without doing up his seat belt in his haste. The stranger took the details of his number plates in a pocket notebook and said. 'Miss Linton, are you ok. You have had a nasty shock.' He made no attempt to touch her but took her heavy briefcase and led her through the foyer and up to her apartment door. 'I am Detective Raymond Chase. I have seen you about. I live near that guy in the same block and noticed he seemed to be around your house and following you in the grocery store.'

He made no attempt to follow her into her apartment. He was the perfect gentleman. 'I have his details

Miss Linton and if he annoys you again just phone your local precinct and I will be down on him like a shot.'

A blinding flash.

Staggering out of the car he held himself upright. He was a fool to have drunk that half bottle of whisky on the plane after no sleep for two days and one small airport meal. It had dulled his thoughts and memories temporarily stopping the nightmares, but it had also impaired his faculties. Tired and grouchy he hailed a cab giving the driver the address and slept again until he got to the house where his Cousin lived.

He was only dropping in for an hour to see his Cousin and then he had to go back to give evidence which might make the difference in catching the men who had murdered his colleague in a particularly vicious manner that had made even a hardened warrior like him used to war scenes blench. He had vomited after seeing his colleague's face and promised revenge and retribution.

Hence, he was taking the night flight back to Summer and started trailing the killers the next morning. His Cousin Mike had said he had good news to tell him. He had not spoken to Collins for over two years, his commitments making him work underground until he gave up his FBI work this year and for three months had been working as a Marshall in the Summer area.

He walked in to a party atmosphere, caterers putting out food and alcohol. He squinted in the dazzling light. He had pulled down the car's window shades. His head was aching, and his eyes were sore. He felt sick in the stomach as the bitter aftertaste of the whisky set in and an ache cut his stomach in half. His clouded brain recognised he needed food and water quick to steady his gut and clear his mind.

He made it to the kitchen where caterers were preparing a buffet. He sneaked some rolls and spring water and took it to the basement where the games room was. After he settled his stomach he would find Mike and find out what the celebration was for. Resting his head against the wall he saw two women enter, one blond-haired and petite, the other a stunning brunette. The latter, nearly as tall as many men; willowy and elegant, exuded confidence and sophistication as she stood holding a baby in her arms.

''Her own,' he wondered but discarded that thought, the baby having tufts of red hair.

''Do you know where Mike is?'' he asked. The women looked at him curiously as if wondering if they should know him. He resembled Mike in facial appearance and build but there the likeness ended. Mike had copper hair while his was as black as coal. His eyes were grey while Mike's eyes were a deep sapphire blue. He had nothing to recommend himself to these sophisticated ladies dressed in party wear. His black tee was crumpled and sweat stained, his leather biker jacket scuffed and dusty as were his jeans. He had a graze over his eye which was forming a scar and a black eye. He looked a dirty mess, but he had only intended to drop in for a few hours and then go back again, after congratulating his Cousin on his good news.

''He has just gone out to get some alcohol and do a few chores,'' said the blond woman. ''He will be back in a few hours.''

''Damn it, I have to catch a plane in three hours. You will have to give him my regards. I am his Cousin Pat, just flown in from Summer to see him. Last time I heard he was chasing that murderess who had belted him. I hope he caught her and gave her her just deserts. He was complaining about a bad headache he said the bitch had given him.''

The reaction to his ill-chosen words was not what he expected. The brunette thrust the baby into the blond's arms and strode to him and poked him in the chest thrusting her face into his. Cold deep violet eyes speared his and she snapped frostily, biting each word out in turn, "that murderess as you so rudely called her is now his legal wedded wife and that is his baby daughter. She is my friend and in future you can refer to her with respect."

She stopped poking him for a minute and stood back as he considered her words. His befuddled mind was still having difficulty taking these facts in. *Mike married. He was as big a skirt-chaser as himself, the eternal womaniser, stating he would never marry. And a baby as well.*

The woman poked him in the chest again her wrath still evident. "Are you going to apologize for insulting my best friend?" she snapped. Her voice had not raised an octave. Quietly spoken, only her eyes showed her wrath. Pat's own temper erupted. He would have apologised but he wouldn't let an itsy-bitsy female make him feel guilty when only his information was out of date.

"Yes Ma'am, when you take your finger out of my chest and treat me with the respect I deserve, or I will treat you as you deserve," he said. She was so close he could smell her musky perfume which fitted her personality so well. He suddenly had the need to show this woman who was boss. When she didn't move back he pulled her into his arms and held her in an iron grip with one arm round her waist and pushed her head up to meet his.

"You were saying Ma'am," he mocked. Eyes sparked again. This was no submissive woman admitting she was in the wrong.

"Well you need to be taught a lesson then," he said. His rational mind reminded him he was behaving badly but the alcoholic haze took over as his macho instincts responded to the softness and curves of a beautiful woman in his arms. He couldn't help himself. He moved closer and took her mouth in his, plundering its depths when she opened in it shock. She fought but gave in when she realised he was too strong and then stood passively still until he let her go, shocked with himself. He pursued women and enjoyed the chase but had never forced himself on an unwilling woman. The desire to shut her up and dominate her had made him forget he was a gentleman.

The lady did not forgive him. She stood back and wiped the back of her hand over her mouth as if to rid herself of a distasteful taste.

She then stared at him for a long moment and like a flash she belted him in the face bashing his previously unhurt cheek and eye. He would have another black eye tomorrow. Her ring had cut his cheek which now dripped with a stream of thin blood.

''Touch me again and I will call the police you, you Bastard. You are as bad as her former Husband,'' she snarled and taking the baby from the blonde's arms she ran upstairs. The blonde watched her go upstairs for a minute and said, ''was that necessary Pat? She was only defending her friend who had been through hell before her marriage.''

Felling defensive and guilty he shrugged. ''That aggression wasn't necessary. A short explanation would have been sufficient for me to apologise. Who is that she-devil anyway?'' He was still shocked at a woman standing up to him and assaulting him. Most women were seduced by his charm and wanted to date and bed him. This woman intrigued him and tantalised all his senses. He wanted to see her again.

Copyright©Dawn Bolton 2017.

Digital publication July 2017.

Cover design by BetBup33

Publisher, Dawn Bolton.

PUBLISHER'S NOTE.